A

NEVER

TO BE TOLD

Book Four
In the
Tales of Avalon Series

BY DAISY BOURNE

For Luke, Canaan and Lantis

First published 2018 in Great Britain by
Text Copyright © Daisy Bourne 2018
www.TalesOfAvalon.co.uk

British Cataloguing Publication data:
A catalogue record of this book is available from
the British Library

This book is also available as an e-book

Illustrations© Caroline Evans
www.carolineevans.net

CONTENTS

MAP 1

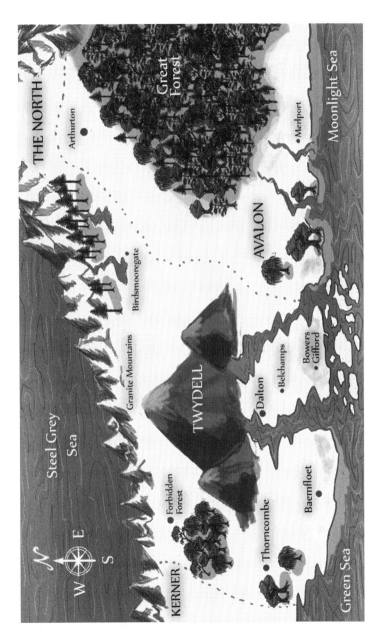

MAP 2

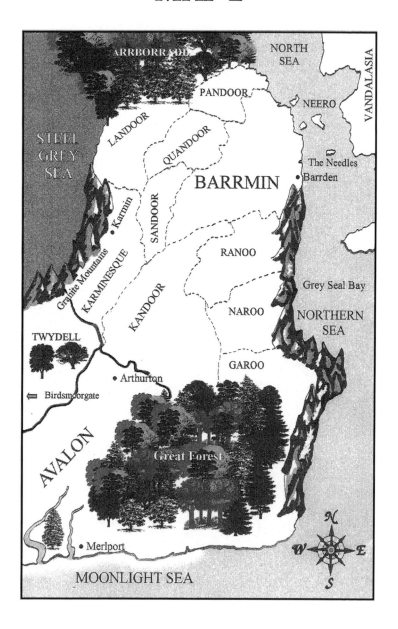

ARRBORRADD

NORTH SEA

VANDALASIA

PANDOOR

NEERO

LANDOOR

STEEL GREY SEA

QUANDOOR

The Needles
• Barrden

BARRMIN

• Karmin

SANDOOR

RANOO

Granite Mountains

KARMINESQUE

Grey Seal Bay

KANDOOR

NAROO

NORTHERN SEA

TWYDELL

GAROO

• Arthurton

⇐ Birdsmoorgate

AVALON

Great Forest

N
W   E
S

• Merlport

MOONLIGHT SEA

Prologue

This is the fourth book in the *Tales of Avalon* Series. If you have not read the first three books in the series, then here is a brief description of the story so far.

The magical people who had formerly lived in Briton are now established in the faraway land, once known as Brewin, now renamed Avalon. Some men and women who had feared for their lives in Briton had also joined them.

The witches and wizards of Avalon amicably referred to non-magical people as plainfolk. The plainfolk referred to witches and wizards as wizzwits. The names did not appear to offend either party.

The Avalonians had thought that they had found a land where they could live in peace and harmony. They had started to build a settlement on the ruins of an earlier one, which they called Merlport, in honour of Merlin, the mighty sorcerer. However, the giants who lived in the Great Forest had warned them that the earlier settlement had been attacked by marauding seafarers, known as Trajaens. The Trajaens had destroyed the Brewin settlement. Those Brewins who had not been slaughtered had been taken prisoner and carried off in Trajaen longboats. Only one Brewin had survived, a young girl named Daisy. It was only their fear of the giants that had stopped the Trajaens settling in what was once known as Brewin.

Aware of the threat, the Avalonians had started to prepare in case of an attack on Merlport by the Trajaens. Men started to practise swordcraft and archery. Wizards and witches practised spells and invented creative charms that would help to protect their new home. Nevertheless, many lives were lost in a subsequent battle. One clever old witch, named Azgoose, cast a spell that created a cloud of pink goo. The pink substance rained down on the Trajaen boats, rendering the savage warriors in the boats helpless for some time, as they tried to free themselves from the sticky goo. It was this delay in the Trajaen advance that helped the Avalonians win the Battle of Merlport.

Azgoose had stood on her broom, shaking her fist in triumph. Alas! She missed her footing and fell headfirst into the sea below. After the battle, search parties were sent out to look for her, but could find no sign of the elderly witch.

PART ONE: THE STRANDED WITCH

CHAPTER 1 - WHERE AM I?

Where am I?

Azgoose continued to cling to the piece of wood that had saved her life by keeping her afloat. She couldn't remember how she came to have hold of it, only that it had been with her for what seemed like days. The wood was slightly rounded and looked like a piece of boat from a wreck. She lay with her body and arms on the wood, the lower half of her body submerged in the sea.

In front of her and to her right, all she could see was sea stretching to the point where it met the sky. She strained her head around to look behind, only to see more water. To her left were tall granite cliffs, but no land on which she could set foot.

She noticed that since she had been drifting, the blue-green ocean had changed to grey and more clouds were beginning to assemble in the sky. It was getting colder and her legs were becoming numb. Her limp body rose up and down with the gentle waves, as they pushed her and the piece of wood onward.

What will happen if the weather turns and the waves grow higher? It'll be no good trying to hold on then. The same thought crossed the old woman's mind time and again.

Every now and again, her fingers ached so much that she lost her grip. She would frantically dig her nails into the wood to try to regain her grasp, only to feel herself sinking into the fathomless depth. When this happened, strange creatures nudged her back to the surface and on to the piece of boat. Sometimes, whilst she was clinging to the wood, she felt their noses pushing at her feet to make sure she continued her journey forward. The creatures must have been some sort of fish because from time to time, they jumped out of the water, gracefully curved their bodies and dived back in again. They had dark greyish-blue bodies that were smooth and without a trace of hair. Wide eyes, which seemed full of innocence, peered out of their large round heads.

A couple of times, the strange fish-like beings had pushed her to the side of the cliff. Azgoose had wondered what was going on, but she soon realised why they had guided her to those points. Rainwater poured down the cliffs. The old woman would put her head under the cascade of fresh water to wash the sea salt from her face. She opened her mouth wide to allow the water to fall inside. She swallowed greedily at each opportunity. However, it must have been at least a day since the creatures had last found her a place to drink.

How I wish I had a drink of fresh water, the old lady thought. *I never appreciated how precious water was when it was plentiful. Now I would give anything for a drink of that cool, clear liquid.*

Azgoose drifted in and out of sleep. On occasion, she let her grip on the piece of wood loosen and her body would slip towards the ocean.

A gaggle of pink-footed geese had followed her on her journey. It was only the attentive care of the geese and the strange sea creatures that stopped Azgoose from drowning.

Sometimes, when she lost her grasp, she would be pecked gently by one of her feathered friends. She

4

would awake, startled to realise her peril, and grab the wood again.

At other times, when her arms ached so much and she felt she could hold on no longer, the strange sea creatures lifted her back onto the wood that kept her afloat.

Now and then, when her eyes were closed, she would hear a soft thump. Upon opening them, she would see the pink webbed feet of one of the birds that were her friends. The goose would drop berries from its beak onto the wood. She would tilt the wood slightly towards her face and grab the berries hungrily with her mouth. Apart from the gifts of berries from the geese, the old woman had not eaten for days.

She continued her journey floating past the granite cliffs, half awake and half in slumber. When her eyes were open, she looked hopefully for a place where she could climb ashore, but there was nowhere. As each day passed, her weary eyes were more often closed than open. *How many days now?* She dreamed of her journey to Avalon. Had her magical flight from Briton to the new land been a dream or did it really happen? Had Avalon been real? Real or imagined, those were happy days in the new land where no one persecuted her for being a witch. She remembered the Battle of Merlport. *Yes, that was real enough.* Even in her present state she chuckled, as she remembered flying high on her broom and creating a cloud above the marauding Trajaens. A short spell and twist of her wand and pink goo rained from the cloud. Despite her semi-conscious state, Azgoose let forth a cackle as she remembered the Trajaen warriors covered in the sticky substance and unable to lift their feet from the decks of their longboats.

Everyone on the beach was cheering me. What a foolish woman I was. I was so proud of myself. Never in my wildest dreams did I think that I would be cheered by humans. In my excitement I wanted to show off. I stood on my broomstick shaking my fist in triumph. I let vanity rule my head. I didn't look so clever when I fell. I could hear the cheers turn to groans as I tumbled headfirst into the ocean. And yes, I remember being struck by an arrow. Instinctively, Azgoose allowed herself to release one arm from the hold she had on the wood. She felt her wound. Her thigh was sore, but it was not as painful as she might have thought.

Perhaps it doesn't hurt any longer because my legs are numb. It's got colder since the sea turned from blue to grey.

It must have only been a graze. The salt in the seawater must be healing the cut. What good is a healed wound if I am only going to drown? But these strange sea creatures and my friends, the geese, must be trying to save me. For sure, I would be dead by now if it were not for them. Is there a purpose in keeping me alive?

What happened to my broom? Another half slumber and Azgoose pictured the riderless broom flying into the cliff. *Ah, I remember when I fell, my poor old broom just kept on flying and shattered when it hit the rock face.*

With a thump, which roused the old woman from her reveries, a goose landed on the piece of boat. A blackberry fell onto the wood. The old woman eagerly lapped it up with her tongue. She savoured the juice from the small fruit before swallowing.

"I need water," she croaked. She hoped the goose or the strange creatures would hear her. "I need water, please," she croaked again, but the goose flew away and the large fish-like beings continued to push her onwards. *Perhaps there is no fresh water nearby. Or perhaps my voice is so weak they cannot hear me.*

Azgoose let one of her hands release its grip from her precious piece of wood. She felt her sleeve to make sure her wand was still in her gown's concealed pocket. It was the same action she had performed over and over again. She felt reassured to feel its long thin shape. *If only I had more strength. I know the spell so well. I could fly to the top of the cliff in no time.*

Azgoose had tried the spell a couple of times when she first fell into the water, but magic requires strength of mind. The stranded witch was disoriented and too weak for her spell to work. Her wound had been sore and was bleeding. The fall had badly shaken her. She had managed to get her wand back into her sleeve for fear it would drop into the water and be lost. *But what good is a wand to a witch who does not have the strength to perform one of her most practised spells? I thought I was so clever, but I was just a foolish old woman seeking glory.*

Tears started to fill the witch's eyes. *No, I will not cry. Feeling sorry for myself will only make me weaker than I am already. Sleep will make me stronger. Or will it?*

She slipped back into the familiar half awake and half slumber that had been her life for what seemed like days now. *I can't continue much longer. I am losing the feeling in my legs and my arms ache so much that I will have to let go soon. Thank you for trying to save me my pink-footed friends and strange sea creatures, but the time has come for me to let go now. Perhaps I will wake up again in yet another new land and my ancestors will be there to greet me. It has been such a long time since I saw my mother. If I pass from this world to the world of those who have lived before me, I am sure she will be there to welcome me.*

Almost as if the sea creatures could read her mind, two swam forward to lift her away from the piece of broken boat and carry her. Azgoose felt as if she was flying. They came from behind and lifted her limp body out of the water and spread it facedown between their smooth backs. Azgoose's head was close to theirs and her feet near their back fins. Each arm hung across one of their bodies. Warm sunshine eased the pain in her aching limbs.

She tried to look into the cloudy eyes of the creatures that bore her. She wanted to look into their souls, but they stared straight ahead and she could see nothing.

After what seemed like a couple of hours of half oblivion on the smooth backs of her rescuers, Azgoose raised her head. *Am I seeing things? Is that a small beach nestling in those endless granite cliffs?* The relief was such that she must have slipped into unconsciousness because the next thing she heard was a man's voice.

"What is it?" he asked.

"An old woman," replied another younger voice.

"How'd she get here?"

"She must have managed to cling to that piece of broken boat."

"Is she alive?"

Azgoose felt someone touch her neck. "There's a pulse, but it's very weak," said the younger man's voice.

"Best let her die. She's the ugliest woman I've ever seen." The older man's voice responded.

"We can't leave her here. Those geese will peck her to death."

"If it hadn't been for the geese we would never have found her. If she isn't pecked to death she'll drown anyway. I've never heard such a racket. There's been no geese hereabouts in my lifetime. I wish I had a bow and arrow. If I could shoot one down, we'd be having a nice roast goose for dinner tonight."

The old woman suddenly felt angry and tried to speak, but only a garbled sound left her mouth.

"We can't leave her here," the younger man bent down. "Help me carry her back to the house, Bert."

"What are you going to do with her?" argued Bert. "We can't feed ourselves let alone another mouth. There's nothing again in today's catch worth eating. Just a few sprats, which are more bone than meat, and a handful of glitter fish. You'll rescue her from the sea only to see her starve and then you'll have a body to bury."

"Then we'll try to catch a goose later. That'll keep us all in food for a while. Come on Bert, give me a hand."

Bert let forth a sigh of aggravation, but two pairs of hands lifted Azgoose off the sand. One took her shoulders, the other her feet.

They carried her away from the beach and along a narrow pathway in between the cliffs. The footpath led across rocks. Each time the pair carrying her stepped up onto a rock or down again, her aching body jerked causing her to groan with the pain.

At last they came to a wooden shack. Someone opened the door and the men lifted her inside.

"We can't put her on the bed, Bert. She'll soak the straw and blankets. Let's lay her on the mat."

"She'll make the mat wet too. It'd been better to leave her outside."

"Can't leave her outside!" The younger man was firm.

"Well it's your house, so do as you will."

"Water, please, water." Azgoose croaked, hoping they would understand.

"I think she's asking for water." A new voice. A boy's voice this time.

They understood me.

She heard the rattle of metal and the sound of water gushing.

Someone lifted her head and Azgoose opened her eyes to see a boy of about ten. The boy held her head while she drunk thirstily from the tin mug he held.

Behind him was a man of about thirty and a little way behind him another older man.

The young voice and the older voice. He called the older voice 'Bert' earlier on.

"Can you speak?" asked the younger man. "What's your name?"

"Gisela," croaked Azgoose. *Where did that come from? Ah, I remember, it was a name I used a long time ago when the Britons accused me of being a witch. I must hide my real identity. These people must not know what I am.*

"Gisela the goose girl," Azgoose croaked. *That's what I called myself. I remember now.*

"Goose woman more like," stated the older man. "How did you get here?"

Azgoose tried to shake her head, but it hurt so she simply croaked, "I don't remember."

"There was a piece of wood near you on the beach," the younger man stated, "a nice piece of wood with carvings. I reckon you were shipwrecked and you used the wood to keep yourself afloat. You must have drifted here on the tide."

"Aye," agreed the other. "I reckon you were taking those nice fat geese to Barrden and got shipwrecked on the way."

Unknowingly, the two men were giving her an alibi.

Azgoose gulped down some more water. "Thank you for your kindness, boy." She tried to smile at the water bearer, but it was too painful. Her lips were cracked and sore.

"Where d'you come from?" persisted the older man. "Were you on your way to Barrden?"

"I can't remember where I come from," lied Azgoose. "I've never heard of Barrden," she replied truthfully.

"Barrden is the capital of Barrmin," the boy cut in eagerly, "even I know that!"

"I can't remember anything," repeated the old woman.

"Dad, if she's lost and has nowhere to go, can we keep her for our new granny? It's ages since our old one died and if we had a new one she could look after the Harries so I could go to work with you."

The younger man laughed. "When she regains her memory I'm sure she will want to catch those geese and find her way to Barrden."

11

"Perhaps she'll give us one or two of her geese in exchange for rescuing her. It would be good to have something other than fish to eat," Bert added hopefully.

Gisela wriggled uncomfortably. *No one is going to eat my geese!*

The younger man spoke now. "We ought to let the old woman... I mean, Gisela, sleep.

"Gisela, you must be uncomfortable in those wet clothes. Do you feel strong enough to change them? Some of my mother's clothes are in the cupboard. I think they'll fit you."

"Please!" Azgoose managed to mouth the word.

"Young Stan, find the old woman... I mean, Gisela, some of granny's old clothes. Bert and I will wait outside while she changes."

Young Stan hurried off through a door to the side of the room.

The younger man took a bucket from the corner of the room and placed it beside Azgoose. "You can put your wet clothes in here. My name is Stan, by the way, but they call me Big Stan and," pointing to the other older man, "this is Bert. Young Stan, the lad who's gone to fetch you some dry clothes, is my eldest son. Those two," pointing to two small children, "are Harry and Harriette."

Azgoose looked around the little house. She appeared to be in the kitchen-cum-living room. She assumed the door Young Stan had gone through led to a bedroom. She noticed the two other younger children standing nearby, staring at her with wide eyes. *They must be the Harries.* She tried to smile at them, but her cracked lips made any movement painful, so she just nodded.

Young Stan hurried back with a bundle of crumpled clothing. "Here you are, granny!"

"She's not your gran, Young Stan." Big Stan stated firmly. "I'll wait outside while she dresses."

"And I'll say goodnight," said Bert. "It's time for me to get back to my own place."

Azgoose raised her hand to bid Bert goodnight.

The two men left the little house together, talking amiably about the day's events. The two younger children seemed to prefer to stand and stare at the new arrival, but Big Stan called to them to follow him outside.

Young Stan showed the old woman a long twill skirt. "There's a nice brown skirt here, granny." The material looked very coarse, but it also looked warm.

"And a nice white, well whitish, blouse." The boy showed her a blouse made of the same coarse material. Azgoose wasn't sure whether it had once been white or had always been a dull creamy colour.

"And a nice green woollen shawl. Granny knitted this. I remember her with her knitting needles. She was so proud of it." The shawl looked as if it had hardly been used. "She liked knitting." Young Stan's face grew sad. "She used to knit us jumpers."

"I'm sorry you lost your gran," Azgoose croaked. The attempt to speak made her cough.

"Will you be our new one?" Young Stan persisted. He went to the kitchen and pumped another mug of water for the old woman.

Azgoose felt a tug on her heartstrings as she looked into the boy's expectant eyes. She accepted the mug and downed its contents greedily. "Thank you, Young Stan." This time her croaky voice was not quite so croaky. "I don't think anyone could replace your real grandmother, my dear, and as soon as I am strong enough I must be on my way."

"Well, if you can't remember where you live, where will you go? You could stay here and be our gran until you do remember." Young Stan was not going to give up easily. Nevertheless, he considered it was time to allow the old lady some privacy while she got dressed. "I'd better wait outside with Dad and the Harries. Please don't take long getting dressed; Dad will need to cook our dinner soon. I'm really hungry and so are the Harries. Harriette's been crying nearly all day. See you later, granny."

The witch wanted to smile, but couldn't. She nodded to the boy and hoped the expression in her eyes showed her gratitude. *I don't think I've felt any affection for a human being before. What a nice young plainboy. I'm much too ugly to be anyone's granny. I wonder whether he would still want me for his gran if he knew I was a witch. Surely not. I hope they don't find out the truth – it's nice to be liked. They are nice people, well, Stan and his family are. I don't think much of Bert. Bert wanted to leave me on the beach to die.*

Pushing herself up by rolling onto her side and then grabbing hold of a nearby rocking chair, Azgoose managed to stand. However, her legs felt like jelly beneath her. She managed to clamber out of her wet clothing before falling into the rocking chair. She carefully removed her wand from the hidden pocket in the sleeve of her wet gown. *Now how will I conceal that in my plainfolk clothing?*

Half sitting and half standing, she managed to put on the dry clothes. After some consideration she pushed the wand inside the waistband of the skirt and tucked the shawl around it. *I'll have to be very careful that the shawl doesn't fall open and reveal my precious wand. I hope I will soon be strong enough to use it so that I can get myself out of here and back to Avalon.*

She was just tucking in the shawl when a knock came at the door and Big Stan gently pushed it open. He politely diverted his eyes in case the old woman was not dressed. "Can we come in yet?"

"Yes, of course. Thank you for these lovely dry clothes."

"Ah, you've found the rocking chair. Well, you just sit there and rest. I have to cook the children's tea." Big Stan stepped towards the old woman and spoke gently. "I'm sorry I can't offer you anything to eat, Gisela. I'm not having anything either. What we brought in today isn't enough to feed the children let alone anyone else."

Azgoose nodded. She watched Stan out of the corner of her eye as he put the day's meagre catch of sprats and glitter fish into a pan. The two smaller children eagerly sat up to the table while Young Stan laid a plate and fork for each of them, including his father.

The aroma of fried fish filled the room for a while, but strangely enough, Azgoose did not feel hungry. The small fish did not take long to cook.

Big Stan served out a small quantity of fish for each of the children. He left his own plate empty. Nothing else was served up. There were no vegetables and no bread. He turned his back on the children eating and pulled up a kitchen chair to sit next to Azgoose. He spoke quietly. "We're all hungry. The sea has been fished so much in the last year that there's nothing left. We had a garden full of potatoes, turnips and carrots, but the king's men have taken the lot."

Azgoose looked shocked. "Why?" she mouthed. Although she tried to speak, hardly any sound came out.

"You really don't know do you? Or you can't remember. A poisonous creeping weed has been strangling Barrmin. It's been growing at an alarming rate and no crops can be grown. The king bought some weedkiller that was also supposed to promote the growth of root vegetables. It was spread through the areas of the country used for farming. In actual fact, it poisoned the soil and the only thing that grew was an inedible vine. It's as thick as rope and it's said to grow a few feet every day. Whether that's an exaggeration, I don't know. But what I do know is that the king has ordered us all to take as much food as possible to Barrden or the forts, where his armies are based.

"We get no payment for the fish we take to Barrden. We have been ordered to take one boatload a week. If we fail, then Bert and I get three lashes of the whip each."

Azgoose raised her brows in surprise. She sympathised with Stan because she too had felt the lash of the whip. It was a long time ago, but she remembered the pain. Back in Briton, humans had accused her of being a witch. She'd been tied to a chair and thrown in a ducking pond. If she drowned, then she would have been deemed to have been innocent, but if she survived the ordeal then she was guilty. As Azgoose was indeed a witch, she floated to the surface on the chair to which she was bound. She was undoubtedly guilty and sentenced to 12 lashes of the whip before being put to death. She suffered the whip, however, before the death sentence was carried out the clever old witch escaped. Azgoose had not done anyone any harm. She set sail on the next available ship to Avalon with many other witches, wizards, fairies and elves – all of whom feared for their lives if they stayed in Briton. She thought she would be safe in Avalon.

The old witch looked at Big Stan with sympathy. *It's bad enough knowing that humans treat magical beings with brutality, but why on earth would they treat each other with such cruelty?*

"The waters around here used to be full of fish," Big Stan continued his tale of woe, "the trouble is King Rabbart pays traders for fish. Foreigners come from all over to fish from our waters. They have bigger ships and deeper nets. We always used to throw the small fish back to let them grow, but the traders take everything. They don't live here so they don't care. They just take the money the king's treasurer gives them. The foreigners get paid for taking the fish from our seas and we get whipped because there's nothing left for us. We only have small boats so we can't travel further out to sea. The traders shouldn't be allowed to fish so close to our shores, but when other fishermen have expressed their anger in Barrden, the treasurer simply ordered them another lash of the whip each.

"And it's not just fish. There's a little village about quarter of a mile further down the path. We used to trade fish in exchange for cheese and butter, but now we have nothing to trade with. Even if we did have fish to trade, the village have nothing to give in return. The king's men have taken nearly all their sheep and cows and left them with hardly enough stock to feed themselves. Now I've heard say that the creeping bindweed is getting nearer to the village each day and nothing can stop it. I heard one of the villagers say that he watched his neighbours try to pull it out of the ground, but ended up with just a handful of leaves. Next he tried to cut it, but the knife couldn't get past the outer layer. They even tried burning it, but it won't catch fire. It seems like we're doomed. We'll all starve to death."

Azgoose shook her head. She could hardly believe what Big Stan was telling her, but she knew that it was true. She could hear his stomach rumbling. She looked at him. He was a big man, but his clothes were hanging loose, like someone who had recently lost a lot of weight.

Stan looked at her. "I do have a little flour left, but I've never been a cook. I tried to make some bread after my mother died, but I just made a gooey mess. I don't suppose you know how to make bread, do you Gisela?"

The delight in Stan's eyes showed bright when the old woman nodded.

"Tomorrow," she croaked. "I haven't made bread for a long time, but I'll do my best tomorrow. I'm already feeling much stronger."

"We didn't think you would last till tomorrow when we found you on the beach. I'm glad you're feeling so much better. I'm just sorry I have nothing to offer you to eat."

"Just give me water and let me sleep in this nice dry clothing tonight. Tomorrow I'll try to get up and around, even if it's just for a few hours, to make some bread." *I can make bread. I'm sure I can.*

Stan refilled the mug and placed it on a stool beside the old woman.

The children had finished their meal and had come to stare at her again. They stood side by side, a few feet away from the visitor. Their eyes were open wide, watching her with curiosity.

"Now children, let Gisela get some sleep and in the morning, if she is well enough, she might make us some bread."

"Hooray! Bread!" three young voices shouted in unison.

"Thank you, granny," Young Stan beamed. He ran to the ugly old woman, gave her a hug and planted a noisy kiss on her cheek.

Harry and Harriette ran towards Azgoose as if to copy him. However, they stopped short. They both decided not to hug and kiss, but to simply stand and stare at her from a shorter distance instead.

"Come on, Young Stan," his father ordered, "leave the old lady alone and help me with the dishes.

"Harry, get the old lady a blanket. When we've finished tidying up, all three of you can get off to bed. An early night tonight and an early morning tomorrow and we'll all go down on the beach and see if we can find some shellfish."

"Yay! Shellfish." Little Harriette clapped her hands.

"I love cockles," Harry chimed in. "Razor fish are better." Young Stan joined in.

CHAPTER 2 - FEEDING THE FAMILY

The light of a full moon shone through the curtainless window, casting long shadows over the room in which Azgoose lay in the rocking chair. She had awoken after a few hours sleep to find herself alone. It was good to be dry and to sleep within the comfort of four walls, but now she could see the outlines of her feathered friends flying past the window. *They are checking that I am all right.* She forced herself to stand. Her whole body ached, but she managed to shuffle her way around the room as quietly as she could so as not to wake the family who slept in the adjoining room. She made her way outside.

Where are my friends?

She heard a gaggling sound and knew her geese were near. She spoke to them in a guttural language of their own. "Keep away, my lovelies, these people are good people, but they are hungry. If they caught you they would eat you. Stay close but out of reach, my beauties."

The geese showed little alarm. They were already aware of the dangers.

"The people who live here would appreciate some of your delicious eggs. Will you lay me some eggs, please? If you give them eggs they will not be so eager to eat you."

The geese made a throaty noise that Azgoose seemed to understand. She bid her friends goodnight and made her way back to the house. Even the short walk outside was exhausting and in the comfort of the rocking chair, she soon fell asleep again.

The sound of Big Stan moving around woke her up. Dawn was breaking, bringing the room to light. She lay in the comfort of the chair watching the dust motes dance in the first rays of the morning sun. She felt much more alert today.

Stan, seeing the old woman with her eyes open, brought her a mug of water and asked how she was. Azgoose, or 'Gisela', as she was known to him, assured him she was much better. He said he was glad she was feeling stronger, but he looked downcast and seemed too depressed to want conversation. Azgoose was disappointed because she wanted to learn more about Barrmin and the creeping weed. More importantly, she wanted to find out whether Stan had any knowledge of the battle that had taken place in Avalon. She was desperate to know whether the people of Merlport had fought off the marauding Trajaens or whether they had been defeated. However, she dared not ask too many questions lest he guess her true identity.

The children woke up hungry and grumpy.

Harriette began to cry. She said her belly was grumbling.

"When will Hubert be here?" mumbled Harry.

"Our gran used to make us porridge for breakfast," Young Stan stated, rather gloomily.

"If we had some oats I'd make you some porridge," his father snapped. "Even I can make porridge."

A knock came to the door, but it opened without any bidding. An elderly man entered. He had an abundance of short white hair and a bushy white beard. He carried a jug. Like Stan, his clothes hung loose, signifying a man who had lost a lot of weight.

"Hubert's brought the milk!" shouted Harry.

"Here you are." He put the jug down on the table. "I've tried to put a bit extra in for the old lady."

He walked over to Azgoose and looked at her with curiosity.

"Good morning. You must be Gisela. I'm Hubert. I'm Bert's father. He told me how he and Big Stan found you on the beach yesterday. How in the world did you end up here?"

Azgoose shook her head. "I don't remember." Her voice was still weak, but much clearer than the previous evening.

"Bert said it was only the gaggling of geese that caused them to notice you, otherwise you'd've been covered by the evening tide. I reckon you was on yer way to Barrden to sell those geese."

Gisela shrugged her shoulders.

Big Stan handed her a mug. This time it was half full of milk. "This is our breakfast. Hubert here has managed to get us some milk."

"Hubert's got a nanny goat," Harry explained.

"Shush," Young Stan admonished him. "The nanny goat's a secret. You won't tell anyone will you, granny? If you do, the king's men will take it."

"I don't know anyone to tell," she replied truthfully.

"Well it would be difficult to hide the fact that we have a goat from her when I'm bringing warm milk first thing in the morning."

"You'll keep our secret won't you, Gisela?" Hubert gave her a big smile and a wink.

23

I like these people. They are like Avalonians.

"Of course I will." She managed a ghost of a smile. Her lips were still sore. Gisela took the mug and sipped the fresh milk. She savoured it on her tongue before swallowing.

"Gisela's going to make us some bread this morning." Big Stan opened a sack. "The flour's a bit on the grey side, but I think it's still edible. Anything's better than nothing."

"Have you got any yeast?" asked Azgoose.

"No."

"Then it will have to be flat bread."

"Flat bread made with grey flour sounds delicious at the moment." Big Stan gave a weak grin. "What do you think, Hubert?"

"Luvverly," agreed the old man.

"We share everything with Bert and Hubert," explained Big Stan.

"And we share our nanny goat's milk with Stan and his family," beamed Hubert.

"Right, let's get out of Gisela's way and fingers crossed, when we get back, we might have some bread to eat!"

"Yes!" three young voices shouted together.

"Goodbye, granny" called Young Stan as he left with his father.

This time Harry echoed his brother. "Goodbye, granny."

"Cheeky little so and so's!" Hubert laughed.

Azgoose had taken an instant liking to Hubert. *Even though he must be hungry he keeps a smile on his face. I like this gentleman.*

"Now, my dear, what do you want me to do to help?" the old man beamed.

"Nothing, thank you most kindly, sir. I'm better working on my own." Azgoose managed a painful smile and hoped she would not make her sore lips bleed.

"Sir! It's a long time since anyone called me sir! In fact, I'm not sure anyone ever did." Laughter came easily to Hubert.

"Well, I won't hold you up. That's my house over there. It's the only other one that's occupied. Everyone else has left. Travelled south to try to find somewhere where that weed don't grow. I suppose Big Stan has told you all about our troubles."

"Yes. I am sorry to learn about that horrible weed and the hunger in Barrmin.

"Now, I must get a move on and try to make this bread. I don't want to hear those dear little children crying with hunger again.

"Perhaps we can talk later when I've finished cooking? I'd like to know more about this place where I've been shipwrecked and about Barrmin."

"Right you are," Hubert touched his forehead in a sign of mock salute, "but don't forget, you know where I am if I'm needed."

Azgoose gave him a little wave. She watched the old man make his way back to his own little wooden dwelling, then she made sure the door was shut.

She looked around. *This place is filthy. It needs a good clean.* She put a chair under the door handle to stop it being opened.

A brush and a mop stood idle in the corner of the room. A scrubbing brush lay in the kitchen window. The witch withdrew her wand from the waistband of her skirt.

I hope I'm strong enough to do this.

25

She uttered some strange words and finished up by saying out loud, "Spick and span, you know you can. Spick and span as fast as you can."

The handle of the pump at the sink started to move back and forth so that water flowed. Azgoose lifted a bucket into the sink and let it fill. The broom started to brush dust and dirt into the corner of the room where a dustpan was waiting to be filled. She lifted the bucket of water on to the floor, ready for the mop to start work. Next, the scrubbing brush went into action in the sink, quickly clearing it of any stains.

Azgoose took a cloth herself and started to clean the table in preparation for her bread making. Now magic may seem simple, but it uses up a lot of energy, so the witch sat down for a few minutes allowing the cleaning process to finish. When the mop finally came to a halt and the scrubbing brush laid itself back in the window, she carefully concealed her precious wand and made her way outside. She took with her a basket she had found. She left the door open to allow the breeze to air the room and the floor and the table to dry.

In the daylight, she could see that the little settlement consisted of just five small wooden dwellings that might better be described as shacks. They were surrounded by the granite cliffs. She recognised the narrow path leading to the small beach along which Big Stan and Bert had carried her the previous night. Another narrow path went in the opposite direction and she supposed this one led to the village.

The settlement was sheltered by the tall cliffs, broken only by the opening for the paths. The clouds were moving fast so it must have been windy elsewhere, but the hamlet enjoyed only a light breeze.

Nevertheless, she observed that the air was colder than it had been in Avalon.

Either the autumn is turning to winter or I have travelled further north than I thought – perhaps a bit of each.

She made her way behind the house to the spot where she had spoken to her feathered friends the previous night. It didn't take long to find eight goose eggs amongst the grass and weeds. She uttered a sigh of relief followed by a louder, throatier sound. "Thank you, my friends."

As she made her way back round to the front of the house she saw Hubert standing on his verandah. Lifting a goose egg out of her basket, she waved her prize at the old man.

Hubert clapped his hands.

Back inside the little house she mixed flour and water and used her wand to knead the dough. Stan had put some wood under the stove ready for her to light. As soon as the stove was hot, she placed the dough in the oven.

When the bread was cooked she tried the doubling spell.

She uttered some words finishing up with, "Make my loaf two loaves." However, all that happened was that two flat loaves appeared, but only half the size of the original larger one.

Oh, dear! I wish I knew Merlin's doubling spell. But how would I have known that I would ever need it?

The little family could smell the aroma of newly baked bread before they got to the house, and quickened their pace. The children started to run.

Azgoose heard their excited voices and quickly concealed her wand. She sprinkled some flour in her hair and on to her shawl to make it look as if she had done the baking without any assistance. Then she put the eggs into a saucepan of boiling water.

Boiled eggs and bread. Not much to offer as a meal, but to this family it will be a feast!

When Hubert saw the family heading towards the house he called Bert. The two of them followed behind with bowls and spoons.

Young Stan, whose face was as bright as a button, laid the table.

Azgoose cut the warm bread into pieces and proudly placed a boiled egg and pieces of bread on each plate. It wasn't a lot and the bread, made with grey flour, wasn't the tastiest, but the eggs were fresh and full of flavour.

"This is delicious," mumbled Hubert with a mouth full of eggy bread.

The children said nothing as they dipped their bread into the egg yolks, enjoying every mouthful and finally trying to wipe their plates clean with what was left of the bread. It was the first square meal they had had in a long time. In fact, it was the first square meal they had had in a very long time!

"Very welcome indeed!" Bert managed to speak, though his mouth was full." Thank you, Gisela."

Big Stan looked around the room with eyes full of surprise. "Gisela, you must have worked hard this morning. You've cleaned the house. I can't remember ever seeing it so clean. And boiled goose eggs, this is really unexpected. There wouldn't have been much in the way of shellfish to share out."

The old witch felt proud of her achievements. She managed a little smile of pride for the recognition Big Stan had given her. The children had brought in a bowl of shellfish that they had picked up on the beach. "I'll bake some more bread later and we can have it with the shellfish," she offered enthusiastically. "There's one egg left so I'll use that to make a cake."

Big Stan looked at her sadly. "The only flour we have is what's left in the sack. Best to ration it because it won't last long. We can only hope that by some miracle we get a good catch of fish when we go out again."

Bert nodded his agreement. "If we do get a few fish then I'd rather let the children eat. It would be better to suffer the whip than have an empty belly or let these children starve."

"Shush..." Big Stan indicated his head towards the children.

Azgoose felt bewildered. She didn't like Bert. He was the one who had wanted to leave her on the beach to be carried away by the tide. It was Bert who had wanted to kill one of her geese so that he could roast it. Now here he was, preferring to suffer the lash of the whip for not taking fish to Barrden than to see the children starve. *He's not a bad man after all.*

The children finished their meal. Young Stan licked the last of the egg from his plate. His younger siblings did the same.

"I'm not a proud man," laughed Hubert, as he copied the children's example.

"Thank you, granny!" Young Stan left the table and coming over to Azgoose, put his arms around her and planted a big kiss on her cheek.

"Thank you, Granny," echoed Harry and Harriette, but they did not offer a kiss. Harriette did approach the old woman though and gave her a brief hug.

Azgoose beamed. *Those young children really do need a woman to care for them. Even an ugly old wretch like me would do.*

Harry stood and watched his siblings but came no closer, though he did give Azgoose a shy little smile before running outside. Young Stan and Harriette followed, leaving the adults sitting around the table.

"Can't you buy more flour?" she asked, but she already knew the answer. She just wanted Big Stan to confirm what she had guessed.

"There are no fish left in the sea, the foreign fishermen with big boats take the lot. We have no fish to sell, so no money. The king orders us to take a boatload a week to Barrden for which he gives us no payment. If we do not have a full boat then he punishes us. The smaller the load, the greater the punishment. Even if we had money, flour is so scarce these days we couldn't afford it.

"To begin with, when the sea was still well stocked, we could get enough fish to take a boatload to the city and still have some to trade with the foreigners on their way to Barrden. The foreigners have plenty of goods to sell to the king. He used to strike a fair deal, but food is so scarce the foreigners can now strike a better one."

Azgoose thought for a moment. "Could you trade goose eggs for flour?"

"We most likely could," replied Big Stan.

"We'd get more for a goose carcass that could be roasted," commented Bert.

"So you might," said Azgoose purposefully, "but a dead goose can't lay eggs. Roast goose might feed you for a day or two, but a goose egg every day would feed you for a lot longer."

"She's right," added Hubert, "the lady's right!"

Lady! Nobody's ever called me a lady before!

Bert grunted. It wasn't clear whether he was agreeing with his father or annoyed with him.

"We ate the goats when we were first short of food." Hubert continued, "We didn't think that the shortage would be for long. That was almost a year ago. Now all we have is one nanny who gives us each a cup of milk for breakfast. We used to have butter and cheese, but not anymore."

"What good's butter with no bread?" Bert added sourly. He didn't expect a reply.

"Well, you and I had better get the boat out and see what fish we can catch." Big Stan had no desire to listen to arguments to which there was no answer.

"Gisela, me and Bert are going to take the boat out to see what we can catch. We'll be home later tonight. I'll cook the shellfish when I get back. I wish I could offer you some, but there's only enough for the children."

"I'll cook the children's tea." Azgoose smiled. "If the geese lay some more eggs I'll do them an egg each too. Do you think you could trade some eggs for some flour?"

Big Stan was thoughtful. "If we take them to Barrden and try to do an exchange there, then the king's bailiff will surely take them from us. He would want to know where we got them from. Tomorrow,

Bert and me, we'll go out early to see if we can catch anything else before we make our way to Barrden. If your geese have laid some more eggs before we go then we'll take them with us. If we see any foreign traders passing, then we'll try to exchange them for some flour. The ships' cooks will always have plenty of flour, but maybe they won't have fresh eggs."

"Good thinking." Bert was in agreement.

Azgoose felt confident. *I will ask my lovelies to lay as many eggs as they can.*

"Now, you two best get the boat ready. I'll wash the dishes." Hubert was already getting the dirty plates together.

"No, I'll do them." Azgoose was keen for the men to leave so that she could put her wand to use again, but Hubert insisted on helping. "You've worked like a busy bee today, the way you've cleaned this house and cooked."

The witch didn't argue and Hubert washed the dishes while she dried them. Bert and Big Stan got the boat ready and the children played outside.

Azgoose felt very tired, despite the fact that her magic had done most of the cleaning and cooking that she had been credited for. "I think I'll take forty winks if you don't mind keeping an eye on the children, Hubert."

"No trouble at all, Gisela. I'm surprised you recovered so quickly and the speed you've done this work in, especially after the ordeal you've been through. I wonder how long you drifted in the sea before Bert and Stan found you?"

And Bert would have left me there! The words Bert spoke when he saw her lying on the beach still stung.

But he was only worried about another mouth to feed. He's not a bad man, she reasoned with herself.

Gisela sat in the rocking chair and fell asleep as soon as she closed her eyes. However, the sound of the children playing woke her. Hubert had taken a chair and was sitting on Big Stan's verandah watching the children play. They were skipping with a piece of rope. The Harries swung the rope whilst Young Stan tried to jump over it. Poor little Harriette wasn't tall enough to swing the rope over the taller boy's head and he was grumbling. The little girl dropped the rope and started to cry.

Azgoose picked up a bowl from the kitchen and went outside. Hubert was trying to pacify the quarrelling children.

"Now then, Harriette. Why don't you come with me to see if we can find some nice tender dandelion leaves? They are good to eat when they are young and tender."

Harriette looked a bit bewildered, but keen to get away from the boys, followed the old lady.

The settlement only covered a small area because of the surrounding cliffs, but Azgoose had noticed some dandelions growing amongst the grass. She showed little Harriette the leaves that were good for picking and those that were too old and bitter to eat. Very soon, the little girl was helping the old woman. The boys followed. They watched and decided that they too would like to help. As they moved around to the back of Big Stan's hut, Harriette pointed excitedly at a large goose egg lying in a patch of dry grass.

"Now tread carefully, my dears. There may be others."

Hubert had followed behind. He fetched a basket and very soon, he too was searching to see if there were more eggs.

"You must have had a lot of geese with you, Gisela."

The old woman didn't reply.

Soon the basket was full.

"I think there's enough to have a little scrambled egg and dandelion salad with our shellfish tea tonight – and still have enough eggs to swap for a bag of flour. Will you look after the children while I prepare tea, Hubert?"

"That sounds wonderful, Gisela. You seem to have brought us good luck."

The children decided to look for more dandelion leaves and eggs, although Azgoose was sure there were no more eggs to collect.

"Why don't you have a look around and see if you can find a four-leafed clover," she suggested to them. "The four-leaf is rare, but if you can find one, it's said to bring good luck. It might help your father and Bert fill their fishing nets."

While Hubert and the children searched in earnest for a four-leafed clover, Azgoose made her second meal of the day. It wasn't a large meal, but there was enough for the children as well as a little for the four adults.

Big Stan was rather worried about the children, as well as himself, eating dandelion leaves. However, Azgoose assured him that they were very nourishing and full of vitamins. Everyone except Bert decided to give the leaves a try and like them or not, they ate the lot.

Hubert again helped Azgoose with the washing up. This time she washed and he wiped. "I can't believe I've stayed awake all day today without nodding off," he confided to her, as he set to work with his drying cloth. "It must be the excitement of your arrival. Big Stan's wife died when Harriette was born. His mother used to look after the Harries while Big Stan took Young Stan with him to work. When his mother died, I used to look after the Harries. Trouble was I kept falling asleep – don't seem to be able to stop myself. Stan was worried that the children would come to harm while I was in 'the land of nod'. Now the older boy stays home to look after the other two.

"I used to have a herd of goats. We ate a few of them at the start of the famine. No one expected it to go on for so long. I lost more when thieves crept up from the village a couple of times and stole them. Can't blame them in a way. Their kids were starving too. The king's men took everything, they even took the vegetables from out of the gardens. Pulled up the carrots before they were fully grown and took the lot!

"I've only got the old nanny left now. I've had her for so long it would break my heart to kill her for a few meals of roast goat. If we ate nanny there would be no more milk. So I understand why you don't want to kill one of your geese. We keep the old nanny well hidden, on top of the cliff. Old she might be, but she still gives us a nice drop of milk each morning. There's a little grassy patch up there and I pick grass from here too so she's well fed – well fed until the poisonous vine reaches us here, that is.

"Steps were carved into the cliff long ago – so long ago nobody knows who or when it was done. We've let bushes grow in front of the steps, but if anyone thought we still had the old nanny they wouldn't take too long to find her."

"I'd like to see the view from the cliff-top," Azgoose put in.

"The steps are very steep." Hubert looked concerned. "I'd be afraid you might slip."

"Oh, I'm quite sure-footed," Azgoose replied, although the memory of falling off her broom handle flashed across her mind as she spoke.

"We'll see." Hubert had no intention of allowing Azgoose to risk walking up the steps.

Azgoose fell asleep in the rocking chair. Everyone must have trod softly around her because she did not wake till first light when she heard Big Stan pumping water at the kitchen sink.

Her limbs ached as she stretched, but she was feeling better as each new day arrived. She had uttered some healing words and waved her wand over her injured leg the previous day. The wound was healing nicely and another good night's sleep had done her a power of good.

She greeted Big Stan, gulped down the mug of water he offered her, picked up the basket and made her way outside.

She returned with a basket full of eggs. She kept back seven – one each – and gave the rest to Big Stan in the hope that he could trade them for flour. Hubert brought some milk. They took a mug each and left the rest for the children.

Big Stan and Bert were soon on their way. Hubert stayed behind to help Azgoose. He lit the fire ready for her to bake the bread she was kneading. This morning, with Hubert around, she did not have the chance to use her wand. She was a bit worried about how her bread would turn out without magic, but the children were delighted to have a boiled egg and home-made bread breakfast again – so was Hubert.

The other two men returned sooner than expected, bringing with them a sack of flour.

"Wonderful," beamed Azgoose. "If we get any more eggs tomorrow I'll bake a cake."

"We saw a large fishing trawler and rowed over. They were taking fish to Barrmen. Said they'd caught them miles away. We asked if they would trade a few cod for some eggs. Thought it was a joke, a couple of fishermen trying to trade eggs for fish. They wouldn't trade, said they'd get a better price in Barrden." Bert scowled.

"Well at least we've got some flour and we'll be eating bread for a while!" Big Stan clapped Bert on the shoulder.

Bert nodded his agreement and half smiled at his comrade.

The two fishermen did not stay long. They were due to set off for Barrden, but with few fish in their little boat. They both knew they would suffer the whip unless they could catch more fish on their journey. Nevertheless, with a hardboiled egg and lump of grey bread to take with them, they departed in better humour than they had for a long time.

CHAPTER 3 - THE STORY TELLER

Azgoose's days in the little settlement, which she now knew was called Grey Seal Bay, grew into a routine. Each morning, Big Stan and Bert would go out fishing. Sometimes, Little Stan would go with them. Hubert milked the nanny goat and Azgoose prepared breakfast.

She cared for the children, cooked and kept the little house clean. Whenever it was safe to use her wand without Hubert or the children seeing her, she cast spells to make her workload lighter. Of course Azgoose's main objective was to make her way back to Avalon, as soon as she felt ready. But the thought of leaving the children without any food made her decision to leave more difficult.

While she was busy, Hubert kept the children occupied by telling them stories. If it was chilly, he sat in her rocking chair in the living room-cum-kitchen. If the weather was fine, he sat on the verandah. If he sat on the verandah, Azgoose kept the door open so that she could hear his every word. The children always sat around the storyteller, listening attentively to the tale he had to tell.

Hubert always started his tale in the same way. "This is your story. The story of the people who lived here before us, but you must not repeat what I tell you. King Rabbart of Barrmin does not want any of our people, the Naroons, to remember our history. But we must honour our ancestors by remembering our true identity. The land in which we live was once called Naroo and we are the Naroons. We may not be able to speak of our history, however we must carry our stories in our hearts and minds."

The children would nod solemnly. They were already in awe of the king, of whom they had heard so much. They knew that their father, Bert and Hubert lived in dread of the king.

"Once upon a time, the land we now know as Barrmin was made up of many different countries, each ruled by different tribes. We lived in the land known as Naroo. We were bordered on one side by a country called Ranoo and on the other by Garoo. Naroo, Ranoo and Garoo all lay between the granite cliffs that border the sea and a much larger country, called Kandoor. Naroo grew onions, turnips, potatoes and carrots, and we had our own flag – a white background with a large basket of vegetables embroidered on it. One of my old friends in the village still has a flag hidden away. If the Barrmen found our flag they would burn it. We were a peaceful country and did not have an army, so when the Barrmen came and claimed our land we had no choice but to surrender.

"Ranoo was famous for its orchards. An apple tree, with an abundance of fruit, was painted on their flag, although they grew pears and plums too. The Garoons bred donkeys and their flag bore the image of a Jack and Jenny.

"As for Kandoor, well, it was a much bigger country and I think they did a bit of everything, so I suppose their flag had a bit of everything painted on it. On the other side of Kandoor was the magical land of Zanadoo."

Azgoose's ears always pricked up when she heard of the magical country of Zanadoo. But whenever she interrupted and asked Hubert what was magical about it, he told her he could not remember.

"The stories were passed down by my father to me and by his father before him. I've never been as far as Zanadoo, but I do remember being told that it was a magical place," the old gentleman apologised.

"I've never travelled further inland than the village and I doubt my father or grandfather ventured any further," he admitted. "I have travelled by sea though. This little beach belonged to Naroo. There's not many beaches in the North so the Naroons were proud of it. We used to travel up and down the coast selling our fish. We never went any further than Barrden, the capital city of Barrmin. We never needed to. Our boat was always full of fish – big fish – we threw the little ones back to let them grow. We always got the best prices in the big city. We earned enough to buy a few of the wares from the traders who filled the Barrden harbour. Ships from many different lands sailed to Barrden to sell their wares. We saw all kinds of people – some had dark skin almost as black as soot, whilst others had skin whiter than my beard, with silvery hair and eyes so pale a grey that you could barely see them. We used to see the fine lords and ladies looking at what the merchants had to offer – fine silk, sweet wine or trinkets from faraway places. Once, I even saw the old king, Rabbart's grandfather, boarding his boat…" And so Hubert began another tale.

"Barrden is a big city now and it continues to grow, though once upon a time it was just plain countryside by the sea. There was a long beach and lots of strange creatures lived there. We know that because they found the bones of giant creatures, the likes of which have never been seen by me, my father, my grandfather or his father before him."

The children gasped as Hubert described the huge creatures with jaws so wide that it could swallow a child in one gulp.

"They say there was a big explosion in the earth. Fire and sparks filled the air and the land opened up, swallowed all the massive creatures that lived there and then spat out the earth again. When the earth dried, it dried solid and formed a hard rock. There were no massive animals and no beach at Barrden – it was all gone. It was just solid rock. They built houses on the rock and there was a big mound and that was where they built the Rock Palace. Men spent hundreds of years digging tunnels and rooms beneath the Rock Palace, but the building on top is built of black marble. They say it's a dark place, cool in summer yet cold in winter. The kings of Barrmen have lived in the Rock Palace for centuries. The Barrmen were a peaceful people. There are no bays big enough for a harbour here in Naroo and no bays at all in Ranoo or Garoo. Apart from Grey Seal Bay and a couple of other smaller beaches, the land is separated from the sea by tall granite cliffs. People used to travel to Barrden to buy and sell goods. Most went by road, taking their vegetables and fruit with them. Us few fishermen, we always used our boats. We enjoyed a trip to the big city."

"If the Barrmen were such nice people, then why did they start attacking other countries and calling them their own?" Young Stan asked the question that Azgoose was just about to ask.

"Ah, that's a story for tomorrow." replied Hubert. "I'm tired now and need forty winks. Will you look after the children for a while please, Gisela?"

"Yes, of course, Hubert. I'll walk down to the beach with them and see who can build the best Rock Palace."

That evening followed the pattern that had now become the old woman's life. The men took it in turn to wash the dishes whilst Azgoose relaxed in her rocking chair. Sleep came easily each evening with dreams of returning to Avalon.

The next afternoon the children asked Hubert to tell them a story.

"You told us that the King of Barrmin won't let us call ourselves Naroons and we know his soldiers took all the vegetables we had. But yesterday, you told us that the Barrmen were peaceful people. It doesn't make sense, Hubert!" Little Stan wanted Hubert to continue the story he had told them the previous day.

Harry nodded his agreement. He too wanted to know the history of Naroo and Barrmin. Harriet never said very much and just knelt expectantly beside Hubert's chair.

"Well, this is the story…" Hubert settled in the rocking chair whilst Azgoose whipped up flour, eggs and a little bit of cream taken from the goat's milk to make a cake. The children nodded, serious expressions had set on their young faces.

"Up in the far north of this land is a mighty forest, some call it an arrborradd, but I'm not sure what the difference is. Fierce tribes of people live there. They paint their faces and wear feathers and bones in their hair. They dress in animal skins like our ancient ancestors used to and they carry weapons. I don't know if they have a real name – we just call them Savages. And it's not just fierce people, no, indeed! There are vicious creatures that live there, tall as giants and with teeth like animals. I've heard 'em called Ogres, but I'm not sure that's their proper name."

"What's a giant?" asked Young Stan.

"Giants are just like us except they're twice, well, maybe three times, as tall. Now let me get on with the story." Hubert was irritated by the interruption. "I'll tell you a story about giants one day, but let me finish this one first."

"The fierce tribes or Savages, as we call 'em, joined together and started attacking Barrmin and other countries in the North. Barrmin was the biggest of all the countries and had the only real sea port. There are other little beaches like ours, although Barrden is the only place with water deep enough to anchor a big ship. The old kings had an army and tried to protect Barrmin, however they were losing the fight. The Savages wouldn't give up. People were leaving their villages and running to Barrden for protection. Barrden's well fortified. It's got a strong castle and town walls made of granite. But as people fled their homes, the Savages took over the land. It was like it is now – a country without any food and relying on fishing, but the city was becoming overcrowded and there wasn't enough food to go round."

"There was a race of people called Trajaens, in fact, there still is a race of people called Trajaens."

Azgoose felt her backbone tingle. She listened intently. The Trajaens were the enemy of Avalon. The same people who had shot her off her broomstick, leaving her for dead in the sea.

"The Trajaens lived in boats on the sea. Now don't ask me how they came to live in boats because that's another story…"

"For another time," the children all said in unison.

"Yes, that's right, another story for another time," echoed Hubert.

"The Trajaens were looking for land that they could call home. Well, the old King Reginald, he said to them that if they helped him fight off the Savages and send them back to the arrborradd in the far north, that he would give them land on which they could settle.

"The Trajaens struck a hard bargain. If they drove the Savages back to where they came from then they wanted enough land to build houses, and to farm. They also wanted chicken, sheep and cattle. The old king had no choice except to agree to their demands. Without the help of the Trajaens then the city and Barrmin itself was doomed.

"Well, the Trajaens fought bravely and many were killed. Even with the Trajaens on the Barrmin side, the Savages were winning. There was one particular Trajaen, his name was Rabbart and he is the great-grandfather of our King Rabbart lll. He slew Savages all around him. Many of the fierce warriors from the arrborradd tried to bring him down, but they all failed. The old King Reginald was so impressed that he gave Rabbart a steel helmet with golden wings.

"Meanwhile, the city walls that surrounded the Rock Palace had started to crumble. Whilst the palace walls were solid granite the city walls were built of small stones and the townspeople knew their homes were at risk. Men on either side were dying in the war that had now gone on for over a year. It seemed as if every time a Savage met his end he was replaced by another, and the Barrmen thought they were doomed. Then one day, the Savages sent a delegation to King Reginald made up of a warrior from each of their tribes. They were like ambassadors, I suppose.

"The delegation said that the Barrmen were brave people, particularly the warrior who wore the steel helmet with golden wings. They said that their leaders wanted no more bloodshed on either side. They made an offer: if the warrior with the golden-winged helmet fought in single combat against their champion and won, then they would retreat. However, if their champion won, they would expect the Barrmen to open the gates of Barrden to them and King Reginald was to give his crown to their leader. They said that all the Barrmen and Trajaens in the capital would have to kneel to the Savages who would take ownership of Barrmin.

"Well, if the Savages won they all knew for sure that the Barrmen would be little more than slaves to them. But if they went on fighting and the Savages won, then it would make no difference.

"The Trajaen warrior who wore the helmet with the golden wings seemed invincible. The Barrmen and the Trajaens felt very confident and joked between themselves at the Savages' foolhardiness. After all, no Savage had succeeded in even wounding Rabbart so far, how could they lose? This was the chance they had all been waiting for. Little did they know that the Savages had lost so many men that they were ready to retreat anyway.

"So, the old King Reginald agreed terms with the delegation. King Reginald and the Savage leaders swore an oath to Mother Nature. They swore that if they did not adhere to the terms, Mother Nature should inflict a punishment on the party breaking them.

"It was agreed that Rabbart, the Trajaen in the winged helmet, would meet the enemy's champion outside the walls of Barrden, at sunrise the following morning. The contestants would only have two weapons each and neither would receive help from any of the onlookers.

"Next morning, Rabbart with an army of Trajaens and Barrmen behind him, marched out of the gate. He wielded his customary two swords – a long sword and a shorter one.

"The army behind him spread out so that they could watch the contest. The townspeople, including King Reginald and his family, watched from the city wall.

"The Savages came forward. Their faces were painted with brighter colours than usual and they all wore ornate feathers in their hair. They looked as if they were wearing their best clothes and ready to celebrate.

"Nevertheless, Rabbart was very confident. 'Where is your champion?' he shouted. 'This is a contest of skill, a fight to the death! It is not a competition to see who has the most colourful finery!'

"Well, a line opened up between the crowd of Savages and out marched a huge Ogre. An ugliest creature than could ever have been imagined. He was four times the size of Rabbart and with a mouth like a wolf's. The Ogre grinned and showed two rows of sharp teeth that could tear a man to pieces if they bit him. The Savages had made the creature a colourful garment. He wore the rainbow-coloured garment over one shoulder and around his loins, the same way the

Savages did. They had even given him a crown of painted feathers. He carried a club in one hand and an axe in the other – both his weapons were nearly as big as Rabbart.

"Rabbart stood awestruck. The crowd behind him groaned.

" 'What trickery is this?' demanded King Reginald. 'You cannot expect a man to fight such a creature in fair combat.'

" 'We, the people you call Savages, are made up of many tribes. Scarryman is one of our people from the Ogress tribe. He has come down from the arrborradd to fight for us,' the leader of the Savages shouted back. 'Is your champion a coward? Will he not meet our champion in combat, as you agreed yesterday? Will you deny the terms of the treaty we made yesterday? If you do, you will all be punished by Mother Nature as well as by us!'

"Before King Reginald could reply, Rabbart shouted his answer. 'I am afraid of no one and will meet your creature Scarryman in combat, but I had not expected combat with an Ogre. Will you allow me to change my weapons before meeting him in single combat?'

"There was some discussion between the Savage chieftains. 'Are you sure you are only going to change your weapons and not run to your longboat?'

" 'I am no coward. I said I would defeat your champion in single combat and so I will!' bellowed Rabbart. 'I will change my weapons and return within the hour.'

" 'Very well,' replied one of the chieftains. 'One hour and no more or we will storm the gates of Barrden.' The Savages would have been quite happy if

Rabbart and the rest of the Trajaens had run back to their longboats and sailed off, because then it would have been easier to defeat what remained of the Barrden coalition. They didn't expect Rabbart to return.

"As nearly an hour passed the Savages started to jeer and shook their fists at the Barrmen. 'Where is your champion? Where is the coward who will not face Scarryman,' they called out. The hour was nearly up and many of the Trajaens had already started to make their way back into the city, ready to make for the harbour before the Savages attacked. The Savages were preparing to advance when Rabbart marched forward. He had replaced his swords with a single spear.

"There were murmurs of surprise on both sides, but then a deathly silence fell on the crowd as Scarryman stepped forward to meet his foe in single combat. The ogre was swinging his club and axe menacingly as he walked. People said that they could hear the giant beast's footsteps echo as he approached Rabbart. Some said they could feel the ground beneath them trembling with each footstep.

"Rabbart took aim with his spear and thrust it at the ogre with all his might. The weapon hit the ogre in the neck. The ogre simply laughed as it tugged at the spear, pulled it from its neck and threw it on the ground.

"The huge beast continued forward to meet Rabbart, who darted around behind it and as he ran, he picked up the spear. The ogre was a big clumsy creature and much slower than Rabbart, who was as lithe as any athlete. He pricked the ogre in the back of its leg with his spear before it could fully turn. Then, quick as a flash, he darted away.

"As the huge creature turned to face the young man it seemed to get giddy and half stumbled. Rabbart ran around him again, this time pricking the back of its other leg.

"The ogre swung back its club only just missing young Rabbart, but as it did so, it almost fell backwards. The Barrmen and what was left of the Trajaens cheered, whilst the Savages started to look worried.

"There was a gasp from the crowd as the ugly creature dropped its axe and started rubbing the wound in its neck where the spear had first struck. The ogre seemed distracted and Rabbart took the advantage to run towards the back of its legs again. This time, he thrust the spear as hard as he could – it wasn't just a prick and blood could be seen oozing from the wound. But this time the ogre swung around, taking the spear still stuck in its leg with it. The defenceless Rabbart tried to run backwards.

"The angry beast raised its arm and swiped its heavy metal club at Rabbart. The club missed the brave young man's head by a cat's whisker, but as he ducked away from the blow, he stumbled backwards and fell. His winged helmet dropped from his head and tumbled to the ground. There was an almighty sigh from the Barrmen. The few Trajaens who were left, turned and started running back to their longboats."

The children and Azgoose listened in awestruck silence. Hubert paused, to give what might have been the end of his tale, momentum.

"The terms of the contest were if Scarryman won, those in the city would bend their knee to the Savages. The Trajaens believed if they could get into their longboats before the Savages could enter the city, then they would not be bound to the terms agreed by King Reginald. Some of those who were running for their lives were shouting insults at the king. They said he was stupid and that he and Rabbart should never have agreed to conditions laid down by the Savages. They were shouting, 'The Trajaen leaders never agreed those terms and it is time for us to go now, you fools!'

"As things turned out, it was the Trajaens who were the fools. They missed the best part of the fight. There was Rabbart on the ground, trying to get up. The ogre tried to raise its arm to strike the blow that would have killed the Barrmen champion, but as it did so it suddenly reeled and fell on its knees. It was still rubbing the wound on its neck with one hand and now it dropped the club and pulled the spear from its leg with the other. It threw the spear aside.

"Quick as a flash, Rabbart was back on his feet. He grabbed the spear and threw it into the other side of the giant creature's neck. The ogre closed its eyes. It rubbed its neck and it rubbed its legs. It fell forward, hitting the ground with its protruding wolf-like snout. The creature was dying. Rabbart climbed on to its back and pulled the spear from its neck, only to strike the creature with its sharp blade again and again.

"Finally, as the hideous creature breathed its last, the champion stepped up on to its head and stood tall. The Barrmen cheered. The last of the Trajaens could hear the cheering as they neared the harbour. They thought it was the Savages who were cheering and continued to run for their longboats.

"Meanwhile, an objection arose from the Savages who menacingly raised their weapons. They shook their weapons at the Barrmen in anger. 'There is no way that your little man could have defeated Scarryman with just one spear', they shouted. 'His spear must have been dipped in poison otherwise those cuts would have been like gnat bites to an ogre.'"

Hubert paused again.

"Well, Rabbart stood on the ogre's lifeless head, calm as you like. 'Yes,' says he. 'We were allowed two weapons each. Scarryman chose a club and an axe. I chose a spear and poison. The fight was fair and I won. You must keep your word and leave Barrmin as you promised. It is known that those who break a solemn oath made to Mother Nature will suffer dire consequences. Your families may suffer a plague or the rains may cease, causing a drought. Who knows what might happen? What we do know is that Mother Nature will punish oath breakers.'

"There were a few angry words and the Savages still stood their ground, shaking their fists at the Barrmen. The Barrmen soldiers loosened their swords and archers appeared on the castle walls.

"Now, as it happened, it had been a close, muggy sort of night and everyone had expected rain. But the rain had stayed off. Now the thunder started to rumble and lightening started to streak in the distance.

"The Savages looked worried. They turned and went and never returned.

"Some say it was Mother Nature who held off the rain that morning so the combat could take place. Some say that it was Mother Nature's anger with the Trajaens that brought forth the storm that followed. It certainly must have made the Trajaen retreat in their longboats treacherous – I'm a sailor and I won't take to the sea in a storm!"

"That's a good story," Young Stan exclaimed. "So what happened next? How did Rabbart become king? Reginald was still King of Barrmin."

"Yes, he was." Hubert nodded. "But the old king had promised the champion whatever prize he asked for and Rabbart asked for the hand of Princess Marjorie in marriage.

"The old king was shocked, so he was. He thought Rabbart would ask for land, gold or even a title, but he never expected the champion to ask to marry his daughter.

"The king was indignant at first. He told Rabbart that his daughter must marry a foreign prince, not a nomad who lived on the sea.

"Rabbart replied that the king had made a promise to him and would suffer Mother Nature's wrath if he broke his oath. What's more, once he married Marjorie he would be a prince and he would live in Barrmen and not on the sea – so how could the king object then?

"Reginald had no choice and to be honest, Marjorie was apparently very happy with the marriage. After all, Rabbart was a champion, a man to be proud of. According to the story, as it was told to me, he was a good looking man."

This time it was Azgoose who interrupted. "What happened to the Trajaens? You said the king had promised them gold and land… somewhere to live."

"Yes, he did," replied Hubert, tapping the side of his nose. "But Rabbart never forgave his kinsmen for leaving him to the mercy of that monster when they thought he had lost the fight. Nevertheless, the Trajaens had fought beside the Barrmen and they returned to remind the king of his promise. But it was Rabbart who doled out their reward. From the day he married Marjorie, Rabbart may not have been king, yet he seemed to take control.

"He gave the Trajaens gold, just as King Reginald had promised. He gave them land too. The gold wasn't as much as they had expected and the land he gave them was a small island. They still live on the island. It's called Neero. It's further north than Barrden and it's a cold barren place. Rabbart gave them a flock of sheep and a few other animals. They say the men built stone huts. The Trajaen women live there in the cold looking after their children and the livestock. The men prefer to be off on their longboats pillaging in warmer climes, or still trying to find a better place to live."

"But, I still don't understand how Rabbart became king," mused Young Stan.

"Well, that Rabbart never really was king, although he did rule – that's for sure. Apparently old King Reginald was walking on the battlements of Barrden Castle late one night and fell over the edge."

Hubert gave Azgoose a knowing nod. Azgoose returned the gesture. *Rabbart probably pushed Reginald over the wall but Hubert doesn't want to say so, in case the children ever repeat it!*

"Rabbart and Marjorie had a baby boy by then, named Rabbart, after his father," continued Hubert. "It was the boy who was really king, but Rabbart the Warrior became Regent until his son came of age. Some of the city dignitaries weren't happy with Rabbart the Warrior being Regent, but Princess Marjorie, or I 'spose she was Queen Marjorie then, seemed happy to let her husband rule."

Hubert paused again. "Some say those dignitaries who objected all came to an unexpected end – hunting accidents, falling in front of horses and carriages..." he sniffed and looked at Azgoose. Azgoose understood.

"How did Rabbart conquer the North?" This time Harry, who rarely spoke, asked the question.

"Another story..." started Hubert.

Azgoose and the children all joined in "... for another time."

CHAPTER 4 - BACK FROM BARRDEN

The two fishermen arrived home, pale and drawn. Azgoose had prepared a bowl of cold water with a little salt to clean the welts made by the whip. She knew that they would have been whipped for failing to fill their little craft with fish.

Azgoose and Hubert had already conspired to draw the children's attention away while she bathed the wounds. She would go to Hubert's house and clean Bert's wounds while Big Stan ate supper with the children. Then Bert and Hubert would take the children out to play while she dealt with the sores on Big Stan's back.

However, before she could treat Bert, the two fishermen had their own story to tell. Despite looking so drawn, they were eager to tell the tale they had heard in Barrden.

"You been telling the kids stories today, dad?" Bert asked. "Well, I gotta better one. There's been one almighty battle down the coast with the Trajaens coming off the worst."

Hubert had already sat down to eat with the family.

Azgoose froze on the spot, where she stood with a pan full of scrambled egg. Then she took a sharp intake of breath and pulled herself together. She tried to look uninterested. She spooned out the hot food onto the plates laid on the table.

"They reckoned they were defeated by magic and skulduggery." Bert continued, "There's a new community with witches and wizards who've moved into that spot in the south. The place where those Brewin people used to live."

Azgoose's hands were trembling as she dished out supper. Fortunately, nobody noticed because they were all engrossed in Bert's tale.

The three children, who usually tucked into their supper with relish, looked at Bert with eyes as wide as saucers. Hubert stared at his son too, his mouth wide open with astonishment.

Azgoose moved around the table, her movements were automatic as she hung on to Bert's every word.

"They reckon ten Trajaen ships went there, to the old Brewin place, with the intention of taking the land for themselves. They'd tried it before but got chased off by some giants. Now these new folk have moved in and joined forces with the giants to drive them away… and a good hiding they gave those villains by the sound of it! Story is that only two of the ten Trajaen boats that set out, came back."

I didn't see any giants. Azgoose didn't say a word but her mind swirled around at high speed. *They must have joined the fight after I left and helped drive off those wicked pirate-like people. Thank goodness!* Azgoose suddenly realised that her fellow Avalonians had been victorious and she let out a loud sigh.

Everyone turned to look at her.

"Are you alright, Gisela?" asked Big Stan.

"Yes, yes," replied the witch, "just trying to take it all in. Surely you don't believe in wizards and witches, do you?"

"Well," Bert continued, "there's been stories for years about ghost ships flying over the Moonlight Sea. Some people said they'd even seen them landing on the water. The Moonlight Sea is on the border of the old Brewin land."

"I always used to think that these people who claim to have seen flying ships must have had a few pints of ale beforehand," added Big Stan.

Hubert and the children continued to listen intently. Supper was forgotten.

"The Trajaens say the new people fly about on broomsticks," Bert stated.

"That's impossible!" Hubert looked at Bert, wondering whether he had found some ale earlier.

"That's what they're saying!" Big Stan supported his friend's statement. "People are getting worried in case they fly up to Barrden. We should be safe here though. We've got pointed roofs on our houses and apparently they won't land on pointed roofs."

Without realising it, Azgoose slammed the empty pan down into the sink. "Ridiculous!" she added. *If I had my broomstick I wouldn't worry about landing on a pointed roof! Besides why would I want to land on a roof when I can land on the ground?* The old woman bit her lip to stop herself telling Big Stan exactly what she thought.

Bert thought that Azgoose was commenting on the idea of flying on broomsticks. "Ridiculous it might sound, Gisela, but that's what they're saying."

The old witch decided to change the subject before she retaliated.

"Now, Bert, your dad said you had a rash on your back and I've prepared some nice cool water laced with herbs to treat it. Shall we pop over to your place and I'll bathe it for you?"

"Yes, please, Gisela. The er... er... rash is really irritating me. I'll tell you some more about these weirdos who've come to live in the South while you bathe my woun... er... rash."

As they walked to Bert's hut, which he shared with his father, the fisherman continued his story. "I can see you don't believe us, but I can only tell you what we've heard from the 'horse's mouth', so to speak. The Trajaens were in port buying cloth to mend their sails. He said that one of those wicked creatures blew flames from its lips and burnt their sails... burnt the boats too."

"But wasn't it the Trajaens who tried to invade their land?" Finally, being unable to hold her tongue any longer, she asked rather more sharply than intended.

"Oh, I don't s'pose anyone will cry for the Trajaens. Wouldn't trust that lot further than I could spit. The worry is these new people, Avalons I think they are called, might attack us!"

Avalonians! She wanted to scream. *Peaceful people minding their own business until the Trajaens attacked us!*

Bert opened the door. Azgoose had never been in the room before and looked around to see bits of wood and lots of shells strewn about the untidy hovel in which the two men lived. She looked around the room with interest, but the sight of Bert's back as he removed his shirt drew all her attention. She shuddered at the sight.

The big man sat on a wooden bench and leaned forward for the old lady to treat his wounds. It appeared as if he had been flogged so often that no stroke of the whip had been allowed to properly heal. Instead, the welts were re-opened week after week.

Azgoose hadn't really found healing herbs. She had looked for some dock leaves but the little piece of land on which they lived, between the sea and the village, was sparse of vegetation. Instead, she had picked some harmless weeds and put them in the water with the salt. The salt would sting, though it would also cleanse. Without a herbal remedy she had resolved to use her wand and magic to heal the wounds.

I won't be able to heal them completely, but I can make them less tender. Even if I could heal them completely I wouldn't be able to because they would know that I used magic.

Although she dabbed the wounds with the softest cloth she had been able to find, Bert jumped at the slightest touch. Cautiously, she drew her wand from the waistband of her skirt. She had a spell to utter and she hummed it like a tune as she scanned the fisherman's scarred back with her wand.

"What's that tune, Gisela?" asked Bert.

"Just something I must have learnt somewhere."

"My back feels much better. Those herbs you used are amazing. They've taken the sting right away."

"Good. I'm glad to hear it. They are still very red though. A swim in the sea might do you good. Seawater has very good healing powers. It certainly helped to heal my leg after…" *careful what I say here,* "… after it was injured."

"Good idea. I'll do that tomorrow when the kids have gone to bed. Big Stan should come too."

Bert put on a clean shirt free of blood stains. "What was that little song you were humming just now, Gisela? Can you sing it again?"

"I'm not sure what it was now," Azgoose lied.

As they walked back to the other hut, Bert spoke kindly to the old woman. "Sometimes, I wish your memory would return, Gisela. Then sometimes, I wish that it would never return because if it did you would leave us. We've been so lucky to have you. You've brought us food, looked after the children and kept my dad company. I know my dad always keeps smiling for the sake of the kiddies, but it's just a front. Before you came, I know how depressed he was when he was on his own – no smiles then. He worries about the future. He worries about the children, me and Big Stan. He worries about our future. Now, with those weirdos in the old Brewin land, he'll have something else to worry about."

Azgoose dearly wanted to tell Bert the truth, but she bit her lip. "Well, as long as the Barrmen keep away from the Avalonians then I'm sure they won't worry the Barrmen." She had intended sounding matter of fact, however the words she spoke came out more firmly than she had wanted.

"Avalonie... what did you call them, Gisela? I thought they were called Avalons."

"Well, whatever they're called. Now come and have your supper," she tried to smile. "It'll be cold by the time we get back."

"Cold scrambled egg, bread and dandelion leaves... a much better meal than anything we had before you were washed up on our beach!

"Thank you for bathing my back, Gisela. I can't believe the difference. Will you show dad the herbs you use to help with the healing?"

Azgoose mumbled as she hurried ahead of Bert back to Big Stan's shack.

Hubert wanted to take the children outside to play, but they wanted to stay with their father and Uncle Bert instead. They wanted to hear more stories about the Trajaens' battle with the newcomers.

In order to help his father get the children outside, Bert bolted down his meal and said he'd race the children to the beach for a paddle.

"It's a bit cold to paddle at this time of the evening," said Young Stan.

"Fair enough," agreed Bert. "I'll paddle and look for shellfish in the shallow water and you can look for shellfish in the rock pools."

Persuaded, the children set off with Bert and Hubert, leaving Azgoose with Big Stan.

"Let me take a look at your back." Gisela fetched a bowl of water, salt and weeds that she had prepared earlier.

As Big Stan leaned forward to allow his almost raw back to be tended, the witch drew her wand from her waistband. Carefully bathing the sore wounds and keeping one eye on the window, she muttered her spell as she scanned the wand over Big Stan's back.

"Sorry, what did you say?" Big Stan could hear her muttering.

"Just talking to myself. How could they do this to you? How could they beat a fisherman for not being able to make a catch because they are allowing foreigners to take the fish from the sea instead? This isn't right, Stan!"

"We all know it's not right, but what can we do? We have no army, no weapons. There are stories, bad stories about people who disobey the laws. The laws might be unfair, but we can't do anything because if we were sent to prison, or worse, who would look after our families? Hubert wouldn't be able to support them for very long. Our only hope is that King Rabbart can find a way of ridding the land of the poisonous weed that's spreading. We'll never return to normal while that weed kills all our crops and poisons the land. It's even killing people and animals. If the king doesn't find a way to destroy the bindweed then we're all doomed. I've even thought about putting the kids in the boat and setting sail somewhere... anywhere... heading south, but even that sounds too dangerous now that witches and wizards are invading!"

The old woman managed to hold her tongue. *Oh, how I wish I could tell him the truth. I'm a witch. I'm a witch. I'm a witch and proud to be a witch! That's how I can find you food and heal your back, well not completely heal your back, but at least ease the pain. I'm a witch!*

"Well that certainly does feel a lot better." Big Stan shrugged his shoulders from side to side. "You're such a clever woman, Gisela. I'm so glad we found you. I know I shouldn't say it but I'm so happy you were shipwrecked and washed up on our beach. Things were very bad before, but since you've been here it's been so much better. I can't thank you enough for all you've done for us."

The big man stood up and leaning forward, placed a gentle kiss on the ugly old lady's cheek.

Azgoose smiled. "Now you go and find Bert and the children while I get those dishes washed. When you get back and the children are in bed, I'll bathe your wounds again."

Another kiss on her other wrinkled cheek this time and Azgoose's grin widened. "Off you go," she chastised the big man.

Once out of sight she put her wand to work again. This time she used her magic to clear the dishes and do the washing up. She still kept one eye on the window though, in case someone returned early. She felt on edge and tried hard to hide her irritation.

When the men and children returned, she pretended to be asleep in the rocking chair. They trod around the house quietly and soon retired for the night.

It was a relief when everyone was in bed. It was good to be alone with her thoughts. She usually found slumber easily, but tonight she could not find the solace of sleep.

She gazed through the window at the starlit sky, trying to sort out the positive things she had heard from the negatives.

The Avalonians had won the Battle of Merlport – that was unquestionably a positive! That victory was more important than anything that had happened to her. She felt jubilant yet infuriated at the way Big Stan and Bert had spoken about her people.

Had the Avalonians sent out a search party to find her? She was sure they had, but having not found her they would have presumed her dead.

She was strong enough to return home now. She no longer had a broomstick. She had taken a look at the kitchen broom, but it had not been made with the spells needed to create a vehicle that could fly. Nevertheless, now she was back in good health she knew a spell that would get her home again. She had known for several days now that she had the strength to perform the powerful spell, which had eluded her for so long. The trouble was she could not bring herself to leave the children. It was even proving to be hard to leave Big Stan, Hubert and Bert. Bert and Big Stan had each kissed her on her cheek tonight – no other adult human had done that before. In fact, the first human to ever show her any affection was Little Stan. She had always liked Hubert. Now she even had a soft spot for Bert – the man who once would have left her on the beach to die.

What could she do? Her mind was in turmoil. She decided to delay making a decision, but a few weeks later the decision was made for her.

A Story Never To Be Told

CHAPTER 5 – BAILIFF BALDROCK

The honks of frightened geese and the sound of men swearing loudly woke the old lady with a start. Her stomach lurched. She pulled herself up out of her chair, making sure her wand was firmly positioned out of sight in her waistband and under her shawl.

Big Stan's long strides beat her to the kitchen door, but she followed him outside at a run.

"What are you doing here, Bailiff Baldrock?" bellowed Stan. "We've nothing left for you. You've taken everything we've got."

"Nothin' left? Then what's these?" A man, wearing a dirty red coat with a wide collar, pointed at the net covering the squawking geese. A group of soldiers were manoeuvring the net to make sure none of the geese escaped. Broken eggs were scattered beneath their feet.

Bailiff Baldrock had weathered skin and greasy black hair. He pulled his thin lips into a malicious grin revealing a set of brown rotting teeth. "Fine geese, just right for the king's table. This isn't all of them though, judging by the number of eggs laying about on the ground and those you barter for bags of flour. Didn't you realise that the Kurtline trader who swapped you a bag of flour for eggs last week was our friend? Didn't you think that our Kurtlinish friends would tell our Treasurer about your little deals? Where are the others, Stan?"

Bert was up now and hurried towards his friend. He pushed in front of Azgoose. The fishermen stood opposite Bailiff Baldrock with clenched fists. Hubert had also appeared. He stood with bleary eyes beside the children on the verandah.

"They're not our geese," responded Bert angrily.

"So who do they belong to then? I thought everyone else had moved out of these forsaken little hovels. Leastways that's what you've been telling me. If there are more fishermen here, then we should expect more than one boatload of fish a week, but you don't seem to be even able to manage that!"

"The geese belong to Gisela. Gisela's a goose woman who was washed up on the beach." Bert explained. "She was probably taking the geese to Barrden, but the ship she was on must have been sunk. There is no one else living in Grey Seal Bay except me, my father, Stan and his kids."

"So you must be Gisela." The bailiff pointed at Azgoose, who now stood a little way behind the fishermen. "Where do you come from, old hag?"

"I don't know. I've lost my memory," lied Azgoose. "I remember waking up on the beach and Big Stan and Bert carrying me to Stan's cabin," she stated truthfully. "I don't deny that the geese came with me although I don't think they belong to me. I remember floating along on a piece of wood and a few geese flying overhead." *That was true too.* "I can't say where I come from or where I was going, but everyone seems to think I was on my way to this place called Barrden to sell the geese – it seems the most likely explanation. I wish I could remember."

"Strange," replied the bailiff. "I've never seen you before in these parts and there's been no news of any shipwrecks either. The only shipwrecks are the Trajaen longboats, torn apart by some strange new creatures who've taken up residence down south.

"The law states that any livestock or garden produce found in Barrmin must be reported to the local bailiff for onward reporting to the Treasurer," the unpleasant man continued.

"I've always thought the law only referred to people living in Barrmin," answered Stan. "Gisela doesn't live here and the geese don't belong to us. We've been expecting someone to come looking for her. People somewhere will be expecting her home by now and will start sending other boats to look for the one that she was on. Either someone will come and find her or her memory will return. In any case, whoever owns the geese will want to know what's happened to them – that's why we didn't dare kill one for dinner!"

Bailiff Baldrock ignored Stan. "Load that lot into the cages, lads," he ordered the soldiers.

A donkey stood in the narrow entrance of the path that led to the neighbouring village. Cages were tied over the donkey's back. The soldiers started to take the geese from under the net and put them in the cages.

Bert started forward with clenched fists raised, but Big Stan held him back. Azgoose stood to his side and pulled on his arm in a similar effort to stop him.

"Let them take the geese," she whispered. "Don't get yourselves in more trouble for my sake."

"It's not just for your sake," mumbled Bert, but he knew he could do nothing so he stayed where he was. "It's the way they come and take everything that doesn't belong to them. None of the bailiffs look as if they go short of food and we know the soldiers don't."

"Search the other hovels, lads," ordered Bailiff Baldrock, "and while you're at it, find that bag of flour too. They're the king's geese now so the eggs they laid are his too. Therefore, the flour they traded for the king's goose eggs rightfully belongs to us... I mean belongs to the king."

This time it was Stan who started forward, only to be held back by Bert.

"We don't know who the geese belong to," Stan spoke angrily. "Whoever owns them might reclaim them one day. When Gisela gets her memory back she will want to go home and then she'll have to explain what happened to the flock she was looking after!" He was more or less repeating what Bert had said.

"In that case, the rightful owner will have to make his case to King Rabbart. I can't see the king being willing to give them back though. As it is, you can make your explanations to the king in person because this time you're going to have to meet him face to face. Each week, you two have got away with failing to bring your boatload of fish to Barrmin. Once a week is all we ask, yet you let us down week after week."

"But there are no fish in the sea!" Bert started to protest.

"Ha ha! Hear that lads? No fish in the sea." Bailiff Baldrock pretended to laugh. The soldiers, although obeying his orders, failed to see the joke and remained straight faced.

A small group of village people had followed the bailiff and the soldiers up the pathway to find out what was going on. More were joining them. The villagers stood at the entrance in the granite rocks watching the soldiers secure the cages. The poor donkey was now overloaded with boxes of geese.

The villagers joined in Bert and Stan's protest.

"You've let the big foreign trawlers take all the fish from the sea!"

"You've taken all our vegetables! You destroyed the plants so we cannot grow more!" the villagers' shouts echoed those of the fishermen.

"Can't you see we're starving?" the villagers cried.

Bailiff Baldrock had the protection of the Barrmin soldiers so the growing angry mob didn't bother him. In fact, he looked as if he were enjoying the hopeless remonstration. He knew there was nothing they could do whilst he was protected by strong, well-fed soldiers. The soldiers might not like him, but it was their duty to defend him.

"All livestock in Grey Seal Bay should have been reported to me," he stated formally, "for onward reporting to the King's Treasurer. You, Bert and you, Stan, have failed week after week to bring a full load of fish to Barrmin. You also failed to report these geese. The Treasurer orders you therefore to attend the king's court at the end of next week for sentence. Bring that old hag with you – she'll have some explaining to do too. A foreigner cannot enter Barrmin without permission."

"She was shipwrecked..." Bert and Stan both started, but Azgoose cut in.

"I will be there, sir. Although I will be able to tell the good king little because I remember nothing."

Baldrock laughed.

"We'll worry about meeting the king when the time comes," she whispered to Bert and Stan, who she could see were finding it difficult to hold their tempers. Both men had clenched fists and clenched jaws.

"Arrive on Friday morning, but be prepared to stay longer. His majesty is out of town. The king's visiting those 'weirdos' who've moved in down south and no one's sure when he'll be back.

"He turned towards the angry mob from the village. "The 'weirdos' down south think they know how to stop the weed spreading. If they can do that we'll happily sell you more seeds and plants so you can grow your own vegetables again."

The comments did not seem to appease the mob.

"If you had taken more care when you took them or saved us some plants we could use as seeds, we wouldn't need to buy anything from you," one called out. His companions agreed. However, they stayed where they were. Nobody wanted a skirmish with fit and armed soldiers.

Some of the soldiers had been searching the little houses within the hamlet. On each occasion they came out shaking their heads – no hidden geese, no hidden food. The exception of course was Big Stan's, where the sack of flour they had traded for eggs was stored in the kitchen. Now one of the soldiers came out on the verandah and called to the bailiff. He lifted a sack with just a little flour left in the bottom. "Here it is, Baldrock!"

"Right, well we'll be off then." A genuine smile swept over Baldrock's mean face. He called the soldiers who escorted him together for their return journey. The villagers stood aside, making a path for the departing bailiff and his men. The king's men marched down the narrow pathway with the donkey and the cages bringing up the rear. The villagers jeered at the procession.

However, just as the overloaded donkey was about to enter the little pathway, which had a tall granite cliff on either side, it stumbled and fell. The cages fell off the poor animal's back and seemed to fly open even before crashing onto the hard rocks beneath them.

There was such a commotion! The villagers cheered as the geese escaped the crates. The soldiers ran back, jumping into the air in an effort to catch the geese as they flew to safety. Not one goose was caught!

Azgoose had moved away from Bert and Stan. With her left hand she had pulled her shawl across her face and appeared to be dabbing tears from her eyes. In fact, she was not crying at all. She was carefully concealing the wand she held in her right hand and using the shawl to cover her mouth as she muttered her spell.

Bert saw her and moved towards her. He thought the old woman was crying and put an arm around her. Azgoose quickly pushed the wand back into her waistband.

"No one's got the geese now, Gisela, look – they've all flown away." Bert was trying to comfort what he thought was a tearful old woman.

Azgoose kept her shawl around her face. She wasn't at all tearful. She was sniggering. *I don't know why I'm laughing*, she thought. *Next week I've got to face the king unless I make my way out of here and back to Avalon. I laughed too soon at the Battle of Merlport and ended up falling off my broom and getting washed up here.*

Once the commotion was over, the cursing bailiff made his way back along the path. Bert, who still had his arm around Azgoose, gently pulled her towards the house.

Surprisingly, the children were not at all frightened. They were on the verandah, still laughing and talking about the spectacle of the bailiff and soldiers chasing after the escaped geese. The villagers had followed behind, hissing and booing at the bailiff's party ahead of them.

"Dad!" called Young Stan. "We've got something to show you." He and Harry ran indoors. The others followed.

Young Stan and Harry had run into the bedroom. Now they appeared again dragging behind them what appeared to be a heavy pillow. Smiling at the onlookers, they then slid a sack of flour out of the pillowcase and onto the floor. The pair were so pleased with themselves they jumped up and down with glee. Little Harriette joined in although it wasn't clear if she understood what the amusement was about.

"They hid the flour," Hubert grinned, "their idea, not mine. The bag of flour the soldier found was the remains of that old grey stuff, the one we stopped using after we traded eggs for fresh white flour."

"And they didn't even get away with the geese!" laughed the children, as they continued to happily bounce up and down.

"Good thing I hadn't milked nanny yet," added Hubert. "If they'd seen the milk they would have known we had a goat and taken her away. Lucky escape all round today!"

Azgoose and the two fishermen were all thinking the same thing. Lucky escape today, but what about appearing in King Rabbart's court next week? Would they be so lucky then?

CHAPTER 6 - COME BACK, GRANNY

"Why's granny going to Barrden with dad and Bert?" asked Young Stan. He, the Harries and Hubert stood on the beach watching the trio set sail.

The dawn light was just cracking the grey clouds as Hubert and the children waved a fond goodbye.

"Oh, she doesn't think she's ever seen Barrden before so it will be interesting for her if she hasn't," Hubert sounded very upbeat. He was very adept at hiding his true feelings. "Or if she has been there before, maybe something might trigger her memory and she'll remember where she comes from."

"If she remembers where she comes from perhaps she'll go back there!" Young Stan sounded alarmed at the prospect.

"When will granny be back?" asked Harriette, looking concerned.

"Maybe not for a couple of days. She and your dad have some business there. She's baked us some bread with that flour you hid though and the geese have been back to lay a few more eggs – so we won't starve while she's away." Hubert tried to sound cheerful.

"But, when?" repeated Harriette, with tears in her eyes.

"Oh, it may be a few days but they'll be back all right," Hubert lied. Like the travellers, he was worried about the prospect of a jail sentence, or even worse.

The trio sat in silence as the boat drew away, contemplating their summons to court.

PART TWO:
THE KING
OF
BARRMIN

CHAPTER 7 - EDWARD THE KING-IN-WAITING

"**B**ut Daisy, you can't go back to the cave!" Prince Edward protested. "It's dangerous!"

"How long did I live there before I met you? I lived there on my own for most of my life and I didn't have two nearly grown lion cubs to protect me then!"

"You need to be here in Merlport, with me."

"Why, do you need protecting?" Daisy mocked him. "I thought the Avalonians were pretty good at protecting themselves."

"No, you know what I mean. Our house is being built and someone should be keeping an eye on what's going on in case my father sends me off on an errand or something." Edward really didn't want his fiancée to go back to the cave in the mountains.

"Yes, I'll be glad when our new home is finished," Daisy conceded in a gentle voice. "I just feel out of place here with my lion cubs. The villagers are nervous of them and afraid they will attack their livestock. Even the men building the house don't like them being around."

"The villagers love you, Daisy," pleaded the prince. "They know how you fired arrow after arrow at the Battle of Merlport, and father and I would probably not be alive now if it were not for your lion cubs. The story of how they brought down those Trajaens who attacked us has been told time and again."

"And I love the villagers," stated Daisy firmly. "That's one of the reasons I'm going home for a few days so they can have a break from worrying that one of my cubs might be around the corner. Besides, there are things I need to sort out in the cave and bring back to Merlport – to my new home in the house up here on the cliffs, away from the village."

"Can't you wait until I can come too? You'll need some help bringing whatever it is you want to bring, back."

"No and no! I want a bit of time on my own. I want to say goodbye to my old home in my own way. You need to be here to help with the building of our house and right now, you should be attending the meeting with the village elders. I wouldn't like to be in your shoes if you're late. You know what your father keeps telling you."

"What, 'Learn to be the leader you will one day be' or 'Listen and learn?' " Edward mimicked his father's deep voice. King Arthur repeated the phrases so often that Edward was fed up with hearing them.

"I was thinking of, 'Don't be late. It is not polite to keep your peers waiting,' " giggled Daisy. She put her arms around her prince who returned her embrace. After a minute or so, Daisy pulled herself away.

Edward knew it was no good arguing with her so he helped her mount her pony and waved goodbye. He took a final look at their half-built house where men were working to put on a roof, before making his way towards the village.

The view from the house would be spectacular. He could see the sea on one side and a green valley on the other. Behind the house was the Great Forest, the home of the giants and where Daisy had lived for a short time with Ursula the Mother Bear, after she was orphaned.

We'll be happy here once the house is built and Daisy can keep her lions away from the villagers and their livestock. Despite being annoyed at Daisy's persistence to visit her old home in the cave, Edward was feeling optimistic.

A cool breeze blew off the sea and he could smell the salt in the air. It rustled through the trees bringing leaves spiralling to the ground. The constant to-ing and fro-ing from the new building was forming a pathway in the cliff. *We'll have to be careful when autumn is in full swing. Those leaves will be slippery and I wouldn't want Daisy or one of the horses to slip.*

As he reached the village he could see his father ahead of him, making his way to the village tavern where the meeting was to be held. He watched the crippled man, leaning heavily on a wooden stick, labour his way to the 'Travellers Rest'. He hastened his step. It would be impolite to arrive too long after the kings and queens of Avalon.

Normally he hated meetings. He would much rather be active than sitting around a table talking, but today was different. It was the first meeting for a long time and Esmerelda would be there.

Esmerelda had recently been elected Queen of the Witches, after the death of her mother, the late Queen Elvira, at the Battle of Merlport. Most humans were uneasy in her presence, but Esmerelda had brought Edward to Avalon and she was like an older sister to him. She was a beautiful young woman with long black hair that shone and a fair complexion that showed no blemish. The young witch's eyes were usually a soft moss green, but when she was excited or angry they turned to bright emerald, often emitting sparks from them. Edward always looked forward to seeing his 'big bossy sister.'

On reaching the back room of the tavern he saw that Allarond, King of the Elves, was already sitting on the table – he was too small to use a chair. Maud, Queen of the Fairies, sat on the other end. Arthur and Edward took seats opposite Esmerelda, the new Witch Queen, and Merlin, the mighty sorcerer.

Edward noticed that Willy the Wood Wizard and Wormald the Wise sat in the corner of the room. It was the place where those being asked to attend to provide information usually sat. *I wonder what those two are here for,* he pondered.

It was significant that Prince Edward sat at the table with the leaders. He had proven himself to be brave and sensible at the battle of Merlport. King Arthur was lame, scarred and battle weary. His son's presence meant that he had been accepted as the future leader of the humans in Avalon.

Allarond pointed his staff at his throat to make his voice louder, on a par with a human voice. Maud did the same with her wand.

"Ah, we're all here now," Allarond looked and sounded very formal.

"What is *that*?" Edward burst out loudly in surprise. His eyes almost popped out of his head, making Esmerelda laugh out loud. Next to Allarond was a piece of parchment with a quill writing on it. No hand held the quill, which between scrawling words, replenished itself from a nearby bottle of ink.

"Erase!" ordered Allarond. Edward's words were erased from the parchment. "Still." The quill stopped writing and remained poised above the parchment.

Esmerelda was still laughing at the look of surprise on the young man's face. The Elf King gave her a hard stare as he explained what the quill was doing.

"Merlin has concocted a spell to enable the quill to keep minutes of the meeting without anyone being tasked to keep notes. The only problem is it writes everything, not just what you want it to write so I suggest we all try to keep to matters relating to the agenda. That means no amusing asides." The Elf King shifted his harsh stare from Edward to Esmerelda – the usual culprits. "We have a lot of business to get through this morning."

"Write!" commanded the Elf King and the quill made ready for work. "Agenda Item One…"

"Er… I have an additional item," King Arthur interrupted.

There was a sigh around the table. No one wanted more items to discuss. The quill became confused as it tried to write the sighs.

"Erase! Stop!" commanded Merlin, who was probably wondering if it would have been easier to write the notes of the meeting himself.

"Sorry," said Arthur, "but this is important. I have a message from King Rabbart lll of Barrmin asking us all to meet him in a few days' time."

"Well, that is important," Allarond conceded.

"Write!" he commanded the quill. "Add 'Meeting with the King of Barrmin' to the bottom of the agenda. Now, let's start again. Item One, Apologies for Absence. We all appear to be here."

"Except a representative from the giants," Merlin stated. "Willy invited them, but it seems they are not interested in meetings unless there is something specifically related to them on the agenda. They prefer to liaise with us through Willy who will receive and deliver any relevant information via the giants' forest master."

"I see, so that is why Willy is here," Allarond peered over the top of his spectacles at the wood wizard, who nodded. "And Willy is nodding his agreement," he stated for the benefit of the quill.

"Item Two, The People of the Forbidden Forest."

"How are the sick wizards and young magical children in the forest," asked Edward. He was genuinely eager to know whether the poorly folk there were improving. "Are they regaining their health?"

It was Queen Maud who answered. "The wizards, young witches, warlocks *and* the fairies and elves who survived are all progressing well. Thank you".

"I'm sorry, I didn't just mean the wizzwits," Edward put in. He could feel his father's critical eyes upon him. "Of course I am concerned about the fairies and elves too."

"We lost three fairies who were unable to survive the ordeal they suffered at the hands of the Kernans," Maud spoke sternly. "They were put in cages to look cute, like colourful birds. They were drugged to render their magical powers useless. It was the drugs, which over time, were the killers. Nobody knows how many of my kind died in Kerner before Merlin arranged their rescue."

"Much the same with the elves," Allarond added with sadness in his voice. "The caged elves all survived I'm happy to say, but there were fewer elves than fairies. It seems caged fairies were worth more than my species... I suppose fairies are prettier." The Elf King managed a weak smile towards Maud. "Of course, as you know, a few of my kind found their way to the Forbidden Forest previously. It was those elves who told us about the cruel practice of caging in the first place. All who survived are content to live in the Forbidden Forest."

Maud nodded her agreement.

"Have they accepted you as their leaders?" asked Arthur.

"There is no reason why they should," replied Allarond looking to Maud for her agreement.

"None at all," the Fairy Queen concurred.

"Maud and I are leaders of the Avalonian fairies and elves. I've no doubt that the Twydell and Kernan members of our species respect us as such, but they are not our kin. Certainly, if they wish to join our clans in the future, we would be delighted to receive them."

Maud nodded again, then for the benefit of the quill stated loudly, "Agreed."

"The three brothers, the members of the Bramble family, are all progressing," Esmerelda added. "Isaiah improves every day. He is even starting to perform magic again. The other two are not responding so quickly, but I am sure they are gradually getting better."

"And so are the children," continued Merlin. "They are eating well. Although the visiting wizards and witches are an enormous help, the poor Bramble women spend almost all of their time caring for the children. The Brambles would be unable to manage on their own.

"One young warlock, Iwan, is a bit of a handful and needs constant watching. He has the knack of creating fireballs, and what with autumn and its dry leaves on the way, we're afraid he will set the forest alight."

Despite the wizard's verbal concerns, Edward detected a look of pride on his weathered face.

"Iwan is going to be a genius," Esmerelda added with a smile. "Tannus is spending a lot of time with him. But you're right; he needs constant surveillance until he can control his power. It only takes the least upset for him to make flames appear. When Tannus is not around Brutuz and Curtuz keep a watchful eye on him and help with his training."

Edward visualised the brothers Brutuz and Curtuz – big and muscular yet kindly warlocks. He had grown up alongside them and knew how much fun it was to be in their company. For a moment, he felt quite envious of Iwan in the Forbidden Forest with his friend Tannus and the popular brothers.

"Item Three, The Human Orphans Who Were Brought to Merlport. An update please, Arthur." Allarond could be very formal when needed.

"First of all, I must say how grateful I am to the Elves of the Forbidden Forest for telling us about these poor unfortunate children. If it were not for them, we would have known nothing of the practice of putting children to work in Kernan mines. I'm happy to say that they are all well. As you know, homes were found for all of them, mainly by the families who had lost their sons in the Battle of Merlport – but there were other families too who offered to take them in. Two of those families have since moved to Arthurton taking the children with them. We'll all be travelling to

Arthurton soon so will be able to check up on them while we are there."

The other leaders looked puzzled.

"Last item on the agenda, Meeting with the King of Barrmin in Arthurton," Arthur clarified.

"Item Four, Building Work."

"All going on nicely," Arthur reported. "Willy has found some nice trees in the forest that the giants have agreed to let us cut, as long as we plant a sapling for each tree felled."

"Is that right, Willy?" asked Merlin. "Working well with the giant forest master are you?"

"Very well," responded Willy from the corner.

"Item Five, Safety of Merlport," announced Allarond.

"I'll ask Wormald to speak on this item, as I have not been here." Merlin looked at his friend who sat in the corner of the room. Wormald stood to make his report.

"I continue to work with my brethren in spell practice. We rehearse spells which stun, and even the youngest warlocks are proving to be adept in this area. Some of our older and more experienced brethren are trying to develop an ageing curse. We thought that if we could rapidly age any would-be invaders it would be easier for our human allies to cut them down."

Wormald spoke for quite a long time recounting the various spells and enchantments the wizards were working on. Edward usually found it difficult to keep awake when Wormald droned on in his usual monotonous tone. Today was different. He listened with interest to the skills his magical friends were developing – visualising muscular Trajaens standing as still as statues or turning into white-haired ancients.

"We are as well prepared as we can be, yet always open to learn about more spells that you may hear of in your travels, Merlin." The white-haired wizard finalised his report.

Next it was Arthur's turn to update leaders on the sword and archery skills practised by his humans. "Men and boys are still practising every evening, and every evening I see an improvement. Many of the villagers come to watch. The combatants are very competitive, which is no bad thing, as they always try a little bit harder when there is an audience."

"Yes, I see the admiring looks from the young ladies when Edward makes a strike on one of his friends with his wooden sword," Esmerelda grinned mischievously at her 'little brother'.

"Unnecessary remark. Erase!" Allarond commanded the quill, as he glared at the Witch Queen.

Edward bit his lip. He wanted to retaliate but decided better of it. *I won't let her goad me.*

"The blacksmiths are making more weapons," Arthur continued. "I'm pleased to say some more smiths, made homeless by the bindweed, have come over the Barrmin border. I am told that many of them wish to remain in Arthurton for the long term. I've not met them yet but hope to soon. More smiths, more men, more weapons!"

"Well, that fits in nicely with Agenda Item Six, The Building of Arthurton."

"Progressing well," Arthur was pleased. "And as I said, we may well all be visiting soon."

"Item Seven, The Bindweed in Barrmin."

"I made a detour on my way here," Merlin spoke on this item.

No wonder he looks so tired. Edward had been surprised to see how pale and drawn the leader of the wizards looked. He had not seen the old man for a while. *That explains his dirty travelling cloak, too.*

"A lot of the work has been done, thanks to Great Grandmother Bramble and her great-granddaughter Heather. They have taught Yzor, Jonathan and I the spells, however we have sworn an oath not to divulge their special kind of magic to anyone else."

"That seems very selfish," Arthur remonstrated. "Surely, the more wizzwits who can perform the spell the sooner the work will be over and done with!"

"Not even Tannus or myself know the spell to kill the bindweed," Esmerelda pointed out. "It is a very similar plant that encompasses the Forbidden Forest and which has kept generations of the Brambles safe. If it wasn't for the bindweed then humans would have entered the forest and destroyed their home. I will not press them to reveal their special magic."

Edward and his father looked grave. They were ashamed of how the magical people had been treated in Briton. Now they had found out that humans in other parts of this new land were just as ignorant and cruel.

"Well said, Esmie," Merlin continued as he watched the busy quill. "There is still bindweed in the large areas surrounding the capital city of Barrden, but most of the plants close to our border with Barrmin have been destroyed. No vegetation grows there yet – not even grass. It will take a long time for the land to recover. The thunderbirds continue to produce rain and that is very helpful, but we cannot guess how long it will take to wash away the poison that the vine has brought with it."

"Well, steady progress at any rate. Agenda Item Eight. The Bindweed in Kerner."

"That is a more difficult subject." Merlin's tiredness was apparent to all. "The weed was not so established in Kerner, as in Barrmin, thank goodness. The Bramble family are very much afraid of entering Kerner or even Twydell. With Great Grandmother Bramble and Heather working in Barrmin, that has left only me to kill the weed in Kerner while Tannus creates rain to wash away the poison in the soil. Great Grandmother and Heather returned once to visit their family and did give us a bit of help, but they are still nervous of the Kernans. I've been trying to persuade Maura and Nora to help, but so far they have both declined."

"Can't blame the Brambles. The Kernans are lucky to have us help them at all after what they did to our people," remarked Esmerelda. "I would have been tempted to seal the border between Kerner and Twydell and let them suffer the consequences. They shouldn't have used weedkiller in the first place without testing it first."

Esmerelda was still angry about the way the people of magic had been treated by the Kernans. The very thought of what had been done to them made sparks fly from her glittering emerald eyes. One spark landed on the parchment, which started to burn. Allarond moved swiftly to stamp on it, putting it out.

"Careful!" he admonished the Witch Queen.

"We'll just have to say, for the sake of the minutes, that work is ongoing."

"Agenda Item Nine. Relationships with Neighbouring Twydell."

"All going well," grinned Arthur.

94

"Rosalie is in Bowers Gifford at the moment," added Edward. "She and Derrick will live there and not in Dalton."

"A good choice," Arthur interrupted. "Gilda has been worried about her. She seems so young to be getting married – it won't be for a while yet though," he added firmly. "Bowers Gifford is a little village on the outskirts of Twydell and not as far from Merlport as Dalton would be. The royal family have a villa there. It's a marshy place by all accounts, close to the sea and the River Twyre. Frederrick keeps a garrison there in case the Trajaens decide to try another invasion, but apparently that's unlikely. There is a race of marsh people who live in the islands around the coast. The marsh people would intervene, weakening any invading army before they reached Bowers Gifford."

"Interesting," murmured Merlin. "I would very much like to visit."

"For the time being though, you have enough to do in the Forbidden Forest," snapped Maud sharply. Edward was surprised because it was unlike Maud to be so aggressive. He noticed the stern look she gave Merlin.

The wizard did not make any effort to refute Maud's remark. The Elf King progressed the Agenda.

"Agenda Item Ten. The Wedding of Prince Edward and Daisy," The Elf King beamed at Edward.

"I think that preparations are well underway. Everyone is very willing to help. Willy has obtained wood to make some tiered seating. Almost every family in the village has said they will bring a plate of something for the feast."

Edward noticed that Esmerelda's eyes had stopped flashing emerald and returned to their natural moss green. She gave him a warm smile.

"I'm afraid that I may not be able to officiate at the exchange of rings service," Merlin stated. He sounded rather disappointed.

"What?" exclaimed Arthur, "I know you are busy in Kerner and the Forbidden Forest, but could you not spare just a few days? King Frederrick of Twydell and Prince Derrick will be attending. They are bringing a marquee as we have no suitable accommodation for them here. The Twydellers are planning to stay for a few days and will be looking forward to seeing you."

"Well, I'll do my best," Merlin didn't seem hopeful. "But in my absence Wormald will preside. I hope that is all right." He gave Edward and Arthur a meaningful look.

Edward and his father turned to Wormald who bowed his head graciously.

"Wormald nods his agreement," Allarond added for the benefit of the hard-working quill.

"Thank you, Wormald, that is most kind," the prince responded politely. His father did likewise.

"The new Agenda Item Eleven. The Meeting with the King of Barrmin. Arthur, tell us your news."

"Well, despite being wary of King Rabbart, I was delighted to receive this message from him," Arthur waved a piece of parchment before reading it aloud.

" 'I would be pleased to meet you, Merlin, and the other leaders of Avalon, at the border of our two countries. I suggest two days after the full moon.' " Arthur went on to explain that it was King Rabbart's acceptance of the magical beings as his equals in Avalon that pleased him most. He said that he had made it clear at the previous meeting that Avalon was not ruled by him alone. The diverse populations in Avalon each had their own leader and the leaders all worked together in harmony.

Arthur's counterparts were also pleased. There were murmurs of approval all round. The invitation was unanimously accepted.

"Wormald, I think you should attend too," Merlin stated.

Wormald nodded sagely. "We do not know these Barrmin people Merlin and I think that we, the wizards and warlocks of Avalon, should accompany you to ensure protection in case of attack."

Trust Wormald to think of that... but he is usually right. Edward turned and smiled at the old man.

However, Arthur had already thought of the risk of meeting the well-armed Barrmen who were not normally renowned for their friendliness.

"I agree with Wormald. If wizzwits who are skilled in defensive spells will kindly join us on the trip to Arthurton then I will ask King Frederrick of Twydell to send some of his men to guard Merlport for a few days. I am sure he will help and he will be interested to know about our meeting with King Rabbart. The Twydellers used to be friendly with some of the little countries that now form Barrmin. He's advised us to be very careful of the people in the North."

"Splendid," Allarond remarked. "Will you liaise with Wormald if there is any problem with your proposed arrangements for Twydell support?"

"Of course," Arthur confirmed. Then looking at Esmerelda, asked, "Has the soothsayer in the Forbidden Forest mentioned the meeting with King Rabbart?"

However, it was Merlin who answered. "No, I'm afraid not. She has lost her powers of foresight. Hopefully she will regain them at some point in the future."

Merlin watched the quill scratch away at the parchment. He seemed to be deliberately avoiding Arthur's gaze.

"Why, what has happened to her?"

"She is pregnant," Merlin told him. "It happens sometimes, when a soothsayer is with child. In this case she is expecting twins so the strain on her is twice as would be in a normal pregnancy."

"Pregnant?" Arthur was puzzled. "But I thought you said there were no men in the Forbidden Forest? The only people who have visited the Forbidden Forest, from what I have been told, are from Avalon. So surely one of our own people must be the father. Do you know who he is?"

Edward noticed Esmerelda looking sideways at Merlin, as she pulled her hat down over her face and tried hard to suppress a giggle. Allarond and Maud glanced at each other. Allarond pretended to cough and hid his smile behind his hand whilst Maud appeared to be inspecting the table beneath her feet.

"It is I," said Merlin whose cheeks had coloured slightly, "I am the proud father of Helen-Joy's twins."

Arthur and Edward looked astonished.

Surely he's a bit old for that sort of thing. Edward looked at Esmerelda who seemed to have read his thoughts. She smiled broadly, as she placed her finger to her lips to bid him keep quiet.

Edward took the Witch Queen's silent advice.

"Erase," Allarond spoke quietly to the quill telling it what to erase and what to write. "Stop."

98

Having got over the initial shock of Merlin's news, King Arthur grabbed the wizard's hand and shook it heartily.

"Congratulations, my friend. I had no idea. Let me see, you have no other children do you?"

"No. None at all and I did not think I ever would have, nor am I likely to have any more. Therefore, I wish to spend as much time with my family as possible. I will attend the meeting with King Rabbart of course, alongside Wormald. After that, I will be spending more time in the Forbidden Forest and thus the wizards must elect a new leader."

Edward watched the smile on his father's face fade. The thought of a new leader of the wizards, after his father and Merlin had spent so many years together, was a great blow to the old king. It was also a shock to him. Edward knew that when his father passed away he would need the support of a trusted adviser himself. He wasn't sure how he would get on with Wormald. Wormald was obviously wise, but Edward did not have the same rapport with him as he did with Merlin.

"Will Helen-Joy not come to live with you here in Merlport? We could build a fine house for you and your family," the king suggested. Edward knew King Arthur was trying to hide the anguish he felt, although the concern in his voice was apparent to all.

"No. Helen-Joy has lived in the forest for a very long time. She will not leave the forest or her friends who dwell there. Nor do I wish her to do so. I must put my family first and the Forbidden Forest will be a good place in which to bring up our children.

"I will arrange a Wizzen – a meeting of all wizards," continued Merlin, "and as soon as a new leader is agreed we will announce it to you all. Fear not, my human friend, I will visit often and provide advice where and when I can."

"Thank you," said Arthur trying to smile, but his face was full of apprehension.

Allarond continued to help the quill erase some sentences and write others.

"All in Merlport will miss you Merlin," stated Maud. The leaders murmured their agreement. "Nevertheless," continued the Queen of the Fairies, "we respect your decision. Helen-Joy needs your care and attention. The children of the greatest sorcerer in the world and the most remarkable soothsayer, certainly that I have ever met, will deserve the best training their parents can give them."

Allarond, having finished monitoring what the quill had written, turned to Arthur. "We will see Merlin on our regular visits to the Forbidden Forest and will carry messages to you and Edward when needed."

Both Edward and his father thanked the leaders of the magic people.

"Any other business before we draw this meeting to a close?" Allarond did not expect any other items and was relieved when no one spoke. "Then the meeting is now closed. Thank you all for attending. Stop!" he commanded the quill, which laid itself idle on the table next to the parchment.

Now that the quill had stopped its work, Edward tried to catch Merlin's attention. Merlin usually left with Arthur for their customary, post-meeting 'jug of ale'. He caught the wizard before he reached the door.

"Will Helen-Joy not come to the wedding?" Although Edward had nothing against Wormald it was Merlin who he wanted to officiate. "Daisy and I would love to meet her."

"No. I am afraid not. She is not a young woman and needs plenty of rest. Never fear, our thoughts and blessings will be with you on the day."

Before Edward could ask any further questions the wizard hurried away, but not with Arthur. Instead, he headed off with Wormald with whom he appeared to be in deep discussion.

Esmerelda had slung her broom, which had a carrying strap attached, over her back and waited outside for Edward. She took his arm in hers and walked with him for a while. When the other leaders were out of earshot she added to Merlin's news. "He didn't tell you that Helen-Joy was one hundred and seven years old, did he?"

Esmerelda burst into laughter. Edward could tell she was enjoying the look of astonishment on his face.

"I didn't realise people so old still…" he couldn't bring himself to say, in front of Esmerelda, the thoughts that were in his mind.

"Oh seriously though," she added, "Helen-Joy is a lovely woman. She doesn't look half her age and she is really good looking. The Brambles love her and she's taken to caring for the unicorns and old pit ponies, which have also made a home in the forest."

"Are you sure she's not a witch?"

"No she's not, but there is certainly something magical about her." Esmerelda decided to change the subject. "Where is Daisy? Up at the new house?"

"I wish she was," replied Edward gloomily. "She's gone back to the cave for a few days.

Esmerelda stopped and looked at Edward, her face full of concern. "Why?" she asked.

"Oh, she says she's gone back to say goodbye to it in her own way. She wants to collect a few things while she's there, but in all honesty, I think she just wants to give the villagers a break from the lions."

The young Witch Queen nodded sagely. "Yes, I have heard a few of my sisterhood expressing concerns in case one of Daisy's pets catches them unawares. They have been practising the stunning spell too, in case of another attack by the Trajaens, but the spell would work equally well on lions."

Edward groaned. He hadn't realised the level of concern Daisy's pets had caused... or perhaps he just hadn't wanted to. The lions were always well behaved when with their mistress.

"Whilst my people and the wizards are all becoming quite adept at the stunning spell," Esmerelda continued, "what can plainfolk do to protect themselves? You have no magic, so no way of dealing with an attacking lion other than killing it."

"The lions won't hurt anyone," Edward insisted.

"Won't they? I remember seeing them maul those Trajaens, although at the time I was very happy to see them protecting you and your father."

"Well, when the house is finished, the lions will be kept away from the village then there will be nothing for anyone to worry about."

"Unless they decide to wander off when Daisy's got her back turned."

Edward sighed. Everything the Witch Queen said was true.

"Sorry, Ed," Esmerelda gave him a peck on the cheek. "I'm afraid I've got to fly." She lifted her broom off her back and mounted it. "I was going to stay at home for a few days, but now I've got to get back to the Forbidden Forest. I need to let Tannus know about the meeting with Rabbart of Barrmin. He'll want to be there. I'll just pop home to feed the cats and then I'll be off. Sorry I can't stay and chat longer. We'll see both of you in Arthurton hopefully and talk then."

"Cheerio, Esmie," Edward wasn't sure if she had heard him. She was up and away in no time. As he watched her go, a small green heart fluttered down towards him. He reached up to catch it, but Esmerelda's parting gesture dissolved in his hand.

Edward made his way back up the cliffs towards his half-finished house. *I'll go to the cave on my way to Arthurton. It's only a little out of the way so Daisy won't think I'm checking up on her. I'll ask if she wants to come with me. I'm sure she would like the opportunity to see the King of Barrmin.* The young man put a spring in his step and started to whistle.

CHAPTER 8 - THE MEETING OF KINGS

Horses whinnied and pawed the ground as they sensed others approaching. King Arthur and Merlin sat astride their mounts with an armed guard behind them. Queen Esmerelda of the Witches hovered high in the air, with King Allarond of the Elves and Queen Maud of the Fairies riding as passengers on her broomstick.

Wizzwits mingled with the humans as they waited for King Rabbart lll and his escort to arrive. There was no reason to expect confrontation other than an instinctive mistrust of the Barrmen leader. The people of magic carried seemingly innocuous weapons in case they and their human allies came under a surprise attack. Some carried brooms ready to soar into the sky if needed and all concealed their wands in hidden pockets within their flowing gowns.

The distant cloud of dust gradually grew larger as it drew nearer the border. At last, the outline of the horsemen, which had caused the dust cloud, could be seen. It was easy to spot King Rabbart and Jaeggar, his adviser, at the head of the approaching party. Both were big men, dressed in black with gleaming silver studwork on their leather clothing. However, they were so much alike that it was difficult to tell who was who until they were in clear view. Rabbart was older than Jaeggar, but a blood relationship seemed likely in their dark similarity.

The town wall of Arthurton, the new Avalonian settlement, was under construction. The wall stood no more than two hundred yards from the border. Workers downed their tools and turned to watch the meeting of kings. No one had any doubt that Rabbart should wish to thank the people of magic who were killing the deadly creeping weed, which strangled his land. Nonetheless, they felt there was more to this visit. No one expected Rabbart to be happy about a settlement being built so close to his border. The King of Barrmin was not noted for his friendliness and he was considered an enemy by the giants who lived in the Great Forest behind Arthurton.

As Rabbart lll and Jaeggar drew nearer, Arthur felt his stomach clench. Although the King of Barrmin raised his hand in greeting, Arthur's instinct told him that this was not a man to be trusted. He wondered what would happen if he died soon and the young Edward took his place on the throne. How would his son fare without Merlin close at hand to guide him? Would Rabbart try to annex the land, now known as Avalon, again? Arthur shuddered at the thought. Nevertheless, the old king took a deep breath and composed himself. He raised his hand and called out a welcome to his visitors.

The Barrmen dismounted. A soldier planted their standard firmly in the ground next to that of Avalon's. The double headed axe, dripping blood on a yellow background fluttered alongside Arthur's black bear, embroidered onto a red background.

The Barrmen and the Avalonians shook hands and exchanged pleasantries. Much appreciated mugs of ale were brought for the travellers who downed the contents in just a few gulps.

Arthur breathed a sigh of relief. *Rabbart looks friendly enough although I would never trust that man.*

"I have a present for you," Rabbart smiled towards Arthur and spread his arm towards a cart pulled by two scrawny horses. It was full of black stones. "It is called coal and is used as a fuel for fires. You need no longer worry about cutting your precious trees to keep warm."

"How on earth do you burn stones?" asked Arthur, confused.

"Let my men put some on those fires where you are cooking what looks like our lunch. Then your co-leaders can watch it burn while you and I have a private chat. After they have seen how well our coal burns, we can all parley. In the future, you may wish to buy some of this wondrous black stone from us."

"As you wish." *I'll take precautions and ask Esmerelda to find a witch to watch this stuff called coal. For all I know it could explode and take the whole of Arthurton with it. No, it won't do that whilst the Barrmen are standing nearby.*

Whilst the visitors enjoyed a second round of ale, Arthur introduced Esmerelda, Allarond and Maud to King Rabbart. Rabbart had met Merlin previously but not the other Avalonian royalty. Merlin also introduced Wormald, explaining that the aged sorcerer would probably replace him as leader of the Avalonian wizards.

"Come, take a seat while our lunch is being prepared." Arthur invited Rabbart and Jaeggar to take seats around the table in the gazebo-like tent that had been erected.

Rabbart took the opportunity to speak. "I wish to thank you, on behalf of my people, for the splendid work you have done in clearing my land of the poisonous creeping vine that has engulfed our farmland. There is still much in the middle area of my country, but I know that your magicians are gradually working their way towards the capital, along with your thunderbirds.

My land, my country – not our land or our country, Arthur mused.

"As a token of my appreciation of your help, please accept this gift, to share as you think fit." Rabbart threw a bag onto the table. He gave his hosts a superior smile as emeralds, rubies, lapis lazuli and beryl poured out of the bag.

"Our mines have started to produce valuable commodities – pretty gemstones and the black stones we call coal. We may have little food, but at least we now have the means to buy it.

"The land that has been cleared of the vine is still polluted. My town councillors report that small patches of grass have started to grow, but the animals feeding on that grass have become sick. Nevertheless, we are still hopeful that the rain your birds create will eventually wash the poison from the soil.

"Your pets are being fed on fresh fish. I have passed a law ordering no one to harm them. In fact," he added with a laugh, "I have made it known that any person trying to render harm to the giant birds will spend a holiday in the dungeons of the Rock Palace."

Esmerelda thanked Rabbart on behalf of the witches and wizards for his gift of gemstones.

"The emeralds are almost as beautiful as your eyes, my lady," commented Jaeggar. Nobody who met Esmerelda could help but notice her sparkling eyes when she became excited or enthusiastic. She was very excited to receive the gemstones.

Esmerelda blushed slightly at the unexpected compliment and murmured her thanks.

Jaeggar was a handsome man. Like his father, he adopted the Trajaen hairstyle for his dark hair – long at the back, but with the sides cut to half an inch. He had dark eyes like his father and tanned skin. Muscles bulged from beneath his leather jerkin. He was clearly a very powerful man. The only feature that marred his good looks was his expression, which was harsh and hinted at cruelty.

On several occasions Arthur caught Jaeggar, out of the corner of his eye, looking at Esmerelda. Esmerelda appeared to react by fluttering her long dark eyelashes at the Barrman. At their previous meeting the King of Barrmin and his adviser had shown a marked dislike towards the people of magic. However, Jaeggar appeared to have changed his opinion. *Is the Barrmen's attitude to wizzwits changing? Is the change due to the effort they have put in to clearing Barrmin of the creeping vine? What is Esmerelda up to? Where is Tannus?*

Merlin thanked Rabbart for protecting the thunderbirds, but added, "They are not our thunderbirds. They are free creatures who simply owed us a favour and who are in need of a new home. It is unusual for people to actually want them to create rain and a great pleasure for them to find themselves appreciated!" Merlin had grown fond of the pair since he had helped them escape the wrath of the Twydell dragons.

Arthur knew that the wizard hoped the enormous birds could find a permanent home in Barrmin where they could fly freely without fear of dragon vengeance.

He noticed that Merlin did not mention that the dragons might still be looking for the thunderbirds.

"Why don't you go and see how the black stones are burning?" Arthur asked his counterparts. "If you don't mind, I'd welcome a few minutes on my own with Rabbart."

Arthur was met with curious looks, but he knew his fellow leaders would not question his actions in public.

The co-leaders started to make their way towards the fires. All except Esmerelda and Edward, who appeared to be having an argument just outside the gazebo. Arthur approached them and overheard Edward remonstrating with the Queen of the Witches.

"Why do you keep smiling at him? If Tannus was here, Jaeggar would have been turned into a toad by now!"

"I don't need Tannus or a 'little brother' to protect me from the admiring glances of a fan. No more than you need me to protect you from all those doting girls who watch you perform your sword craft each evening," Esmerelda laughed.

"Esmie, you're leading him on…"

"Stop this!" snapped Arthur. "Act your age! Both of you!" then he whispered, "King Rabbart will hear you if you're not careful.

"By the way, where is Tannus? I thought he would be here in Arthurton with the other warlocks."

"Oh, he's pretty busy at the moment," Esmerelda gave Arthur a wide smile as she turned and made her way towards the fires. Edward tagged along beside her.

Arthur noticed Jaeggar looking around as he stood beside one of the fires. His gaze stopped when he saw Esmerelda approaching. *Oh no, I hope Edward holds his tongue. I'm sure Esmie is only amusing herself.*

Perhaps it's a good job Tannus isn't here. I can't imagine Rabbart being very happy if a jealous warlock turned his adviser into a toad... and the armed Barrmen soldiers outnumber ours.

A large black dog had followed Arthur and Rabbart into the tent earlier. It was now stretched out on the ground behind their seating. Arthur commented on the fine dog Rabbart had brought with him.

"It's not my dog," said Rabbart, "I thought it was yours. If I knew who it belonged to I would ask if I could buy it. A strong cur like that would make a good guard dog."

"I'll find out," said Arthur who would have liked to have bought the dog for himself. He sent one of his men to speak to George, the leader of the new settlement at Arthurton, to find out who owned the dog.

"So what is it you need to speak to me about that you do not wish my peers to hear?" asked Arthur, as he poured Rabbart another mug of ale. "You realise that we are joint leaders of Avalon and there is nothing about our land that should be discussed without my peers being present," he added sternly.

"Yes, of course. You have made that perfectly clear. What I wish to discuss is the possibility of a marriage between your son Edward and my eldest daughter Isla. Such a marriage would strengthen the bond between our two countries."

Arthur was taken aback. He had little knowledge of Rabbart and did not know that he had a daughter of marriageable age. "Yes, such a marriage would indeed strengthen the bond between us and I am honoured by your proposal. But I am sorry; Edward is already promised and will be married within the next two weeks."

"To whom?" demanded Rabbart, as he brought his fist down with such force that the mugs jumped up from the table, spilling their contents. For a second, the affable look on Rabbart's face turned to one of anger, but he quickly regained his composure.

"To Daisy," replied Arthur, who was rightfully concerned by Rabbart's behaviour. "The lovely fair-haired girl over there, practising archery with my men."

Rabbart turned to see a line of archers, including some of his own men, who appeared to have entered a competition.

"The girl dressed like a soldier?" Rabbart looked horrified. "Your son, a prince, is marrying a girl soldier?"

"Yes," replied Arthur firmly. "I am sure Isla would have made an admirable wife and it would have been an honour to be joined with Barrmin. But Edward and Daisy love each other. Their union has already been arranged."

"You would prefer your son to marry a commoner rather than a princess?"

"It is nothing to do with my preferences. I do not command my son. I cannot stop what has been promised. Daisy is the last of the Brewins. She and her pet lions saved my life. She is a remarkable young woman. Please do not underestimate her."

Rabbart looked back at Daisy who was carefully drawing her bow. She released an arrow that hit the bullseye. The men around her, including the Barrmen, applauded. As if on cue, Leo trotted over to his mistress and nuzzled her hand for attention.

Rabbart raised his eyebrows. Hitting the centre of the target was no mean feat for any archer – a girl archer made the achievement even more noteworthy.

The sight of a nearly fully grown lion trotting up beside her and allowing her to ruffle its shaggy mane was even more extraordinary.

"I see what you mean," said Rabbart. "That must be her pet lion."

"It's one of them. She has two. Daisy has a way with animals."

"And she obviously has a way with princes as well." Rabbart could not hide his disappointment. "Your inability to accept my daughter's hand in marriage to your son is a loss to both of us. But there are others who seek the honour of joining with the House of Barrmin."

Rabbart forced a smile as he continued, "I am disappointed, but you say this girl saved your life. I can see that you are a man of honour, Arthur, and I respect that."

Arthur was about to explain that the fact that Daisy had saved his life had nothing to do with his permission to allow Edward to marry her and that he would not force any marriage. However, he decided against any further argument. Peace with the King of Barrmin was more important.

"You are, of course, invited to the wedding. We have no grand castles in Merlport or indeed anywhere in Avalon, but it will be a merry occasion."

"Thank you, that is most kind," Rabbart managed to affect another strained smile. "Let me show you the coal. It must be burning by now." He stood up, signifying that the private talk was over.

The two kings strolled over to the fire where the coal had been laid. Rabbart politely slowed his pace so that Arthur could keep up. The black dog, tail wagging, padded along behind.

Fingers were pointing at the coal, which had been pitch black pieces of stone before being put on the fire. Now the stones were glowing red and all who stood around the fire could feel the emanating heat.

"This is incredible," one of the cooks exclaimed. "This coal stuff is burning well and lasting much longer than wood!"

"It doesn't create high flames that burn the roasts," commented another.

"Feel the heat coming from that fire." Esmerelda's eyes glowed a luminous green as she gazed in amazement at the radiant stones. "Any coven would be proud of a fire like that."

Jaeggar stared at the Witch Queen. He seemed to be fascinated by the changing shades of her green eyes.

Rabbart's earlier annoyance seemed to dissipate. He listened with satisfaction as the Avalonians admired his black stones known as coal.

Later, he and Jaeggar enjoyed partaking of the food with the Avalonian leaders, some of which had been cooked on the coal fires. The table had been laden with a splendid meal, but when finished, the table top was turned. Good food was replaced with parchment and quill. The parley had begun.

The Barrmen wanted to buy food to make up for the loss of produce they had suffered due to the contamination of their land. In exchange, they were willing to sell coal and precious stones from their mines. They watched in half astonishment and half amusement as the quill recorded the agreements being made. Deals were done and hard bargains struck during the meeting.

Much to both Arthur and Edward's annoyance, several smiles had been exchanged between Jaeggar and the Witch Queen during the meeting.

At the end of the parley, Rabbart surprised the Avalonian leaders by announcing, "My daughter is to be married in one month's time and you are all invited to the wedding."

Arthur looked mystified. Only hours earlier, the King of Barrmin had offered his daughter's hand to Edward!

Rabbart saw Arthur's puzzled expression and laughed. "I have three daughters," he explained. "Three beautiful daughters of whom I am very proud. The only woman I have ever met whose beauty compares to that of my daughters is Issyluna, my wife. Our second daughter, Delphine, is betrothed to Duke William of Vanddalasia. My wife is the only daughter of King Xargon of Vanddalasia and William is the highest ranking lord. One day, William and Delphine will rule Vanddalasia, which is a far bigger country than Avalon and Barrmin combined.

The King of Barrmin went on to tell the Avalonians about the vast kingdom that lay on the other side of the North Sea. He described it as a cold place with snowy mountains and little arable land. In the past, the Vanddals had bought supplies of meat, vegetables and fruit from Barrmin. Now, with the shortage of food in Barrmin, the Vanddals had increased their fishing. Both countries currently relied on traders from other lands to bring supplies of other commodities.

"Traders or Trajaens?" Arthur considered asking the question but decided to keep quiet.

"Yes, I remember you said at our previous meeting that you were related to the Vanddals." Arthur sat back,

115

deep in thought. "What do the Vanddals trade in return for food supplies?"

"A mixture of things," responded Rabbart blandly. "My father-in-law may be king of Vanddalasia, but it is our ministers who do the negotiating. The Vanddals are skilled fishermen, with strong vessels that can sail into the rough, cold seas further north. They bring us fish. They also have mines that bear copper and tin and they have smiths who are skilled in making weapons.

"Xargon will no doubt seek a supply of coal to keep his palace warm. Vanddalasia is a bitterly cold place. If you come to William and Delphine's wedding, you will meet him. I have no doubt he will attend the wedding of his granddaughter. I am sure that he will look forward to taking the opportunity to meet all the leaders of Avalon."

"He may wish to buy some of your salted meats," Jaeggar added. "I think it is something traders cannot supply the Vanddals with."

"I would like to think we could trade with the Vanddals," added Arthur. "We certainly look forward to meeting your father-in-law."

"And naturally, your beautiful wife and daughters," added Maud quickly.

Throughout the meeting the black dog lay on the ground inside the tent. Occasionally, it raised its head as if listening to all that was going on, then laid it back down again and went back to sleep.

George had been hovering outside the tent waiting for the meeting to finish. When he saw that it was over he caught Arthur's attention. "We have no idea who the dog belongs to. It appeared yesterday. Nobody has seen it before. Most probably it belonged to one of the families who left their homes in Twydell or Barrmin, and got lost".

Arthur would have liked the fine dog for himself. However, having upset Rabbart over the rejection of a proposed marriage of a Princess of Barrmin to Prince Edward, he thought the dog might offer some compensation.

"The dog doesn't appear to belong to anyone," he told Rabbart. "It seems to be a stray. If you want it and you think it will go with you, then take it."

I hope it prefers to stay here. Arthur would have been happy to keep the handsome dog.

Rabbart called to the dog, which pricked up its ears and padded over to him. He stroked its silky coat. The dark King of Barrmin and the vicious looking black dog seemed well suited. When the goodbyes were said, the dog followed its new owner without hesitation.

❀ ✦ ❀ ✦ ❀ ✦ ❀ ✦ ❀ ✦ ❀

The Kings and Queens of Avalon regrouped to discuss the Barrmen's visit.

"So what was the private chat about?" Queen Esmerelda of the Witches asked Arthur. "What was it that the plainfolk could not discuss in front of the wizzwits?"

"He offered the hand of his eldest daughter Isla to Edward."

"What?" Edward looked startled. "I don't care how beautiful his daughters are. I am marrying Daisy."

"Don't worry. I told him that you are promised to Daisy." Arthur knew that a marriage between Barrmin and Avalon would have been a good alliance, but he felt proud of his son's loyalty to Daisy.

117

Edward gave a sigh of relief. Esmerelda gave him a warm smile. Her eyes were the colour of moss.

"I have invited him and his family to the wedding, although I am doubtful if they will come, especially as the giants are also invited.

"However, I wish we had found out more about the House of Barrmin before he arrived. It was embarrassing inviting him to a wedding in ten days time. It was like an afterthought, which in fact it was. We never considered inviting him before and I never realised that he had any daughters. I did explain that we had no fine palaces for them to stay in, perhaps he thought that was the reason we had not invited him earlier."

"I would like to know more about him," said Maud. "He may be good looking, but I don't trust him."

"Good looking?" Edward asked, screwing up his face. Arthur and Selogon looked equally puzzled.

"From a woman's point of view, yes," confirmed Esmerelda. "Very good looking, and so is his adviser Jaeggar. That doesn't mean to say that I like either of them though. I agree with Maud. I wouldn't trust them an inch. They send cold shivers down my spine."

Edward gave an audible sigh of relief. "Jaeggar spent all afternoon looking at you. It was very unpleasant to watch!"

"Are you jealous of him, plainboy?" goaded the Witch Queen.

"Stop this!" Arthur sounded exasperated, "I don't care what they look like. In my opinion, that black dog was better looking than either of them. Now if you two have finished squabbling we'll get back to business. I will ask George to gather some of the migrants from Barrmin together. We can ask them questions about the king, his family and Barrmin so we can learn as much as we can before going to the Barrden wedding."

"Do you think Jaeggar is his son?" asked Allarond, as he sat waiting for George to gather together some of the former Barrmin inhabitants.

"Almost certainly. Probably a son born out of wedlock," Esmerelda looked unconcerned as she filed her nails. "Not only do they look alike, but they are almost telepathic. Didn't you see the looks passing between the two? They talk to each other with their eyes."

"I only saw Jaeggar looking at you," Edward responded sarcastically, but the rest of the company ignored him. "It's a good job Tannus wasn't here."

Maud ignored Edward's comment. "I wonder what his daughters look like. I wonder if they have copper skin and black hair like their father."

"None of them could be as lovely as Daisy," Edward stated firmly. "Rabbart has most likely exaggerated their beauty. They are probably all quite ugly."

George entered the tent first. He seemed a little nervous, which was unusual for him. "I've brought a few of the Barrmen and Barrwomen, but please be careful. The people from Barrmin are reluctant to talk about King Rabbart. Some suspect that he has sent spies to join us. They are afraid to say anything untoward about him, as they still have relatives in Barrmin and they are worried about repercussions."

Allarond nodded his head sagely. "Thank you, George. We will take care. Please invite the people you have brought in to meet us."

The cool evening was drawing in and the flaps on the tent had been lowered so that it formed an enclosed room. The small group of former Barrpeople entered with trepidation, but they were greeted warmly.

Arthur thanked them for coming. He explained to them that King Rabbart had invited the Avalon leaders to the wedding of his daughter Delphine to William, Duke of Vanddalasia. He said the Avalonian leaders wished to know more about the House of Barrmin. They also wanted to learn about Barrden, the capital town in which the marriage would take place, before they travelled.

"What is the climate like?" asked Maud tactfully, leading the questioning. "Will we need warm clothing or should we take our summer wear?"

"It depends on the time of year," replied one of the women. "The summer is much as it is here, but in Barrden the winters are colder. I visited the capital once in winter, when I was a child. It was bitterly cold and I was glad of a woollen coat. I'd take warm clothing if I were you, my lady."

"Thank you, I'll do just that. What is Rabbart's castle like? Is it grand?"

The men looked at each other and responded each in their own way.

"The Rock Palace is an impregnable fortress."

"It is a large castle built into a high rock. I've heard it said that many millions of years ago something called a volcano exploded. The volcano burnt itself out and is no longer dangerous. Legend has it that the castle was built into the rock whilst the earth was still warm and is now set into hard stone."

"One side overlooks the sea. The other three sides look out over the town. The views from the tallest towers must be magnificent."

"Do the princesses of Barrmin have copper skin and black hair like their father?" asked Esmerelda.

"No," replied one of the men who had recently been to Barrden to deliver Arthur's message. "His daughters take after his wife. Queen Issyluna is tall and fair like the Vanddalasians. She is said to be the most beautiful woman in the world and I can believe it. I saw her when I took your message to King Rabbart, sire. Her loveliness took my breath away, but she looked very sad.

"Rumour has it that he has imprisoned his youngest daughter because she tried to run away. I don't know if that is true, but I saw a beautiful girl with long hair, the colour of straw in sunlight, looking out of the window of a tall tower. I wondered if that was the young princess. I saw the other two girls with their mother. You would think that they were twins because they are both tall and have their mother's pale complexion and graceful countenance, but one is fair like her mother and the other has dark auburn hair. It is said that Duke William chose the second daughter rather than the eldest because he liked the unusual colour of her hair. The people of Vanddalasia are all fair."

"Why would the king's daughter want to run away?" asked Allarond.

The people from Barrmin remained silent.

Esmerelda tried another question. "Do many people from Barrmin have copper skin and black hair? I noticed that almost all of the king's escort were pale skinned like you and I."

The people looked at one another. They knew of the recent Battle of Merlport and looked anywhere rather than at the Avalon royalty. Finally, one replied.

"King Rabbart is a descendent of the Trajaens, my lady."

The response was met with a hush.

"But they must learn about Rabbart, especially if they are travelling to Barrden," the man stated firmly.

"King Rabbart's great-grandfather, Rabbart the Warrior, married the then King of Barrmin's daughter. He had fought many battles alongside the Barrmen and was a brave man. He was given the Princess Marjorie's hand in marriage, as a reward. The old king died and Rabbart the Warrior became Regent until his son became of age. His son and all kings after him have been called Rabbart."

The man continued, "The north was made up of several smaller countries, but over time the Rabbarts of Barrmin annexed those smaller countries. When I was a child the land I lived in was called Kandoor, which was one of the last to fall to the Rabbarts. The Barrmin army is strong and we had no soldiers of our own to match them. Our leaders surrendered without a fight so Kandoor became part of Barrmin. Things didn't really change much. In fact, I don't think things changed at all except that our taxes were raised. I've been Barrman rather than Kandoran almost all my life and I don't feel much different. The biggest problem has been the weedkiller-cum-fertiliser we were given to use. It bred the poisonous bindweed, but you can't blame the king for that. He would never have given it us if he knew the problem it would cause. He didn't do much to help us when the famine began though, not until he agreed to let your people destroy the weed."

And is Rabbart a good king in other ways?" Arthur asked. "Is he a brave warrior like his great-grandfather?"

There was a long silence before one man responded, "Rabbart is a shrewd man. He is a strong ruler. If his subjects obey his rule then they have nothing to fear. I like it here in Avalon. I hope the alliance of Avalon and Barrmin will be strong and that peace will prevail, but King Rabbart is not a man to fall out with. The only battle he ever lost was against the giants of the Great Forest when he tried to annex Brewin, or Avalon, as it is now called." The man tightened his lips and folded his arms to indicate that he had said enough. His comrades remained silent.

Arthur was about to dismiss them, but Allarond asked another question to make sure that the meeting did not end on such a serious note. "Tell us about the people of Vanddalasia. I am really looking forward to meeting King Xargon."

The Barrmen knew very little about the Vanddalasians except that they were skilled fishermen who often brought their catches into Barrden harbour.

"One thing I would say," added one of the women. "I've heard people here call them Vanddals, as they often get called in Barrmin. They call themselves Vanddalasians. I don't think the Vanddalasians would be happy to hear you refer to them as Vanddals."

"Thank you," replied Merlin. "I had no idea we were not referring to the people of Vanddalasia by their correct name. You may have saved us much embarrassment. This has been a very useful meeting. Thank you so much for your help."

123

"Just one more question," called out Esmerelda, as the group was leaving the tent. "Is Jaeggar related to King Rabbart?"

"He may well be," smiled the woman who had told them about the Vanddalasian name. Much to the annoyance of her comrades she added, "It is said that Rabbart has several children who look like him, but they are not the children of Queen Issyluna."

The former Barrpeople bowed and curtsied before leaving. Then they went about their business, building their new homes in Arthurton. However, they all wondered inwardly whether there had been an ulterior motive for King Rabbart's visit. They each knew the history of their own small countries that now formed part of Barrmin.

A Story Never To Be Told

CHAPTER 9 - THE HOUSE OF BARRMIN

It was a two day journey to Barrden. King Rabbart and his escort made their way across barren land. Occasionally his people came out to watch the procession. Their faces were sullen. They bowed or curtsied, as would be expected, but none cheered. The king did not care. He was a king who ruled by fear rather than love.

It was decided to spend the first night in a small village inn. The overnight stay had been arranged by his sergeant, with just a few hours notice. The innkeeper had rushed around trying the best he could to make his king's stay a comfortable one. It was well known that the king was quick to show his displeasure if arrangements were not to his liking.

The king and his adviser were given a table away from other customers. However, local people soon made themselves scarce when the king and his armed guards arrived. Rabbart and Jaeggar sat away from the guards who had taken over the vacated tables. The two spoke in hushed tones. The black dog lay a short distance away.

"It was a pity you gave them the bag of stones before that old fool, Arthur, turned down the chance for his son to marry the lovely Isla," Jaeggar remarked.

"Don't be impertinent!" Rabbart snapped. "The King of Barrmin is expected to reward those who have been of use to him. Besides, his magical friends still have a lot to do and are actually doing a good job.

Fools as they are to help us for we would not have done the same for them. The stronger your neighbour, the weaker your kingdom."

"I liked that witch," commented Jaeggar, "her eyes were fascinating. I couldn't stop looking at her."

"So I noticed," replied Rabbart dryly.

Bowls of soup arrived with loaves of fresh bread. Rabbart complained loudly that his soup was little more than water. It was a broth that had hardly any meat or vegetables.

The innkeeper tried to explain that supplies of food were short due to the poisonous bindweed that had destroyed the local crops. Despite being fully aware of the circumstances, Rabbart was not sympathetic. The king had not been in a good frame of mind throughout his journey to Avalon. He had done his best to hide his foul mood right through his visit. Since his daughter's marriage proposal had been turned down by Arthur, his temperament had worsened.

He told the innkeeper that he should have made sure he had obtained sufficient supplies to feed his sovereign ruler and demanded that he bring the next course.

"It is a pity they are saving Kerner from the vicious weed," Jaeggar dipped his bread in the watery soup.

"Kind hearted fools," Rabbart continued. "It wouldn't have taken much for us to sail over to Kerner and relieve Jeffrey and his hungry army of its stony kingdom."

"What would we do with a land full of poisonous bindweed?" asked Jaeggar.

"The bindweed may not have sealed the mines. It didn't in Barrmin. It just attacked the arable land."

The two ceased to talk as the landlord brought a roast chicken and a few carrots.

Rabbart cut a leg of chicken, bit a piece of the meaty thigh and spat it out. "This chicken is an old broiler bird. It's as tough as a boot!" he bellowed.

The landlord apologised and again tried to explain the shortage of food. Rabbart tossed the chicken leg to the black dog, which skilfully caught the bone in its mouth. "Your food is only fit for dogs," he told the landlord, as the worried man bowed low and backed away.

"I'd like to know if Jeffrey has gudgers working in his mines." Rabbart commented.

"Ah, one of our spies gave me a useful piece of information today," Jaeggar continued to chew at the other chicken leg. "She got chatting to one of Arthur's escort. Apparently the man was with Merlin when he forced Jeffrey to release the children who had been working in the Kerner mines. He told her there was talk of strong creatures taking the place of the child workers."

"Really?" Rabbart looked interested. "I'm glad at least one of our people seems to be earning her keep. When are you likely to get spies into Kerner again?"

The adviser shook his head. "It's been difficult getting anyone inside the border since we sold them the weedkiller. They don't want to trade with us and don't welcome strangers."

"Curse that interfering idiot Merlin. Why couldn't he have left the Kernans to starve? After all, Jeffrey didn't do his magical 'weirdos' a lot of good did he? Keeping the wizards in prison and shutting the little people in cages. Well, at least we got a good price for the fertiliser. They paid us more than it cost us."

129

"It cost us dearly in food," Jaeggar commented, as he gave up on the piece of chicken and threw it to the dog. The dog caught it in its mouth, dropped it on the floor, sniffed it and left it where it was.

"Look. Not even the dog is interested in this tough chicken." Jaeggar chuckled.

Rabbart ignored him. He continued to seethe with anger at the rejection of his daughter's hand in marriage. "I could have easily taken over when Arthur died. A young and inexperienced son-in-law like Edward would have relied on a strong father-in-law such as I."

"Especially with the old man's departure being hastened and Merlin out of the way," Jaeggar smiled. "My spy told me that Merlin is going to live in some forest the other side of Twydell. Apparently he has a wife there who is expecting twins."

"A lost opportunity," replied the king shaking his head. "We may have lost Edward, but don't forget, there is still Derrick of Twydell. He may be promised to Arthur's daughter, but he is not married yet. Maybe the Avalon girl could meet an unexpected end."

Jaeggar laughed.

"Have you got any more information worth sharing?" asked Rabbart.

The advisor shook his head and called the landlord to the table. He complained that the ale was weak. The innkeeper apologised, stating that there had been a shortage of the hops and barley needed to make a good brew. Jaeggar called over one of the guards and ordered him to give the innkeeper six lashes of the whip. He then demanded a jug of wine.

One of the serving maids brought a jug of the landlord's best wine. She begged that the landlord be spared the whip. The pretty girl pleaded that food supplies were scarce everywhere. With tears falling down her cheeks she said that they had tried their best to please their beloved king, but it had been very difficult at such short notice. She begged the king to be merciful.

The red wine was palatable and Jaeggar reduced the landlord's punishment to five lashes of the whip.

"How benevolent," laughed Rabbart. "Well, apart from some fair trading, one good thing to come out of today is the dog. Handsome creature isn't it?"

"It is indeed," Jaeggar nodded, as he glanced at the black dog. Its smooth coat shone and its powerful muscles rippled as it stretched out on a rug.

"I could see the disappointment in Arthur's eyes when he told me I could keep it. I think I'll call it Rover. Good name for a stray. That poor old cur Fido has had its day. It's grown too fond of Issyluna. It snapped at me the other day when I hit her."

"A dog that has lost its loyalties is no good," Jaeggar agreed. "Perhaps we could have some fun with poor old Fido and young Rover."

"We think so much alike, my son." A cruel smile passed over Rabbart's handsome face.

Next day, the party arrived at the Rock Palace in Barrden, the home of the House of Barrmin. Queen Issyluna and her daughters Isla and Delphine stood on the palace steps to welcome the king. They stood together graceful and serene, dressed in fine silks and quietly waiting for the king to approach.

The Lady Kyrsteen, Rabbart's sister was also awaiting the arrival of the king and Jaeggar. She was tall and broad, much like her brother. She had black, short-cropped hair. Her copper skin was well cared for, yet her features were hard. Nevertheless, she was still a striking woman. She had a good figure, emphasised by a fitted waistcoat studded with silver, and tight trousers. Kyrsteen rushed forward to greet Rabbart and Jaeggar in the courtyard. With their same dark colouring and black leather clothing the three looked very much alike.

"I have good news for you, brother. Robin the Hay Warden has been caught! We were not sure if you would be back today or tomorrow so I have ordered a gallows to be erected in the town square, ready for a hanging on Sunday morning. Your court will meet on Friday for his trial. After you find him guilty I thought you might like Saturday to sit him in the stocks and perhaps give him a little flogging? What do you think?

"You know my tastes admirably, sister." Rabbart dismounted and took her in his arms, kissing her warmly.

"Where is the hay warden now?" Jaeggar asked.

"He is in the Western Tower. In the deepest dungeon, from which there is no escape. I have men walking him up and down the cell constantly. He will hardly be able to mutter a coherent word at Friday's trial."

"And yet not a mark on him! I like your style, my dear sister."

Jaeggar looked up at the top of the tower overlooking them.

"Luena held at the top of the tower like a damsel in distress and the hay warden at the very bottom."

Jaeggar laughed as he strode forward and put his arm around his aunt.

Kyrsteen returned the hug and kissed Jaeggar on the cheek. Then she turned back towards the steps with Rabbart on one side and Jaeggar on the other. Issyluna and her two daughters waited patiently in the doorway.

As Rabbart approached, the three bowed their heads and curtsied. Kyrsteen simply walked on ahead with Jaeggar, ignoring them. The king released Kyrsteen's arm and turned towards his queen and princesses. He took each of them by the hand in turn and raising them to their full height, gave each a kiss on the cheek.

In the entrance hall, a servant rushed forward with tankards of ale for the king, Jaeggar and Kyrsteen. Kyrsteen and Jaeggar took their tankards and waited for Rabbart to finish greeting his queen and daughters. When the king was ready they made their way to his parlour. The black dog trotted along beside Rabbart. The queen and her daughters followed.

"Where did you get that fine dog?" asked Kyrsteen.

"It was a stray," replied Rabbart. He went on to tell his sister the story of how he was sure Arthur would have liked to have kept the dog.

As they entered the parlour, another dog got up from its comfortable basket. The dog looked similar to Rover, but it was less muscular and its once black face was turning grey. It growled at the newcomer. Rover bared his teeth and let forth a warning snarl. The older dog lowered its head and tail and backed away.

Rover stood triumphantly beside his new master, wagging his tail.

Rabbart laughed. "So the old cur has had his day." Then he turned to his sister, "What other news?"

"Issy's father sent seven boats of fish to help ease the hunger in the town. I've taken three boatloads for the palace. Soldiers need to eat. The rest is being sold in the town."

"My father sent the fish to be shared amongst the poor," the queen spoke gently and looked at her husband with pleading violet eyes.

Her answer was a punch in the stomach. Rabbart did not like his wife's interference in what he regarded as administrative matters. She half expected the blow, as Rabbart often hit her. However, he never hit her where a bruise might show and rarely hit her in front of their daughters.

Fido growled and leapt in between the queen and her husband before he could strike again. Rabbart and Jaeggar drew their swords. Their movements were so swift it seemed as if they acted in unison.

Rover growled, but seemed confused as to what side he should take.

"Get back," the queen managed to whisper an instruction to Fido, as she gasped for breath. Still bent over from the punch, she struggled to push the old dog back to its basket. Isla and Delphine came to her aid forcing Fido back while their mother, still clutching her stomach, tried to straighten herself.

"I told you that dog had lost its loyalties," Rabbart said through gritted teeth, as he and Jaeggar put their swords back in their scabbards. "We'll starve the disloyal beast and Rover and then take them down to the beach. Let them show their master which is the strongest. The poor can eat what's left of Fido's flesh when Rover's finished with him and the sea can wash away the old cur's blood."

Kyrsteen and Jaeggar raised their mugs to show their agreement to the king's suggestion, but the queen was visibly upset.

"No," cried Issyluna in a croaking voice. The poor woman was still bent over from her husband's punch, but she was determined to speak. "That dog has been faithful to you for twelve years or more. You cannot just cast him aside because you have a new pet."

"Do not tell me what I can and cannot do!"

Rabbart made to strike his wife again, but this time Delphine and Isla stepped in front of their mother to shield her. Their lovely faces were white with fear and tears filled their eyes. They knew that their father had a foul temper, although they hardly ever saw it. On the occasions that his temper flared they were sent to their rooms and neither their mother nor their servants ever spoke ill of him.

The king was visibly shocked. Not just by his daughters' actions, but because he had foolishly allowed them to see a side of himself he chose to hide whilst in their company. Rabbart seldom made mistakes. He stepped back and regained his composure. He rarely lost his temper in front of his daughters but the strain of the past few months was beginning to take its toll. His kingdom was suffering famine and his youngest daughter Luena had tried to run off with a mere hay warden. Now, the King of Avalon had turned down his offer of Isla's hand in marriage to Prince Edward, thereby thwarting his plans to take over the arable land of Avalon.

"Let us take dinner," Rabbart ordered. "We have suffered long days on the road with little to eat. The last good meal we had was in Avalon. I am tired, hungry and bad tempered."

The queen, managing to straighten herself, called the servants to lay the dining room table with the meal prepared for the king's homecoming. While they waited for dinner she and her daughters listened as Kyrsteen told her brother and Jaeggar of her triumph in catching the hay warden.

"He was hiding in the city all the time," she told them. "No wonder we could not find him anywhere on the road to Karminesque. He was still here. He had covered his hair with mud so that his blonde locks could not identify him. But one day, he was standing outside looking up at the window while Luena was leaning out. The guards had seen him there before and approached him. Once they got up close they recognised him and grabbed him.

"What a fool! If he had an ounce of sense he would have fled the city."

Isla whispered to her mother, "Except he probably really loves Lue and wanted to be near her."

Queen Issyluna responded with a "Shhhh."

Delphine looked as if she was going to say something, but the door opened. The head servant announced that dinner was ready. Delphine stayed silent.

As they followed the king, Lady Kyrsteen and Jaeggar into the dining room, Issyluna put an arm around each of her daughters. The girls looked at their mother with worried expressions on their faces.

"Please. No arguments," Issyluna whispered to her daughters.

"What news of Prince Edward?" asked Kyrsteen, as she took her place at the table. "Are we to look forward to another wedding?"

"Don't upset him again," Jaeggar cut in. "Edward is already promised. We'll tell you about it later."

Isla looked at her father expectantly, but he said nothing.

Servants rushed to fill the table. Rabbart and Jaeggar gulped down mugs of ale whilst the food was being brought in. The two were so hungry that they grabbed food from the plates before the servants had time to lay them on the table. Kyrsteen sat at the far end of the table opposite Rabbart, where in any other household the king's wife would have sat. Isla sat beside her mother and Delphine beside Jaeggar.

One plate contained a large roasted cod, which had come from the boats that King Xargon had sent to relieve the hunger in Barrden. However, Rabbart did not much like fish and having just argued with his wife about the Vanddalasian fish supplies, ordered the servants to take it away.

"I am sorry the gift my grandfather sent does not please you," Isla spoke gently.

Queen Issyluna squeezed her daughter's arm, willing her to hold her tongue.

Rabbart was surprised that his usually quiet and obedient daughter made such a remark. The ill-tempered king brought his fist down on the table and glared at his wife who sat beside him.

"Who has taught my daughters to be so disrespectful?" he demanded.

Delphine responded before Issyluna could. "No one has taught us to be disrespectful, father. We have minds of our own. We see our people starving. Aunt Kyrst has taken the food our grandfather sent to feed the poor for our table instead. Now you have turned it away. I am sorry father, but it seems so ungrateful."

The Lady Kyrsteen glared at Delphine and was about to utter a retort, but she saw Rabbart lift his hand to silence her.

"Indeed you are right, Delphine." Rabbart's face strained a smile as he tried to control the foul mood he felt. He knew that Delphine would soon be married and living in her grandfather's kingdom. He had no wish to part from his daughter on bad terms and he certainly did not want Delphine to tell her grandfather tales of an unhappy household.

"I apologise for my behaviour tonight. I am tired and disappointed. I had wished to come home and tell my beautiful daughter, Isla, that I had arranged a good marriage for her. It pains me much to tell her that Prince Edward is already promised to another. A girl who would pale into insignificance in the presence of any one of my daughters."

"I am disappointed too, father," responded Isla. "I seem so unlucky. The marriage you arranged with Prince Igor of Kurtlin seemed a good one. I never met Igor, but I would have been a dutiful wife and it would have been pleasant to have lived in a country where the sun shone every day. I was sad when the prince took ill and died. When Duke William chose my sister instead of me I was upset, but pleased for Delphine. Nonetheless, I am happy here with my mother. We all miss our sister Luena. Soon Delphine will leave us. My mother needs me."

Queen Issyluna gave a little gasp and smiled at her daughter. "You must never give up an offer of a good marriage for me, my dear. Your first duty is and always will be to your kingdom."

"Your mother is right." Rabbart knew his wife always did and said the right thing. He was trying hard to swallow his pride and hide his temper. "If an offer comes of a good marriage you must take it. I love your mother dearly and will always care for her."

Delphine and Isla, who sat diagonally opposite each other, exchanged concerned looks.

"Come, we have good food on the table when there is a shortage elsewhere. We should appreciate what is in front of us and what our cook has worked hard to prepare. Let us eat and not argue on the day of your father's homecoming." Issyluna was always the peacemaker.

Rabbart looked at her. He knew how lucky he was to have Issyluna as his queen. However badly he treated his wife, her behaviour was always impeccable. The only fault he could find in Issyluna was that she had never borne him a son. A king needed a son and heir and he constantly reminded his queen that she had failed him.

Disappointed that he did not have a legitimate son, the king was nonetheless anxious to maintain a good relationship with his daughters. He was a cunning man who knew that he could use his daughters to forge good relationships with other countries. It was always his ambition that he might, through their marriages, gain influence or even control of prosperous lands.

Soon Delphine would be married to Duke William. Whilst the princess still lived at home she was under her father's rule. This was the first time he had seen her as an outspoken woman with views of her own. Now the king was unsure where her loyalties would lie when she went to live in Vanddalasia.

Rabbart decided it was best to hold his tongue over dinner in case he lost control of his temper again. He let Jaeggar relate the story of the trip to Avalon.

Jaeggar had never known his real mother, whom he was told had died at birth, so Kyrsteen had brought him up as her own. He was as close to Kyrsteen as he was to his father. Jaeggar spoke mostly to his aunt, although the rest of the family listened intently.

Isla wanted to hear about neighbouring Avalon. While she was sad to learn that Edward was already engaged, it didn't stop her wanting to hear more about the prince and his fiancée. When Jaeggar said that Arthur had invited them all to Edward's wedding, she jumped at the chance to go.

"Father, may we attend the wedding, please? I would love to see Avalon and all those strange magical people. I would love to see Edward. If he is ugly I might not be so vexed that he turned me down."

Rabbart laughed and gave his daughter a warm smile. "I think it would be most appropriate for you to attend, Isla, my dear. Let Edward see what he has rejected and let him be not just disappointed, but truly heartbroken. His darling Daisy is a handsome wench, but she would be merely a shadow in your presence."

When Rabbart showed genuine warmth to his wife or any of his daughters, the pleasure was felt by all of them.

"We will have some fine clothes made to wear," Issyluna spoke enthusiastically. "There is no shortage of silk or velvet."

"We could each dress in the colours of Barrmin, but in a different style. Luena could come too, couldn't she? You will have forgiven her by then and released her from that locked room," the queen looked pleadingly at her husband.

Rabbart grasped his wife's wrist and pulled her nearer. He kissed her hand. "It is difficult for me to refuse you anything when you look at me with those violet eyes, more beautiful than any gemstone. But I cannot allow you to go. I will not attend and I cannot bear to think of being in this castle without you.

"Avalon is a dangerous place for me. I barely cross the border without having to watch for any sign of the giants. I do not shy away from a fight, but another battle with those monsters is the only one I would avoid.

"Kyrsteen will go with Isla. It is safer for her to attend than Jaeggar or me. I do not believe the giants would attack women. Isla and her aunt will travel by ship, which will stay in the harbour at Merlport. They will not stay overnight in Avalon, but return to the ship as soon as the wedding celebrations are over."

Issyluna gave a sigh, but did not argue. She suspected that before the end of the evening, she would have to endure another quarrel with her husband. She did not want to upset him further at this point.

"May I go, father?" asked Delphine.

Rabbart took Delphine's hand and kissed it. He now held Issyluna's hand in his left and Delphine's in his right.

"Ah, how I would love the Avalonian 'do-gooders' to envy two of my beautiful daughters. They could not fail to see the mistake they have made by rejecting a marriage with the House of Barrmin. However, although I do not believe you would come to any harm in Avalon, I cannot risk you leaving Barrden so close to your own wedding. Besides, you and your mother have many arrangements to make for the forthcoming ceremony."

"What about Luena?" asked Isla gingerly.

Issyluna sighed. This was the dreadful argument she had been expecting.

"Luena will remain under lock and key until after the hay warden has been hanged. After that, she must remain under close watch," snapped Rabbart. Without thinking he increased the grip on Issyluna's and Delphine's hands so tightly that they both winced. He released them, almost throwing their hands away. Picking up his mug he quenched his anger with ale.

The queen took a deep breath before she spoke. "Why must he hang?" she asked. "He is just a foolish young man who fell in love with a beautiful girl. He is well liked by the people of west Barrmin. Could we not simply exile him?"

Rabbart thumped the table with his fist, but it was Kyrsteen who answered. "You are such a soft-hearted fool, Issy. You would get on well with the kind-hearted idiots in Avalon! A man cannot simply run off with the daughter of the king and get away with exile. He must be put in the stocks, flogged and hanged. I've already arranged the gallows to be erected and people do love a good hanging." The dark woman sniggered at the queen's discomfort.

"Kyrst is right," Rabbart snapped. "We will talk about this later when we are alone. I forbid any more discussion on this matter while I am trying to enjoy my dinner and the company of my family."

Jaeggar tactfully changed the subject by continuing his stories about the people of Avalon. Despite the king's ill temper the family were amused to hear about a quill that wrote on its own and the Witch Queen, whose eyes flashed emerald.

"I have invited them to Delphine's wedding," Rabbart told his wife, "so you will have to find somewhere for them to stay. The witch is coming too and bringing her boyfriend. I don't think they are married, but perhaps that kind don't always wed. Merlin is also coming, but leaving his wife at home. I don't know what you will do with the little people, presumably they'll sleep in the flower bed."

Jaeggar and Kyrsteen laughed at the idea of guests sleeping among the flowers. "Will they want beds in the flower beds?" Kyrsteen quipped.

"Perhaps we should send one of the secretaries to Merlport with Kyrsteen and Isla," the queen spoke with the sense and dignity of a lady of her rank. "The secretary can make enquires as to the sleeping arrangements so that we are sure to offer the correct hospitality."

"Issy," Rabbart took his wife's hand and kissed it again, "always the perfect wife."

The king gulped down one more mug of ale, pushed his plate away to signify that dinner was over and stood. "Come Issy, I have had a long day. It is time for us to retire."

The rest of the family rose to bid the king and queen goodnight. Then they too made their way to their chambers whilst the servants cleared the table.

The two dogs had remained quiet. Rover had spent most of the evening stretched out on a rug near the fire. He too was weary from the journey. Fido had remained in his basket. As the room emptied the younger dog got up and moved towards Fido. The old dog trembled as Rover approached.

CHAPTER 10 - THE PRISONERS IN THE WESTERN TOWER

The tall stranger trod cautiously, staying within the shadow of the castle wall. His black cloak concealed him well in the midnight darkness.

Extra guards had been put on duty outside the tower. The additional guards were not only to ensure Robin's confinement, but also to make him lose heart at the sound of so many feet.

As the stranger approached the entrance, two guards crossed their spears to block his way. However, half way through their "Who goes..." the stranger pointed a finger at them, mumbled some words and the guards fell into a deep slumber.

The stranger quickly leaned one of them against the wall. A sharp tap from a short stick on the guard's shoulder made his body rigid against the wall. The other one was pulled over to a nearby bench on which he was made to appear as if he was sitting. He whispered in the ear of each that they had not seen him, they had fallen asleep on duty and best not admit their folly to anyone or they would be punished.

A group of soldiers heard nothing unusual as he moved stealthily towards a cavern, where they were throwing dice. Candlelight flickered long shadows against stone walls. Within the gloomy room the stranger seemed to merge into the wavering shadows.

The men were so engrossed in their game that they did not see him pour a phial of sleeping draught into their jug of drinking water.

Keeping close to the wall, the shadow made his way up the spiralling staircase to the top floor, where Princess Luena was imprisoned. A severe-looking woman was her only guard. She sat in a comfortable chair outside the locked room. Her chin was resting on her chest – the gaoler was already taking a nap.

The stranger relieved the woman of her keys as he whispered a sleeping charm into her ear. The woman fell into a deeper slumber.

Luena looked startled to see the oddly clad man who opened the door to the room in which she was confined.

"Shhh… I am here to help you and Robin."

"Who are you?" Luena did not know whether to trust the tall stranger, who was dressed entirely in black and wore a scarf over his face and head. All she could see were brown eyes in a pale face and a strand of long black hair. He did not sound old and he moved with the agility of a young man.

"I am a friend who has heard of your plight and wish to help you and Robin escape before it is too late. I must be quick in case the guards awake. If I am able to return on Friday night before Robin is flogged and too ill to travel, will you be ready to leave?"

"Flogged? Is that what they intend to do to him? I have seen the scaffold being put up. I thought father and aunt Kyrst would have some cruel measure in mind before they hung him. Poor Robin – and it is all my fault. It was I who asked him to take me away. His only crime was to fall in love with me."

"Why did you ask him to take you away?"

"I met him when father let mother and me go with him when he visited the provinces. Robin lived in a place known as Karminesque. Everyone there seemed so happy. I fell in love with Robin the moment I set eyes on him. He came to Barrden a couple of months ago to beg my father for help to feed the people in Karminesque, because their crops had failed and there was no food."

"I know all about the poisonous weed," interrupted the stranger. "Tell me about how you came to run away with Robin."

"Well, I didn't," sighed Luena. "My father is trying to arrange a marriage to a foreign prince for me. I don't want to live an unhappy life like my mother. Isla and I went to a school to give some kitchen leftovers to the children. We would have liked to have given them proper food, but Aunt Kyrst forbade it. Robin saw us and while Isla was talking to the children, I went over to speak to him. He wanted to ask for my help getting food to Karminesque, but when he saw how unhappy I was, he asked me what was wrong. I told him and next thing I know, he offered to meet me that evening to take me away.

"Someone must have seen us talking and told aunt Kyrst because when I went to meet him, I was followed. Father's soldiers surrounded us, but I challenged them. 'Obey me, a Princess of Barrmin, not my aunt!' I ordered. 'I am here to make a gift to the people of Karminesque. How dare you intervene?' The poor men were confused. I gave Robin a bag of jewellery and told him to take it to help buy food for the starving people. I then told the guards to escort me back to the palace, and left Robin standing there.

"When we got back to the palace, aunt Kyrst was furious. She ordered the guards to be punished. I felt very guilty because they were only doing their duty, doing what I ordered them to do!" Tears trickled from her blue eyes as a soulful cry left her lips.

"Hush. I have heard the rest of the story. You must be ready on Friday night. Do you have any dark clothes? A black dress and a black cape plus a hat or scarf to cover your golden hair? You must be unrecognisable."

"My mother and sisters are not allowed to visit me, but I can send them messages. I will ask them to bring me dark clothing. I have a mourning gown and cape and a black veil."

"Your message must not convey any mention of our plan!" The stranger spoke sharply. "If your father or your aunt have the slightest inkling of an escape, then all will fail."

"I will tell no one. I promise. I do not know who you are, but I have no other hope. I have to trust you."

"Be ready to leave late Friday night or in the early hours of Saturday morning."

The stranger left quietly, locking the door behind him and replacing the keys on the gaoler's belt. The woman stirred and he placed his hand on her head, gently adjusted the cushion on which she was resting, then sent her back into her land of dreams.

Luena watched out of the small window in her door. She mouthed a 'goodbye' and 'go with care' as she watched the stranger begin his descent down the winding stairs. He passed the ground floor where he had put a sleeping draught in the guards' drinking water, and could hear them snoring. On his way he had either avoided the other guards on duty or put them to sleep. They would wake up when they heard the next shift arriving and be sure to make themselves seem as if they had been awake and alert all night.

At last the stranger reached the lowest depths of the tower. As he crept down the last few stone steps he could hear Robin's groans from the cell below. Two men sat outside resting, enjoying a mug of ale, fresh bread and a large meaty fish. They had just finished their turn of walking the prisoner back and forth in his cell to rob him of sleep and were building up their strength for their next shift.

They were so intent on their supper that they did not see the silent stranger approach. When he pointed his short stick towards them, they simply fell asleep on the stools they were sitting on. Before entering the cell he whispered dream commands in their ears.

Inside the cell, gaolers paced on either side of the prisoner, holding him up and forcing him to walk, even though his legs were buckling beneath him. When they saw the stranger at the door they dropped Robin to the ground.

"Who are you?" asked one, before his knees bent and like his colleague, lay snoozing on the stone floor.

Robin fell too. He looked anxious and exhausted as he struggled into a kneeling position.

"Don't worry, I am a friend," said the stranger as he put the two guards into comfortable positions. If anyone checked up on them it would look as if they had decided to break from their duties and take forty winks instead. No one would guess that their slumber had been imposed.

"Who are you?" Robin repeated the gaoler's question.

"I am a friend. The gaolers have a supper of ale, bread and fish. Try to drink and eat something. You will need all your strength. The stranger fetched the meal that the two men outside the cell had been eating.

Robin gulped the ale thirstily and crammed food into his mouth.

"Slowly," advised the stranger. "If you have not eaten for a while you will make yourself sick."

"How did you get in here?" Robin asked, between mouthfuls of food. His eyes echoed the caution he felt. "How do I know this is not a trick?"

"You don't. You have no choice but to trust me. Do you know anyone else who would put your gaolers to sleep?"

"No," then after a moment's thought, "where is Luena, is she well?"

"Apart from fearing for your life, she is in good health. I have just left her."

"How did you get in here? It is impossible for an intruder to get in or out of the Western Tower!"

"Not for me," replied the stranger, "but we must be quick. If the sergeant checks up on the gaolers we are both doomed. He will wake up all the guards and I cannot play the sleeping trick on too many people at the same time.

"If I help you escape, is there somewhere safe where you and Luena can go?"

Robin looked wary. "You are Rabbart's man. You are trying to trick me into telling you if I have any friends who would be willing to hide us!"

"I am not Rabbart's man. I can understand why you are suspicious, but if you do not trust me, what other chance do you have?"

Robin sighed. "If you can help me escape there is a place in which I can find refuge, but if I tell you where it is then I put other lives in danger. You must tell me who you are before I can trust you."

"Rabbart intends to have you flogged in public, before putting you in the stocks and then hanging you. You have been found guilty before your trial is heard. He may well decide other means of torture before or after the trial. If you give him my identity then I too put others at risk."

"Are you a wizard?"asked Robin. "I have heard that Brewin, the place now known as Avalon, has been taken over by magical people. Are you one? I will never tell Rabbart whatever he does to me."

"Whoever you think I am you must trust me." As the stranger spoke, he heard footsteps on the stairs. Quick as a flash he darted through the doorway. At the bottom of the stairs he pressed himself back against the wall so that he could not be seen by anyone coming down the steps. As the sergeant placed his foot on the floor, the stranger reached out and grabbed him around the neck with one arm. With his free hand he held a short wooden stick to the man's head.

This time, the stranger stroked the man's neck and whispered in his ear. "You have checked the hay warden's cell and all is well. You must return to your room where you will become very tired. You need to put your head down for well-deserved respite. If you see any of your men asleep on your way back then have pity on them. Let them have their rest; they have worked hard and are weary. When you wake up you will remember nothing of this visit."

"You are right," mumbled the sergeant. "I am tired and I need forty winks or I'll fall asleep on the job."

"It'll do no harm," affirmed the stranger.

"No harm at all," repeated the sergeant as he turned and walked back up the stairs.

Robin watched from the floor of his cell. He shook his head. "That was incredible."

The stranger stood still.

"Quickly, tell me how you came to be in Barrden and if you have somewhere to go. You must be quick."

"I may be a fool, but I will trust you with a well-kept secret. You are my only hope. There is a land called Zanadoo. It is hidden in the mountains between Karminesque and Twydell."

"Where is Karminesque?" asked the stranger.

"It is to the west of Barrmin. It was a small kingdom before it was annexed by Rabbart's father. I was born a prince of Karminesque, but when it was certain that our land would fall to the Barrmen, my parents gave me to a family who had lost their child.

"My parents told the Barrmen soldiers that I had died. They checked the coffin of the child I replaced and believed that it was me who lay inside. I was brought up as a hay warden, but many of my people know my true identity.

"The kings and queens of Karminesque knew the secret of Zanadoo. Rabbart ll was not sure if Zanadoo was a legend or whether it was a real place. The Trajaens who made up his army tortured my parents to find out the truth. They died stating that Zanadoo was only a myth. My guardians who brought me up know where Zanadoo is, but all the paths, bar one, were sealed when Karminesque surrendered to the Barrmen. Few people know the only open path, but I am one of them.

"I saw Luena once when her father visited Karmin, the small town where I live. I fell in love with her at first sight and she with me. That was a year ago, but I have thought of her every day since. I came to Barrden recently to plead for food. All our crops have been killed by a creeping bindweed that has left the soil poisoned. I went to King Rabbart to beg for help, but he simply told me he would provide food only if we had the money to pay for it. I left trying to think of a way of persuading the king to send food to Karminesque. I was wandering around the town trying to form some sort of plan, when I saw Luena in a coach. I ran after it. She was visiting a school. She saw me watching her and came over to speak to me."

"I have heard the rest," stated the stranger who was worried in case any of the guards were waking. "Do you have anywhere to go?"

"Yes. I will take Luena to Zanadoo and we will live there," Robin stated firmly.

"Make yourself comfortable and I will put you to sleep. It will probably be only a few hours rest, but at least it will be some respite. I will do my best to return on Friday night. That is the night after your trial and before they plan to put you in the stocks and flog you. Try to keep your head clear and impress upon the court that you meant Luena no harm. But be careful, say nothing of tonight."

"I won't," promised the hay warden.

Robin took one more swig of ale before making himself as comfortable as he could on the stone floor. The stranger placed his hand on Robin's head. Robin fell into a welcome slumber. Then to safeguard himself he added, "You will adhere to my instructions, but will remember nothing of this visit until you see me again."

After returning the jug and empty plate to its original place, the stranger slipped away past the sleeping sentries and out into the darkness of the night.

A Story Never To Be Told

CHAPTER 11 - KING RABBART'S COURT

The trio said little during their journey. The waters were grey and slightly bumpy. To the west, the granite cliffs stood tall and harsh and after a time, they all looked the same. A cloudy sky and biting wind emphasised that winter was on its way.

Why am I doing this? Azgoose asked herself. *I could be gone from here and my geese with me. Now I know that Avalon is safe and free from invaders I could return. But I can't go. I can't leave Big Stan and Bert to face the consequences of my actions albeit I never intended to bring them trouble.*

I've escaped from humans before. She gave a sigh of satisfaction. *But if I go now what will happen to Big Stan and Bert? Will they suffer my punishment as well as their own if I leave them?*

I wonder why the king went to Avalon?

The group from Grey Seal Bay had discussed the subject several times since Bailiff Baldrock mentioned that the 'weirdos' had said they could rid the land of the poisonous bindweed.

I don't need to go to Barrden to find out; I could simply fly back to Avalon. Azgoose debated with herself. *No. I must stay with Big Stan and Bert. I must keep my wand well hidden. If the Barrmen know that there are magic people in Avalon, they may recognise my wand and know that I am a witch. I need to take care. Harbouring a witch could cause my friends even more trouble than they are in now.*

157

The old woman's dilemma was reflected in her face. Bert and Stan thought her anguished looks were caused by a fear of meeting the cruel King of Barrmin and the punishment he might dole out.

I will stay, she finally decided. *I can't leave my friends now. I just hope that I can return to Grey Seal Bay to care for my grandchildren again. They call me granny so I will be their grandmother. If I return!*

Hour passed hour as the little boat continued its journey. Tall ships could be seen further out at sea, but all heading for or leaving the same destination. It was almost noon when they finally arrived at the port of Barrden. The Rock Palace loomed ahead, dark and menacing against a dull sky. In contrast, the harbour was dotted with the colourful sails of the merchant ships as they were brought into port.

The port was busy with trading vessels, but the harbour master signalled the little boat away from the foreign ships that were unloading. They were guided into the outlet of a river where, with the help of a customs official, they moored up.

"Ah, the Grey Seal Bay fishermen," commented the customs officer, who wore the same dark red coat as that of Bailiff Baldrock. He looked much like Baldrock except he was stouter. The officer nodded towards Azgoose, "And that old crone must be the goose woman.

"Not much in the way of fish again this week. That's three lashes of the whip each, but we'll deal with that later after the king has sentenced you for stealing the geese and their eggs."

"But we didn't steal any geese, Bailiff Grimshaw!" protested Stan.

Azgoose touched his arm. "Let it be, Stan," she said gently. "Let me tell the king my story."

"Well, you'll be doing that today," the bailiff stated cheerfully. "King Rabbart arrived home yesterday. He doesn't usually hear the court for a day or two after his travels and when he does, it's normally first thing in the morning. Today's different. He's having an afternoon court because he's eager to sentence that Robin the Hay Warden to swing on Sunday."

"If he hasn't heard the case, then how do you know the man will hang?" asked Bert. "That's what you mean, isn't it, when you say he'll swing?"

"Because the king's sister, the Lady Kyrsteen, is already having the gallows built!" Grimshaw laughed. "The young fool tried to kidnap the Princess Luena, the king's youngest daughter." The bailiff laughed even more heartily.

"Tried to kidnap the king's daughter!" the two fishermen echoed in astonishment.

"Yep. He'll not have much time for you, the good king won't. He'll hear the case and then he'll pronounce sentence himself. There will be no jury for any of you today."

"Now that could be good for you because if the king's going to pronounce a hanging, then he might be more lenient on the other cases he hears today. On the other hand, his mood might be such that any punishment he deals out is worse.

"Better get a move on or you'll be late. As soon as the bell tolls you'll know the king is on his way. His Highness won't be happy if he has to send out a couple of his guards to look for you.

"I'll look after your boat for you. Nice little boat you got. Perhaps he'll confiscate it if you can't pay the fine, or perhaps I'll just have to take it into custody if he puts you in the clink." The bailiff's smile widened.

"You…" Bert started towards the laughing red coat, shaking his fists. Stan and Azgoose, fearing the penalty for hitting a king's official, held him back.

"Don't let him goad you," Azgoose whispered to Bert. "He's doing it on purpose to cause more trouble."

"Gisela is right," Stan helped her physically turn Bert around. "Come on mate, let's get this over and done with."

The trio made their way towards the court, but as they started off along the quay, they heard Grimshaw's voice again, "Hope to see you later. Ha ha ha!"

Bert and Stan marched ahead, anxious to be out of the reach of Grimshaw's voice, but Azgoose stopped to tie up the strings that held her shoes together. As she bent over, her shawl fell forwards covering her head and arms.

A sudden splash and yell for help made the fishermen turn around. The bailiff was in the water. He obviously couldn't swim because his arms were flailing helplessly in the dirty seawater.

"What happened?" someone shouted.

"He must have lost his footing and fallen in," someone else called out. "Quick, throw him a rope!"

A younger man in a dark red coat ran towards Grimshaw who was now coughing and spluttering filthy water. He grabbed a spare mooring rope and threw it towards the drowning man.

Azgoose stood up, took one look behind her at the distressed bailiff and then strode forwards.

"Come on lads or we'll be late. Let's not risk any more of the king's displeasure."

Despite all, Bert and Stan were smiling. "That was odd," Stan shook his head in disbelief.

"Everything's odd about this place lately," Bert followed his friend.

After weaving their way around mooring ropes on the quay and avoiding the men carrying goods from the ships, they reached Main Street. It was uphill to the court. The walk might have been interesting in other circumstances. Small, grey stone houses bordered the narrow streets, which were strewn with men, women and children begging for food.

Traders, wearing oddly fashioned garments, walked around the beggars. On occasion, they cast coins to outstretched hands. It was not just the traders' garb that was unusual. Some men had skin the colour of ebony, others brown like the Trajaens. There were also men who had skin whiter than milk and eyes so pale they could barely be seen against their light complexions. Muscular soldiers in black leather uniforms on well cared-for horses kept beggars away from the traders' goods.

Meanwhile, mules pulling carts full of various wares headed upwards towards the castle. The cartwheels rattled on the cobbled streets, but the sound was broken by the toll of the court bell.

"The king's on his way to the court. We'd better get a move on." The fishermen moved ahead quickly, but soon realised that the old woman could not keep pace.

I'd be faster than them if I could only use my wand. She grimaced.

By the time they made it to the court the building was packed. The fishermen reported to a clerk in the entrance hall who ticked their names off a roll.

"You're case number 29. The king is hearing case 23 already. He's dealing with them all very rapidly today… or rather, Lady Kyrsteen is."

The clerk called a guardsman. "Help these people make their way to the front. They're case 29 and we don't want the king losing his temper because they're late."

The guard grunted. "We don't want a display of the Lady Kyrsteen's temper either. Come on then," he indicated with his hand for the trio to follow him.

The court was full. A press of people filled the rooms. Even with the soldier pushing people aside, the way forward was not easy. Azgoose could see a large, dark-haired man sitting on a very high and ornate chair. Beside him sat a woman of similar stature and colour.

At the base of the king's throne lay a sleek black dog. It looked relaxed, its eyes closed as if it were asleep.

I suppose that's his throne and that must be his sister, Kyrsteen. It can't be the queen. Hubert said she was fair. As they drew closer she could see that the man had a stern, heartless face. He had a dark, neatly trimmed beard and dark brooding eyes. His sister had the same colouring – she could have been beautiful, but the harshness of her demeanour spoiled her good looks. As the trio grew closer they could hear the case in the process of being heard by the court.

"Six months rowing the king's galley," ordered Kyrsteen. The king nodded. The man tried to say something, but was hauled away by the guards. They dragged him back past the trio as they pushed their way forward. Azgoose could see terror in the man's eyes.

A man accused of killing a rabbit and stealing it from the King's woodland wasn't given a chance to speak. "Six lashes followed by a day in the stocks, once a month for six months," the Lady Kyrsteen snapped. "Next."

"Case number 27," called a clerk in a black court robe. A group of children aged between about 8 and 12 were brought forward by the guards.

"These urchins were found emptying the palace bins," the clerk stated.

"The boys are to be sent to work cleaning the stables for one year," snapped Kyrsteen. "The girls are to be sent to the guardhouse to scrub the stairs and the latrines."

"Er… they were only looking for leftover food…" the clerk stated.

"Do you argue with me?" The look of anger on Lady Kyrsteen's face was terrifying. The spectators could almost see the clerk tremble and expected the heartless woman to order him to be punished too. However, a sudden hush fell over the audience.

The crowds were voluntarily moving apart to make a pathway in their midst. As they did so, they pressed against the people standing at the sides of the hall. Azgoose strained her head to see what was happening. At first she could see nothing, but as the Barrmen bent low or curtsied she set eyes on the loveliest woman she had ever seen. She had fair hair pinned in spirals around her head and she wore a deep green velvet grown. She walked with a rare grace and dignity in front of two younger women. Her steps were such that it seemed as if she floated rather than walked. The two younger women were almost a mirror image of the first except that one had deep auburn hair. The blonde girl wore green, like the older woman, whilst the other wore a purple gown that was almost the same colour as her eyes.

As the women passed, the audience rose to their feet again, but as they did a ripple of applause could be heard. It started at the back of the hall and as those who had knelt stood, they too clapped their hands, so that the applause grew gradually louder. There were whispers of "Bless you," or simply, "Your Majesty," from the crowd.

"It's the queen," mumbled Bert. He fell to his knees, as did the others around him. Azgoose reluctantly copied their example. *I've never knelt to a human before, but I suppose that as I'm pretending to be human, I'd better not be the odd one out.*

The king stood and stared in disbelief as he watched the three approaching women. He had never allowed Queen Issyluna to attend court. His sister had always sat at his side on the lesser throne during council or court meetings. He and Kyrsteen's thoughts on punishment concurred whilst he had no doubt his wife's ideas would be different.

Rabbart knew his wife was loved by the people, yet even he was taken aback by this show of affection. The court echoed with applause for his wife and daughters.

As the royal ladies reached the area in front of the thrones, they each curtsied low in front of the king.

"My dear wife," Rabbart allowed his surprise to show, "what are you doing here? I know you are concerned about the trial of Robin the Hay Warden, but there is no need for you to trouble yourself. The Lady Kyrsteen and I will deal with the matter fairly and squarely. Guards, escort the Queen and the Princesses back to the palace."

The queen, however, signalled to the guards to stay where they were. The guards looked confused, as did the courtiers and clerks who sat at desks below the throne.

"My dear beloved husband," the queen's voice was almost musical, but it was also clear and carried across the hall. "I know you and the good Lady Kyrsteen, who takes my place on my throne, seek only to relieve me of the burden of the court hearings. Nevertheless, the boy Robin is accused of kidnapping my daughter and it is natural that I should wish to be here. So, I will stay.

"Please stay where you are Lady Kyrsteen. I will stand here." The queen smiled sweetly at her sister-in-law. If the smile was not genuine then the queen was well accomplished at performing it.

Kyrsteen, who had made no attempt to move from the queen's throne, glared at Queen Issyluna.

Princess Isla looked with sadness at her aunt sitting on her mother's throne. Princess Delphine, however, returned Kyrsteen's malicious glare.

Clerks hurried to bring the royal ladies chairs on which to sit, but they continued to stand.

"Er… shall we postpone cases 28 and 29, sire, and move straight to case 30, the Hay Warden case?"

"No, continue," The king ordered. He wanted time to think. It was rare for his wife to disobey him and he had no wish to argue with her in public. Added to his dilemma was the fact that his wife's father, the mighty King of Vanddalasia, was expected to attend the forthcoming wedding of his daughter Delphine to the Duke William. Vanddalasian ambassadors were in Barrden to prepare for the visit and Rabbart did not want news of a public quarrel reaching his powerful father-in-law. He had no wish to quarrel with Delphine either. One day, his second daughter might be Queen of Vanddalasia and he wanted to influence her, not alienate her.

"I don't think you finished hearing the last case," Delphine put in. "Didn't the clerk say these poor children were looking for food in the palace bins?" She smiled kindly at the children who knelt huddled together at the base of the throne. They looked at the royal ladies with wide eyes full of awe.

"Poor hungry mites, they must have been really starving to be looking for scraps in the bins." Princess Isla crouched beside the children. She patted one little boy on the head, then took a little girl's hand and stroked it gently.

Lady Kyrsteen gasped with aggravation. She was about to say something, but the king raised his hand to quieten her. Other than silencing his sister he sat still and wordless.

"I agree with the Lady Kyrsteen," Queen Issyluna stated. Kyrsteen raised her eyebrows in surprise whilst the princesses stared at their mother in puzzlement.

"We should find these poor little children places at the palace. The boys? Yes, I think two or three hours a day learning how to groom horses will give them skills they will use in later life. But the girls? Well, I think they are far too young to clean latrines. We will find places for them in the kitchen where they will learn culinary skills. All our staff are well fed and these children will enjoy meals with our other servants." She looked at her husband who nodded to indicate approval.

"Take them back to the palace please, guards, ensure that the stable master and the chief cook are aware of my orders. Tell them to make sure the children are bathed, given clean clothes and fed. They are to be given beds for the night and they can start work tomorrow."

The guards moved forward to take the children, but the queen commanded them to wait.

"Have you written all that down?" she asked the clerk with a warm smile. The clerk looked at the king as if expecting him to overrule the queen's instructions, but the king remained still.

"Yes, your grace."

"Good, we don't want any mistakes." She turned back to the children. "I shall come and visit you to check that you are being well cared for."

"So will we," Delphine added. "My sisters and I will make sure you are looked after properly." She glared at her aunt who returned the look with a face full of malice.

The children were ushered away by guards, but turned to look at the kindly women. There were several murmurs of 'thank you' from them as they were led away. One small child even waved goodbye. There was a soft buzz of approval from the crowded hall.

"Next is case number 28," the clerk stood with a piece of parchment in his hand. A gruff, gaunt-looking woman with matted hair was pushed forward. "This woman was found to be growing carrots in her window box. Bailiff Stone confiscated them and the woman threw a pot of urine at the bailiff."

Before Kyrsteen could issue sentence, Delphine spoke. "What a good idea. Growing vegetables in window boxes. Everyone should do it until we are sure the weed has stopped growing."

"Many of us have used window boxes for carrots and peas," replied the woman. She was the first prisoner to be allowed to defend herself so far that day. Prior to Queen Issyluna's arrival, none had been allowed to speak. "But no sooner do our plants start to grow then the bailiffs find 'em and steal 'em. I got a family to feed, but whatever I do to try to grow food the bailiff soon finds out and takes it."

"They are under orders to do so," snarled Kyrsteen. "If the soldiers don't eat they will be too weak to defend us if we are attacked!"

"They won't be defending my family," answered the woman. "We'll all have starved to death if something isn't done soon."

Many of the crowd quietly echoed their agreement with the woman.

The queen realised that her husband had not yet told the people about his successful trip to Avalon. This surprised her. She spoke clearly and calmly. "We hope that something will be done soon. I am pleased to tell you that my dear husband has something to tell you all when the trials are finished."

She looked at her husband who nodded his agreement. He had had no intention of telling his people his news, other than issuing orders. Nevertheless, he accepted that in the present ill will that surrounded him, it would be prudent to tell his people of his plans to resolve the famine. Rabbart ruled by fear, his wife ruled by love. In any other circumstance he would not have allowed her interference, but his people were hungry and unhappy. The court was packed and his guard outnumbered. Now was not the time to make a fool of a popular queen.

"Let us finish with this wretch," he stated firmly, "and then I will give you the good news." He wanted his wife and daughters to be gone before Robin's trial and hoped, without much confidence, that by telling his subjects about his trip to Avalon now, he might win the crowd's favour.

The queen looked at the prisoner before her. "The bailiffs are under the king's orders and must not be hindered in their work. In future, if you have a complaint about a bailiff you must take it to the clerk of the court and ask him to speak to the Treasurer."

"But what good would..." The woman started to speak, but this time the queen silenced her.

"However, you have created an innovative idea to provide your family with food. How many children do you have?"

"Five," replied the woman nervously. "One is a newborn baby."

"You poor thing," commented Princess Delphine. A look of compassion filled her face. "It must be extremely difficult to feed such a large family during this famine."

"Clerk," the queen stated firmly, "arrange to have this poor woman's window box repaired and give her seeds enough to plant the box again. In the meantime, instruct my palace cook to provide the woman and her children with potatoes, carrots and flour."

"Thank you, your Highness," the woman fell to her knees again and started to sob tears of gratitude.

Kyrsteen hit the side of the queen's throne with her fist and let out a sound of exasperation. It looked as if she was going to rise and spill forth her ire, but her brother placed his hand over hers and she remained seated and silent.

King Rabbart rose to his feet. The black dog, which had been asleep at the base of the throne, stood too and stared at the crowd in front of him. It was as if he wanted to warn them that he was his master's protector.

"You are too kind, my love," although the king's lips smiled, the gesture was not reflected in his eyes. "You are right though. If every person in the city had window boxes full of edible plants, then they would certainly not starve. I will arrange to have our carpenters help our people make window boxes."

The queen clapped and a small ripple of applause filled the hall.

He looked away from Issyluna and straight at the crowd standing in the hall. "My good wife is correct. I do have an announcement to make. I hope that I have set plans in motion to bring this terrible famine to an end."

The onlookers gasped while the king continued. "However, it will take time. I know the Vanddalasians did not deliberately sell us the weedkiller that has caused so much devastation."

The crowd sighed. Issyluna's cheeks turned red. However, the crowd showed her no malice.

"Indeed you are right, sire," she said curtseying once more before her husband. "My father would never have wished this terrible poisonous vine on even his worst enemy. He was not to know that the weedkiller had been so badly contaminated. Mother Nature knows that he has tried to make up for this awful mistake by sending shiploads of fish to our port each week. The fish is good and our soldiers and staff remain strong, ready to defend our realm."

Rabbart did not like his wife's reminder that the food sent by her father was given to the palace and his armies. Nevertheless, his lips continued to smile.

"My people, you will be aware that I have been away this last week. I have travelled to the south of our land where I have met the new inhabitants of Avalon – a land we once knew as Brewin."

Azgoose had listened intently to all that had gone before, but now her ears were even more alert, absorbing every word the king spoke.

"The Avalonians are a strange people – they are a mixture of humans like us and odd magical creatures. The female of the magical species are called witches, whilst their male counterparts are known as wizards. These wizards and witches fly on the handles of broomsticks – a most bizarre sight."

A murmur of shock ran through the audience. Many had heard the rumours from the Trajaens who had visited the port and doubted the truth. Now they were hearing the story of magical beings flying around on broom handles directly from their king!

"Told you so," Bert whispered to Azgoose. Azgoose said nothing and tried to keep a blank expression on her face.

The king continued. "There are also some rather attractive little species known as fairies and elves. Some of these seem to have wings and can fly too, but appear to be quite harmless.

"I trust no foreigners and it is our law not to allow foreigners to enter our land without permission. Nevertheless, I have made a pact with these Avalonians."

There were stirrings in the crowd.

"They have demonstrated to me that they can kill this poisonous weed. They fly around it on their brooms waving sticks, which they call wands, and muttering strange words."

Again, the crowd stirred.

"Extraordinary as it may sound, the weed shrivelled up in front of my eyes and died."

A low hum ran through the crowd again, this time followed by a clapping of hands. Smiles started to appear on drawn faces that had had no reason for merriment for a long time.

"The witches and wizards of Avalon are led by a king called Arthur."

That's not true! Azgoose was irritated. *We are not ruled by humans. Elvira is my queen!* She did not know that Elvira had died in battle.

"I agreed with Arthur some weeks ago that these strange wizard and witch creatures be allowed into Barrmin to destroy the weed. Soldiers delivered despatches to the towns and villages, where the magicians have been working, ordering that no harm must come to these creatures... these wizzwits, as the Avalonians call them. Although I gave my word that no harm would come to them, I ordered our army to keep a watchful eye whilst they performed their tricks. Now, as their work brings them nearer to the city, the same orders will be issued in Barrden and the surrounding area.

"Regrettably, the ground is still poisoned in the areas where the bindweed has been prevalent. Even the grass that has managed to push its way to the surface is poisoned. We are still unable to feed our livestock in the southern part of my kingdom."

The smiles that had started to adorn the faces on the audience faded.

"But, all is not lost. King Arthur and I have come up with an idea that will gradually weaken the poison, until one day our land will be free of this curse. Arthur has found two enormous birds called thunderbirds. These giant birds bring heavy rainfall and thunder storms with them when they fly. I have persuaded Arthur to let these birds regularly fly over the contaminated land. I believe that the rain they create will gradually weaken the poison in the soil and one day, our land will be green and fertile again."

Queen Issyluna started to clap and soon all the court followed her example. Even Azgoose applauded, although she was a little bewildered.

So, Rabbart has met Arthur. But what are these thunderbirds? I've never seen or heard of the like!

King Rabbart's smile at last became genuine as he listened to the applause. However, he raised his hand in a gesture to bid the crowd to stop. "I have not finished yet. The work in clearing the bindweed is nearing Barrden. These weird beings will be approaching on their broomsticks shortly. The humans refer to them as wizzwits, so we shall do the same. In order for these wizzwits to do their work, I have issued the same orders as I gave to those living nearer the border. I have promised King Arthur that no harm will come to them in Barrmin. The thunderbirds are not to be harmed either. They are rare and we will seek others like them that can be trained to provide rain when we need it. Let me tell you now, any person harming a wizzwit or a thunderbird will be brought before me for punishment. You know that I am a fair and merciful king, but believe me when I say that I will show no leniency to any person who disobeys these new laws."

Someone shouted, "Three cheers for King Rabbart the Third."

The king beamed as the crowd raised their voices in unison. His sister looked on with a haughty pride. The black dog barked its approval. At first the cheers were not loud, but gradually the volume rose.

Then someone else shouted, "Three cheers for the lovely Queen Issyluna."

The court raised its voice again. This time the cheers were so loud they echoed off the walls and throughout the hall until the sound could be heard outside. Rabbart looked bewildered, but politely remained standing and joined in the clapping.

The Lady Kyrsteen, who had a face like thunder, continued to be seated. Her hands did not move.

Azgoose noticed that Bailiff Grimshaw had joined the group of officials in the court. He had found dry clothes and was holding a leather bag. He took his seat at the side of a man wearing a bright red coat. He placed the bag between them. The two exchanged knowing glances.

"Now," boomed the king, who felt confident that the crowd was no longer so surly or aggressive, "we shall begin the trial of Robin the..."

"Ahem," the clerk coughed, "er... there is still one other case to be heard, sire," he spoke apologetically, with his head bowed, "or shall we postpone it?"

"No," Rabbart replied irritably as he sat down again. "Get on with it."

"It's the people from Grey Seal Bay," the clerk explained. The guard who had escorted them to the front of the court pushed the fishermen forward. Azgoose followed, standing a little way behind. Then the three fell to their knees before the royal party.

The clerk continued. "The bailiffs report that these two fishermen, Stan and Bert, were ordered to bring just one boatload of fish to Barrden each week, but each week they fail to do so.

"Now they have been found to be harbouring this... foreigner." He pointed at Azgoose. "A flock of geese have also been found at their residence, yet these were not reported to the bailiff."

Azgoose was conscious of Bailiff Grimshaw's wide grin. *He can't wait to hear what punishment is levied upon us. The worse the punishment, the happier he'll be!*

"Rise," ordered the queen, and the three prisoners stood.

"Do you not know how hungry the people in Barrden are?" Her expression was stern and her tone was cool. "Why did you not deliver your fish each week?"

"That's an easy question to answer, yer majesty," Bailiff Grimshaw stood up. "They're selfish, that's why. They'd rather grow fat on the fish they catch than share them with their fellow Barrmen."

"That's not true!" Bert, Stan and Azgoose responded in unison.

"Let the prisoners speak!" commanded the queen, with a disdainful look at the Treasurer.

Kyrsteen gave out a loud sigh of boredom.

"Please, your majesty," Azgoose hobbled forward as if her back were bent, "these men are not fat. See how their clothes hang on them. They might have been big men once, but until I arrived... until I was washed up on the shore that is, they were hungry and starving and so were their three little children."

"But, why?" demanded the queen. "Let the men answer for themselves."

"The seas have been trawled to the point where there are few fish left in the sea," Stan explained. "The big foreign trawlers used to stay far out at sea. Now they bring their big nets in near the coast. There's Kurtliners, Malovians, Grendulans and other foreign ships. They take everything."

Bert supported his friend's statement. "We used to be able to catch a boatload almost every day – cod, haddock and mullet. We could bring four or five boatloads a week to Barrden and sell another load to the local villagers. We used to throw the little fish back in so they would grow, but the foreigners take the lot!"

"The place we live is called Grey Seal Bay," Stan added. "Neither we nor the villagers used to eat seals ourselves. We didn't need to eat them – we had plenty of fish and the villagers grew vegetables and kept goats. The seals were more like pets. We gave them each a name and even fed them the fish we didn't want. I suppose that's why they used to gather there. Then one morning, we found the foreigners clubbing them. They took what they killed and sold the meat in Barrden market. The seals that were left swam off and never returned. There used to be dolphins and porpoises as well. I suppose there's not enough fish left in the sea for them to feed on hereabouts, so they've found another home. We haven't seen any seals, dolphins or porpoises for near on a year."

The queen was about to speak again, but her husband stopped her. "You say foreigners killed seals on our beach and fish off our coast?"

"Yes, sire," Stan responded. "We reported the seal clubbing to the bailiff, but he said it was the Treasurer's friends just having a bit of fun. As for the big ships, they've fished our waters clean. I've heard more than one trader boast about the big price they get for locally caught fish in Barrden. But we get paid nothing for what we catch."

"Is this true, Treasurer Coyne?" the king asked the man sitting beside Bailiff Grimshaw. "Do foreigners fish our waters and then sell us our own fish at a high price?"

"No. No, your majesty. Of course we don't buy our own fish," he shook his head and feigned a laugh. "They are just making excuses and it's not just the fish," he exclaimed, trying to change the subject. "Ask them about the geese they kept and failed to report. They are just greedy, sire."

"Explain yourself!" the king commanded.

"Please may I explain?" asked Azgoose, as she shuffled forward.

"Who are you?" bellowed the king.

"My name is Gisela, sire. I was washed up on the beach at the place they call Grey Seal Bay several weeks ago. I couldn't remember where I came from. These two gentlemen found me and took me in. They think I was probably shipwrecked. It is true a flock of geese seem to have followed me. The fact that they followed me must surely mean that I am responsible for them. But I don't think I own them. I've lost my memory you see."

"If she owned them she might have been dressed better," Stan cut in. "When we found her on the beach she was dressed in rags. She wore a very strange robe, the likes of which I've not seen before."

"Where did we get our last supply of geese from?" the king questioned the treasurer, who paused before answering.

"I believe it was a Thalakanese trader, sire."

"Does she look Thalakanese to you?"

"I'm not sure, sire."

The king looked at the old woman. "Well, her hair may be grey now, but it looks as if she was once dark and her skin is quite brown."

Azgoose's skin was normally pale, but the time she had spent outside with the children had given her a tan.

"Does the name 'Thalanakia' mean anything to you? Were you bringing a fresh supply of geese from Thalanakia?"

"That name means nothing to me, sire. I'm sorry, but I don't remember anything except floating in the sea and holding on to a piece of wood for what seemed like days. Then I woke up on the beach with Stan and Bert standing above me. They were so kind to take me in. They could have left me for dead instead of helping me and having another mouth to feed. I'm just sorry that I've caused them so much trouble. I must have cared for the geese well because they stayed close by. They started laying eggs in the grass outside Stan's house, where I've been living since they took me in. I look after his children now, at least for the time being till I get my memory back and return home.

"The geese never settled in Stan's yard. They'd lay an egg and then fly off. We were afraid to try and catch one to roast in case the owner came looking for them. He would have been angry to find that we had stolen one of his flock and demanded that we be punished."

"Quite," agreed the king, who now looked at Bert and Stan. "Nevertheless, you should have reported the geese and this foreigner to the customs officer at Barrden."

"We are sorry, your majesty." Stan lowered his head. "We didn't realise that we should report the geese because they weren't ours. We didn't think to report Gisela. We should have reported her and we didn't. We most humbly beg your pardon."

"Please forgive them," Azgoose fell to her knees begging. "I didn't mean to cause them any trouble and I didn't know I wasn't supposed to be on your land... and I didn't even know it was your land. These poor boys suffer three lashes of the whip each week for not bringing a boat full of fish because there's none in the sea anymore... and now I've just caused them more trouble."

King Rabbart knew that the crowd were in better humour than they had been for a long time. He could tell from their expressions that they sympathised with the fishermen and the old woman before him. He did not want to spoil the mood before pronouncing sentence on Robin the Hay Warden.

"Well, my dear wife, what would you have me do with these three?"

The queen looked surprised that her opinion was sought. She was still standing beneath the throne.

The black dog had got up and was sniffing around the floor nearby.

"The foreigner and the geese should have been reported, as our king rightfully states. However, it seems these men have suffered three lashes of the whip each week through no fault of their own. I think they have been punished enough."

The crowd murmured their agreement.

The king nodded. "So be it. But what about the woman?"

"She is not from Barrmin and was not aware of our laws. If she was not a good carer of the geese then they would have soon flown away, but they stayed close to her. That is a sign that she is a good person."

She smiled a charming smile at Stan who seemed spellbound by her radiance. "You say this woman currently resides at your dwelling?"

"Yes, she's been looking after my two younger children. My older boy usually looks after them, or Bert's father, but he's old and keeps falling asleep. Since Gisela's been with us she keeps an eye on them and she cleans and cooks... eggs, that is... that's all we have."

"Well, my lord husband, I suggest that the woman, Gisela, remains at Grey Seal Bay until she regains her memory. The geese don't belong to the fishermen so they have no right to kill them, but I see no reason why they can't keep the eggs. The eggs will pay Gisela's rent."

"You are too generous, my dear wife, but if that is your wish, then so be it. You know I can refuse you nothing." Again, the smile on his lips did not reflect the look in his dark eyes.

The fishermen fell to their knees beside the old woman and thanked the queen and the king profusely.

"Out of the way now," the clerk ordered the kneelers. "We have another case to hear yet. Call Case number 30 – Robin..."

"Wait!" the king commanded. "Anxious as I am to hear the next case, let us finish this one first."

Azgoose felt her stomach lurch. Like the fishermen, she had started to rise, but now they looked up at the king in alarm. The king, however, was not looking at them. Instead, he was glaring at the treasurer. The black dog was sniffing the leather bag that Bailiff Grimshaw had placed between himself and Treasurer Coyne.

"I wish to know why we are paying foreign fishermen high prices for fish caught in our own waters." The king's face was full of malice.

"We don't!" stated the treasurer firmly. "Those men are lying, sire. I beg you not to listen to them!"

"Why do you think my treasurer pays a high price for fish?" asked the king, turning a stern face towards the fishermen."

"Sire," said Stan, who fell back on one knee, "when Bailiff Baldrock came to our hamlet to catch the geese, he told us that he knew the geese were there because the treasurer's trader friends told him that we had swapped eggs for flour. All the traders boast about the good price they get for fish in Barrden."

"Then I will inspect the accounts to see whether there is any truth in this matter," the king responded.

"It... it is true that the sh... shortage of f... food has pushed up prices, but that is only to be expected in times of famine." Treasurer Coyne had started to turn pale and was beginning to stammer.

"Push the price of home-grown food up," the king responded, "but it should not affect the price charged by traders."

The black dog, which had been sniffing around Grimshaw's leather bag, now grabbed it by the handle and started to pull it away. Baldrock bent forward to stop the beast, but Rover snarled and bit him on the hand. The bailiff pulled back in fright. The dog looked extremely ferocious as it bared its teeth and growled at the bailiff. It grabbed the handles of the bag in its teeth and dragged it from under the table into the middle of the floor.

"What's in that bag?" asked Rabbart.

The clerk, who had no intention of going anywhere near the dog, simply stared at the bag.

Princess Isla approached the growling dog warily. "Rover, good boy, let me have the bag. Rover, please."

"Sit, Rover!" ordered the king. The dog obeyed its master's command and sat down on its haunches, still holding the handles of the bag in its mouth. Rabbart looked proud of his ferocious pet. "Let Isla have the bag, Rover. Good dog."

Rover immediately allowed the bag handles to drop from his mouth.

Isla took the bag and looked inside. She lifted out a round of cheese enclosed in an orange coloured rind.

"We don't produce cheese that looks like this," the princess looked puzzled.

"It is cheese from Malovia," said the queen. "That is the only country, as far as I know, that uses an orange rind."

"There's a chicken in here too." Isla lifted a plucked chicken by its neck from the bag. "That must be what Rover could smell." She handed the chicken to the clerk who stood hovering around the strange scene. He looked rather bewildered as to what do with the chicken, but decided to push away his papers and put it on his desk.

"What's this?" Isla finally took out a money bag. She held it up for her father to see.

"Open it!"

The princess did as her father bid and gold coins poured out onto the floor. The clerk hurried around the floor, bending as he picked them up.

"I was only thinking to myself, before I left for the south, how well fed and well groomed all your family appeared." Rabbart looked directly at the Treasurer. "I have no doubt that you have paid a higher price than necessary for foreign goods and been rewarded by the traders in gold and other perks. Guards, take Coyne away and search his house for more illegal food and money. Do the same with Grimshaw. In fact, you are to search all the customs officers' and the bailiffs' homes. Any food you find is to be confiscated and shared between the poor. The gold is to be brought to me."

A spontaneous round of applause started from the floor, but the king raised his hand to stop the show of appreciation.

"Henceforth, no foreign ships may fish within five miles of our land. My warships will guard the coast. Any fishing vessel found within the five mile limit, other than those owned by Barrmin fishermen, will be taken and impounded in Barrden harbour. Make sure our foreign traders are aware of this new Law," he ordered the clerk, "and tell them to make no mistake! I will not treat those who break my laws with leniency.

"Furthermore, before any trader leaves Barrden port today they are to be levied a tax of a further ten gold coins for each night they have spent in our harbour. In future, they must pay this daily fee to use our port or they will not be allowed to dock or to trade with us. I now know that I have been robbed by these foreign traders and their deviousness will not be forgotten!"

"But sire," one of the king's councillors sought his attention, "we rely on the foreign traders for food! If we tax them they may take their wares somewhere else."

"We no longer rely on them! Did I not mention that Barrmin will be buying food from Avalon in the future? Well, I tell you now. The animals, which used to live in our plains and valleys, have moved from our poisoned grasslands to the sweeter pastures in Avalon. Avalon has agreed to supply us with vegetables and meat in exchange for coal. The coal costs us nothing except the labour in our mines. We will no longer be so reliant on goods that come by sea.

"Another new law. This time for our Barrmin fishermen."

Stan and Bert looked concerned.

"All small fish caught are to be thrown back in the sea to grow," commanded Rabbart.

The Grey Seal Bay fishermen smiled and this time it was they who led the applause, which resounded throughout the court.

"Enough!" commanded Rabbart. "You two," he pointed to the fishermen, "will remain in Barrden in case more information is required of you. Report to the clerk each day until he gives you permission to leave."

"Yes, sire," the fishermen duly responded.

"Now, Case number 30 has waited too long. Bring in the prisoner."

A Story Never To Be Told

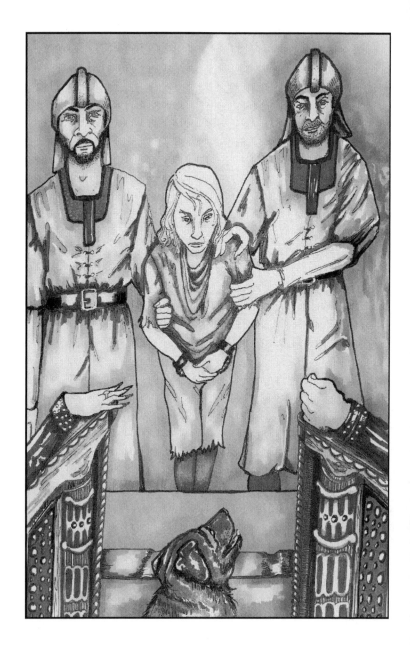

CHAPTER 12 - THE HAY WARDEN'S TRIAL

"That was a result," Bert gave a sigh of relief. "Shall we stay to hear the young lad's trial?"

"Yeah, can't miss this and we're in the front row." Stan responded.

Good. Gisela thought. *This is very interesting.*

"You alright staying, Gisela?" Stan asked the old woman, as an afterthought.

Azgoose nodded.

Two burly guards, who must have been the biggest soldiers in the king's army, brought in a fair-haired youth. Even though he was pale and drawn and his blonde locks fell over his face, his handsome features were still apparent. Robin looked so weak that the two soldiers who stood either side of him appeared to have to hold him up.

Azgoose's heart went out to him. *The lad looks so small and helpless between those stony-faced brutes. I wonder whether the people here in the court feel sympathy for him too?*

"Case number 30," the clerk of the court announced, unrolling a piece of parchment. "Robin, a hay warden from Karmin, a village in Karminesque. Robin the Hay Warden is accused of attempting to kidnap the Princess Luena and steal her away. The princess's father, our good King Rabbart lll and her mother, our good Queen Issyluna, have been ill with worry. It is only thanks to the efficiency of the Barrmin army that the princess has been returned safely to her home in the Rock Palace. Robin is also accused of stealing the queen's jewellery, which was found in his possession when he was captured.

"Robin the Hay Warden, do you plead guilty or not guilty?"

"Not guilty," stated the fair-haired lad, who did his best to stand straight.

"Not guilty?" bellowed Rabbart, slamming his fist down on the arm of his throne. No one had ever seen the king so angry and they had seen him enraged many times. His dark features became menacing. "You stole my wife's sapphire necklace and earrings and then tried to make off with my daughter and you tell me you are not guilty! I sentence you to a public flogging tomorrow followed by spending the rest of the day in the stocks. On Sunday, you are to be hanged by the neck until you are dead!"

Kyrsteen smiled for the first time since Queen Issyluna and her two daughters had appeared.

"But I love her and want to marry her. Lue was coming willingly," pleaded Robin.

"Lue? Who is Lue?" demanded Rabbart, banging his fist down again, and this time the arm of the throne was heard to crack. "You will refer to my daughter as Princess Luena. In fact, you will not refer to her at all because I will hear no more from you. Take him away!"

"Please, wait," Queen Issyluna fell on her knees before her husband's throne.

Robin's guards faltered, not sure what they should do. They decided to wait.

"My dear lord, my beloved husband. I beg your forgiveness. I gave the sapphire necklace and earrings to Luena. I should have told you because you gave them to me once, long ago, as a gift to show your affection for me. I did not tell you and I am sorry."

Rabbart simply became angrier. "What difference does that make, you fool?" The crowd muttered their disapproval at the king for referring to his wife as a fool. The king, however, had reached the state where he cared little for what the court thought. "The charge is that he stole my daughter and jewellery from the palace. It matters not whether the trinkets belong to my daughter or my wife!"

The queen rose gracefully, keeping her head bowed.

"King Rabbart, my husband of twenty three years, you are known for your wisdom and fairness."

A slight murmur rippled through the court, but it was not one of agreement.

Azgoose looked at the queen full of admiration, wondering what her next move would be.

"Our Laws affirm that prisoners have the right to state their case. Please let this boy tell his side of the story."

"He already has told his side of the story!" Rabbart had turned scarlet with anger. He stood up and glared at his wife.

"The woman's mad!" Kyrsteen sneered.

Grumbles of disapproval stirred in the crowd.

Rabbart thrust his arm backwards and struck the Lady Kyrsteen across the face. "How dare you refer to my wife in those terms!"

It was the first time Rabbart had ever struck his sister. This time a murmur of approval went through the court. It was known that Rabbart beat his wife, but it was also known that he held his sister in great esteem. Kyrsteen was not at all liked.

The King of Barrmin took a deep breath and regained control of himself. He sat down again.

Kyrsteen sat still. Her face was expressionless. A trickle of blood was seen to emerge from her lip.

The queen ignored the incident and instead, stole the opportunity to continue. "My lord, I have taken the opportunity this morning of speaking to the Princess Luena…"

"You what…? I left orders that no one was to speak to her!"

Issyluna curtsied low. "I beg your pardon, my lord, but she is my daughter too. I ordered her guards to unlock her room to let me and her sisters enter."

Princess Isla and Princess Delphine moved to either side of their mother and like the queen, curtsied low.

"I left orders that no one was to enter Luena's room!" bellowed Rabbart. "Why did you not seek my permission to speak to her?"

It was Delphine who answered. "You were in discussion with the Lady Kyrsteen and we thought better than to bother you." She glared at Kyrsteen. "After that, you left for the court so we had no opportunity to seek your permission father. Please forgive us."

Queen Issyluna rose to her feet and looked pleadingly at her husband. "I needed to speak to her to find out her side of the story. She tells me that she intended to leave willingly with this young man. They intended to wed. She is a foolish girl to think that she, a princess, can marry a commoner.

"My lord, I have failed you. It is my duty as a mother to explain to my children that a princess cannot choose a husband. It is a princess's duty to marry a man chosen by her parents, a choice to benefit her country." She turned to the prisoner in the dock. "A princess does not marry for love. If a princess is lucky, as I have been, to marry a fine prince whom she falls in love with, then she is indeed fortunate. A princess's duty is to her country."

Turning back to her husband she continued, "Both our elder daughters are aware of their duties. Alas, I have failed you in that I have not tutored our youngest daughter as well as I have trained her sisters."

Princess Delphine spoke next. "My dear father, I beseech you on behalf of my sisters and myself to take pity on this foolish young man. He deserves to be punished, but I beg you to spare him the rope. Instead, deport him. I will ask my future husband, Duke William of Vanddalasia, to take him as a bonded servant. Vanddalasia is a cold place, but there are a few valleys where it is warm enough to grow grass and make hay. My future lord and husband will find a place for Robin and make sure that he does not return to Barrden."

"Will he indeed?" Rabbart was seething. "I do not remember bringing a hay warden into your marriage negotiations with Duke William. I remember no reference to the Duke taking a thieving hay warden off my hands as part of your wedding dowry.

"Enough is enough. I will hear no more. Robin the Hay Warden, who sought to kidnap a princess of the realm and steal her jewellery, you are sentenced to death as per my earlier instructions."

King Rabbart rose and stepped down from his throne. Kyrsteen followed. His wife and daughters curtsied low as he passed them by. He did not bother to give them the slightest glance. He marched past Robin looking straight ahead as if the boy did not exist.

The guards, who would not leave the court ahead of their queen or princesses, stood awaiting the royal party to pass before taking Robin back to his cell. They were surprised when the queen and her daughters stopped to speak to the prisoner.

"We have done our best to save you and I am sorry we have failed," tears sparkled in the queen's eyes. "My husband is resolute in his decision and we can do no more. You are young and foolish, as is my daughter."

"How is Lue?" asked Robin. "You said she was locked in her room."

"The Princess Luena is in good health, but sad. Her sisters and I will do our best to comfort her. Be brave, Robin. It will soon be over." She turned and left.

The Princesses followed, but as they did they each kissed their hands and then placed them on Robin's face. "From Lue," whispered Isla.

A Story Never To Be Told

CHAPTER 13 - THE DOG FIGHT

It was a grey evening. Clouds scudded across the sky as the courtyard echoed with the sound of horses hooves. The fine horses belonging to Rabbart and Jaeggar had rested since their journey to Avalon, but now they were brought out of the stables ready for their masters' pleasure. They were joined by a third horse, another black stallion that belonged to the Lady Kyrsteen.

The three were flanked by half a dozen mounted soldiers plus a kennel master and his assistant, each of whom brought a hungry dog. Rabbart had not kept the dogs hungry for as long as he would have liked. Nevertheless, he considered that Rover was sufficiently vicious and jealous of Fido to be ready to prove himself.

Rabbart, his sister and his adviser were delighted when the two hungry curs started snapping at each other and had to be pulled apart.

Queen Issyluna ran down the steps towards her husband. She fell to her knees. "Please don't do this!" she begged, tears rolling down her face. "Fido has been your faithful pet for years."

The king ignored her and signalled the party on. The horsemen made their way around their distraught queen, but Kyrsteen could not resist steering her stallion towards Issyluna. "The problem is that he is faithful to you now and not his master," she teased. "Fido is old and useless, as you will one day be. Fido's time has come. But be positive, dear sister-in-law, his carcass will be put to good use. We will give it to our starving subjects who you worry about so much."

Kyrsteen put her horse into a fast trot to join her brother who led the procession down Barrden Main Street. Many Barrmen stopped and stared, but none cheered as the party passed. Rabbart and his companions ignored the people who watched them go by. At the bottom of the hill, next to the harbour, lay a long stretch of beach. The guards watched as the three black stallions and their riders galloped along the beach back and forth to exercise their horses. All were skilled equestrians who could command a fast pace without risk or fear. They enjoyed racing against each other.

They were laughing and breathless as they returned to the spot where the dogs were being held at a safe distance apart. All three were delighted to see Fido and Rover growling and baring their teeth at each other.

"Release them!" ordered the king, and the dogs were set free.

They snapped and grabbed at each other and poor old Fido received a sharp scratch from Rover's paw, which left an open wound on his side. But the old dog wasn't finished – he suddenly jumped at Rover who turned tail and ran.

Rover headed towards the cliffs at the far end of the beach. It was remarkable just how fast the beast could run. Fido gave chase. The king and his companions turned their horses and followed.

At one stage it looked as if Fido and his master were catching up, but Rover headed towards some rocks. Rabbart and his followers had to dismount to continue the chase.

Rover and Fido leapt over the smaller rocks into pools of seawater, but other rocks stood out of the ground like giant needles. It was difficult for the onlookers to see what was going on. They could only catch glimpses of the dogs as they darted between the tall needles.

Rabbart had no intention of getting wet, but Jaeggar made his way across the rocks along with the guards. One of the soldiers cursed as he slipped on seaweed and fell on his backside.

By this time, Rabbart was raging. "Kill that cowardly black cur of a dog – the young one, not the old one!"

Jaeggar and the remaining soldiers made their way across the rocks and pools, but the dogs were too far ahead to catch. Fido was jumping from one flat rock to another in his effort to catch Rover. Eventually, they reached the point where the beach narrowed as it met the cliff and both disappeared from sight. It took a while for the soldiers to reach the cliff edge. The water had become deeper and a whirlpool made any further attempts to follow the pursuit too dangerous. They stood watching for signs of the dogs.

"Look" shouted one, "there's the old dog!"

Fido was swimming back towards them. There was no sign of Rover.

Soldiers and dog made their way back to the king, who was furious.

"Cowardly dog! What a waste of time bringing it back to Barrden and feeding it!"

"We didn't feed it, sire," interrupted the kennel master, "we kept 'em both hungry, just like you ordered."

Rabbart had remounted his horse and from his higher position kicked the man, who stumbled to the ground. "Fool. I meant I fed it on the journey and when it first arrived."

"I even gave it my chicken leg," put in Jaeggar. "Pity we hadn't left it with poor old Arthur. Anyway, there's no sign of it now. The cur must have swum away and with a bit of luck, it will have already drowned. There's a swift current over there and a whirlpool."

"If it is still alive, I'll give a gold crown to anyone who catches the beast and brings it to the palace. If it is returned, *you*," he pointed to the kennel master, "will cut its throat. I don't want to see it again."

"Yes, sire," the kennel master was shaking the sand off his trousers.

"Now you can deal with Fido. Cut his throat and let the hungry have his remains." Rabbart had no intention of returning to the palace with Fido. He wanted to punish his wife and did not want her to know that Fido had fought off the new dog, of which he had been so proud.

The kennel master was shocked, but he took his king's orders seriously. "I'll take him down to the water and do it." He tied the rope back on to Fido's collar. "It'll make less mess down there."

"Whatever way you wish," snapped Rabbart, as he nudged his horse into a canter and signalled his party to follow.

Only the kennel men were left on the beach.

The kennel master's assistant offered to help his senior perform the foul deed. He knew that the older man had always been fond of Fido. However, his offer was rejected.

"No thank you, lad. I've known this old chap since he was a pup. He was once as sleek and agile as that Rover. I'm proud of him seeing off his replacement, though the truth is I'd have liked to have had both of them back at the kennel.

"I'll carry out the order myself and say goodbye in my own way. You get back to the palace and if the queen asks, tell her that I made sure Fido's end was quick and painless. "

At the tug of the rope, which acted as a lead, Fido followed obediently to the water's edge. The old dog's greying face looked up wistfully into the man's eyes. They had known each other for a long time. The man looked behind to make sure his assistant had left the beach. He looked around to make certain that no one else was watching and then released Fido. "Go on boy! Swim away. I know you can do it, I saw you swim just now."

Fido hesitated as if he knew what was being said to him. "Go on. Don't worry about me. I doubt whether the king will check who I gave your body to. I'll have to lie to the mistress though. She'll be very upset to think I've killed you. You meant a lot to her. Now quickly, off you go and don't come back!"

Fido nuzzled the kennel master's hand, before swimming off towards the whirlpool at the base of the cliff.

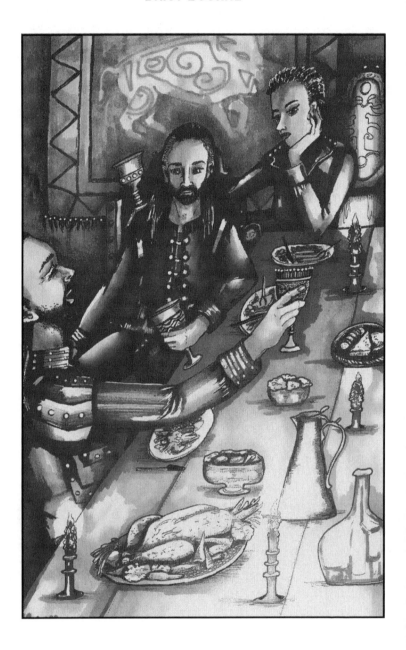

CHAPTER 14 - THE LAST SUPPERS

Queen Issyluna and her daughters were too upset to take dinner that night and asked to be excused. King Rabbart had already seen the tears streaming down their faces. Part of him was pleased at the women's anguish because he felt that they had made a fool of him in his own court. The other part of him wanted no more quarrels with his family, particularly Princess Delphine, who would soon be free of his dominance. If his scheming went according to plan, his daughters might one day be queens of other countries. Were he to retain their respect, he might be able to exert power and influence.

"You are excused. I want none of your miserable company tonight when I have so much to celebrate. I love you all dearly, but you are all weak women, too kind hearted for your own good."

Kyrsteen was disappointed not to have her sister-in-law's company over dinner. She would have enjoyed taunting the queen about her failure to save Robin and the loss of Fido.

Whilst Issyluna and her daughters retired to their chambers, Rabbart, his sister and Jaeggar enjoyed roast chicken with a variety of vegetables washed down by some of the best wine from the royal cellars. The meal was followed by the cheese with the orange rind that had been found in Bailiff Grimshaw's bag, accompanied by sweet liqueur.

"After the hanging we will ride out to see how far those weirdos from Avalon are getting along. They must be nearing the city now."

"A perfect suggestion," replied Jaeggar. "I don't want to be within earshot of your good wife and the lovely princesses while they're wailing with grief. It's been bad enough tonight."

"Will you join us, sister? You will enjoy watching the wizzwits at work. And the sight of those giant birds is breathtaking. I wouldn't mind one as a pet."

"Now there's a difficult choice. Stay here and wallow in the good Queen Issy's grief or see the magic that shrivels up the evil weed. I'll have to think about that one."

"What are you going to do with that little minx Luena?" asked Jaeggar. "You know I wouldn't mind marrying her. She's a pretty little thing."

"You can't marry her," snapped Rabbart. "I know you have waited a long time for a wife. I have been selfish inasmuch as I have appreciated your company and the protection your combat skills give me. Never fear, I shall find you a good marriage – and soon. I had thought to marry you to a lady of Vanddalasia to keep an eye on Delphine and help her rule, if the right time comes.

"Now, I wonder about a marriage in Twydell. I have had no time for old King Frederrick, but he is very old now and it cannot be too long before his son will take the throne. He is not married yet to the young Avalonian princess. We need eyes and ears in Twydell. We also unquestionably need eyes and ears in Avalon."

"That witch with the green eyes was rather nice… and she's a queen."

Kyrsteen almost choked on her liqueur. "Marry a witch?"

"Well, Arthur did! Wait till you see her, Aunt Kyrst. She is stunning."

"Stunning indeed," laughed Rabbart, "but I gather she is spoken for by some wizard."

"So is Prince Edward," Jaeggar responded, "yet that hasn't stopped you scheming to get rid of the girl soldier to make way for Isla... or Luena. Talking about Luena, are you going to set her free after the hanging?"

"Yes, into her mother's care during the day, but we will keep a watchful eye on her. I will place a guard outside her room at night to make sure she doesn't try to run off again."

"Why not release her into my care?" Kyrsteen asked.

"I need to heal the wound with Luena and there will be no healing while she is in your charge, sister. She is my daughter and one day, she will be expected to make a good marriage. Perhaps we need to find something in Robin's past that will make her realise what a fool she has been."

"Is there anything?"

"No, Aunt Kyrst, but I'm sure my father will find something." Jaeggar sat back in his chair allowing a wide smile to spread across his dark features.

Luena's supper lay untouched on the table in her locked room. She could hear her gaoler's keys jangle as the grim woman tucked into her own meal outside the door.

Her mother and sisters had tried to visit her when the trial was over. Rabbart had forbidden the meeting. Instead, he himself broke the news that Robin would hang. He tried to explain that he had no choice but to issue a death sentence. However, Luena had broken into such uncontrollable sobs that he was afraid she would choke and he called for the royal physician to try to console her. The physician gave Luena a sleeping draught, which she pretended to drink. He left only when he was sure that Luena had calmed down.

As soon as the physician had gone, Luena sent a message to her mother and sisters via the gaoler. The gaoler, however, was under orders to deliver all messages to the Lady Kyrsteen who chose whether to pass them on or not. She laughed when she read the princess's parchment asking for her black mourning gown and veil, and tore it up.

Luena sat in an armchair. The room was comfortable enough, with a soft bed and a selection of books that Kyrsteen had chosen for her, but they remained unread. Food was delivered to her room each mealtime. During the first few days of her confinement, Luena had picked at the food. Although she found it hard to eat she had tried to do so. She had wanted to stay strong in the hope of attending the trial to plead for Robin, or even escaping.

She had thought of the dark stranger many times over the last two nights. At times, she wondered whether her lack of food and all the worry had created an hallucination. Yet his presence and words had seemed so real.

She waited in hope that the stranger was not just a figment of her imagination.

Like any condemned prisoner, Robin had been asked what he wanted for his last supper. It was a day early, but the prisoner was to spend the next day and possibly the whole night in the stocks. Therefore, the head gaoler had decided to provide Robin's last supper tonight.

Condemned prisoners never enjoyed their last meal and rarely ate it. The gaoler usually had it for his own supper, which is why he never failed to ensure that the tradition was adhered to.

Robin wanted nothing. All he asked for was water. However, the head gaoler had not wanted to miss out on a fine supper so he ordered a slice of ham, some cheese and an apple.

The prisoner sat looking miserably at what was to be his final meal. He felt no temptation to eat. He had no memory of the stranger who had visited previously.

Azgoose and the fishermen had returned to their boat. It was still moored at the mouth of the river, away from the larger vessels. They were preparing to spend the night on the little craft before reporting to the clerk of the court in the morning. The trio were tired and hungry, but it had been an eventful day and they were in good spirits.

The sound of footsteps alerted them to someone approaching. They were surprised to see the young assistant bailiff who had rescued Grimshaw from the sea earlier that day. He knelt down on the wall and leant down towards the boat.

"Here you are, take this. It's only a watery vegetable soup, but it's still warm and better than nothing."

"That's a very welcome surprise," Bert took the pot the young man offered and passed it first to Azgoose.

"I wish I could give you more. You've done us honest bailiffs a true favour. We knew that some of our officers were corrupt. It has not been possible to do anything about it because the dishonest men, those who shamed our office, were all promoted to senior positions. They had the protection of the Treasurer. Those who complained were dismissed or worse still, accused of things of which they were not guilty. And as well as losing their jobs they were put in the stocks."

"Have the king's men searched the Treasurer's house?" asked Bert.

"Yes, and found not only a pantry full of food, but also an outside store brimming over with all sorts of foreign goods. A large sum of money was found too along with many valuable items. I guessed a long time ago that he was taking gifts in exchange for paying higher prices –more than was necessary. He was also probably selling some of the gifts he took from the traders.

"My home was also searched, but there was nothing there that should not have been. It has only been the homes of senior officers in which hoards of food and other gifts were found."

"Where's the Treasurer now?"

"In gaol, along with his wife. The Grimshaws and other senior bailiffs are in there too."

"What about Bailiff Baldrock?" asked Stan, as he took a turn at sipping the hot soup from the pot.

"It'll take a few days for the news of today's happenings to reach him. I'm sure the king's men will get to his house before it does. After you mentioned his name in court the clerk made sure that soldiers were sent straight away. The clerk is a good man.

"I'm Bailiff Watson, by the way. I'm in charge of the harbour now so it will be me you are reporting to on your future visits to Barrden."

"Well, it's good to meet you Bailiff Watson." Bert had taken the pot and gulped down the last of the soup that Azgoose and Stan had left him. Before handing back the pot, he shook the young man's hand vigorously.

Thanks and 'good nights' were said. Azgoose and the fishermen settled down in the small boat. It was uncomfortable, but with warm soup in their bellies Stan and Bert soon fell asleep. Azgoose rose quietly. She mumbled a sleeping spell in Bert's ear, then crept across and uttered the same words in Stan's. After climbing the short ladder to the top of the wall she made her way back to the street and up the hill.

CHAPTER 15 - STRANGER THINGS HAPPEN

Azgoose kept close to the houses that lined Main Street, so that she was swallowed in shadow as she made her way up the hill. She passed the court and climbed further until the outline of the palace loomed above her in the darkness. It was a gloomy night. The only light was that shining from the candles in the palace windows and burning torches either side of the castle gate.

A fine drizzle moistened the streets and the people of Barrden stayed indoors.

The walk up the dark street had already made her eyes accustomed to the night. She could make out a cluster of trees opposite the palace and tiptoed her way to a place behind a trunk, where she was confident the guards would not see her.

Patience was one of Azgoose's virtues and she stood as still as a statue. She concentrated her gaze on the palace and put all other thoughts out of her mind. It was an hour later when something caught her attention. The city was infected with rats and mice and she had seen several since her arrival, but there was something different about the one that was inching slowly down the pathway from the castle gate. It wasn't scurrying and it kept looking around. It appeared bigger than a mouse yet smaller than a rat. She decided that it must be a type of mouse because it seemed so timid. She lost sight of it as it made its way behind the guards, keeping within the shadow of a lower wall. But as the creature looked towards the trees where she was standing, Azgoose knew immediately what was going on.

The mouse was slowly crossing the road towards the trees when Azgoose became aware of a pair of green eyes stalking the small creature. The ginger tom, which owned the eyes, remained rigid. It kept its body and tail close to the ground ready to pounce as it surveyed its intended victim. It tensed its muscles and leapt at the mouse, which instead of running, turned and stared in horror at its attacker.

What transpired was that it was the cat that became the victim. A goose suddenly flew down from the trees and attacked the cat. A series of events then took place – the cat let out a succession of yowls, the mouse at last ran to the safety of a hollow in a tree and the two guards on duty at the lower wall drew their swords, looking around for the source of the terrible din. At the same time, two other soldiers walked from the gate down the path, heading towards the guards on duty.

One of the guards turned back to what he thought was his approaching colleagues. "All's well, it's only a large bird attacking a cat," he laughed, as he put his sword back in its sheath.

"Big bird," stated the other as he too put his sword away. "Must have been a seagull." He too was laughing, but the smiles were wiped off both faces as they looked at the newcomers.

"Who are you? I don't recognise… that's Robin, the…" but it was too late. The taller of the newcomers touched the guard's neck and he fell into a slumber.

The other drew his sword and opened his mouth to call for help, but Robin hit him in the throat. However, Robin was still weak and the punch had little effect. He made to hit the man again, but the man was already stock still. The second punch made him fall rigid to the ground.

Robin's taller companion sat the sleeper on the wall and left the other lying by the side of the road. He took Robin by the arm and led him towards the trees.

"Hello, Tannus," Azgoose smiled. "Good evening, young man," she acknowledged Robin.

"Azgoose!" Tannus wrapped his arms around her for a brief hug. "Thank you! I thought it must have been Yzor who stunned the guard. How long will he hold still?"

"Not long. Stunning isn't my speciality so you best hurry. Your other companion is hiding in the hollow of the tree. I'm guessing it's Princess Luena."

"How did you know?"

"Never seen a mouse with blue eyes before. Seemed as good a guess as any. When I saw you in court yesterday, I knew you were up to something and I wondered whether you were planning a rescue."

Robin was on his knees looking for the girl he loved. It didn't take long to spot the two blue specks looking up at him. He gently picked her up and kissed her furry head.

"Quickly!" Tannus pulled Robin through the trees along a pathway.

"How long will Luena be like this?" asked Robin, who was rather worried that the woman he loved had been turned into a mouse.

"Not long. I've never turned a princess into a mouse before. In fact, I've never turned any human into anything before. I experimented turning a dog into a mouse a couple of times yesterday. The spell lasted less than an hour."

"Where are you going?" asked Azgoose, as she hurried along behind.

"Yzor is not far away with two broomsticks. He's waiting at the point where the castle wall meets the cliff. I'm hoping Luena doesn't turn back into herself before I can get her up to the top of the cliff. It will be a lot easier carrying a mouse than trying to fly two on a broomstick. It'll be hard work as it is because Robin will have to share with one of us."

Azgoose realised that there was not enough time for more questions and kept pace with the two men.

Robin started making gentle sounds at Luena, but Tannus told him to be quiet.

At last they reached the spot where Yzor waited in the shadow of the cliff with two broomsticks. He looked surprised to see Azgoose, but welcomed her with a warm smile and embrace once he had recovered from the shock.

"Have you got a broom?" he asked her.

"No, but I'm not coming with you."

Tannus and Yzor looked at the old witch.

"Never mind me. I'm at a place called Grey Seal Bay between Avalon and Barrden. If I go now, then my friends, who you saw in court with me, will be asked about my whereabouts. I can't risk them being punished because they can't explain where I've gone. Besides, I've got a family to look after now."

Tannus nodded. "Yes, I heard what you had to say. We'll be in touch."

Yzor was already on his broom and had levitated it into the air a few feet above the ground.

Tannus mounted his broom and told Robin to sit behind him. He was beginning to rise into the air with Robin hanging on behind him, when he hesitated.

"How did you recognise me... in the court?"

"You looked just like your father. Even when he was old and grey he could still transform into a handsome-looking black dog."

Tannus started to laugh, but a commotion could now be heard in the distance.

"Hurry," Yzor snapped.

"You won't get far flying two on a broom." Azgoose looked worried.

"There are two thunderbirds waiting at the top of the cliff," Tannus told her. "Don't transform into a goose again until you're clear. Yzor's pets would relish a nice goose."

"Goodbye, Azgoose, it's good to see you. Someone will be along to that Grey Seal Bay place soon." Yzor would not delay further and his broom lifted swiftly into the air.

"Thank you, Azgoose," Tannus whispered, and Robin echoed his thanks as they rose more slowly.

Then Tannus stopped and lowered his broom. "May I beg one last favour?"

Azgoose listened to the request before shooing Tannus and his passenger on their way.

"I'll try to slow the guards down," she stated as she hurried back towards the palace, careful to keep out of any glimmer of moonlight. She was grateful that it was a cloudy night full of gloom.

Hiding behind a tree, she pointed her wand towards the road and the feet of the approaching guards. One stumbled and as he did so, tripped another who followed him. It only delayed the troops a few seconds, but a few seconds, she decided, was better than nothing.

Fortunately, the soldiers were looking for their quarry at ground level. None had thought to look upwards otherwise they would have seen some movement at the top of the cliff. Azgoose was relieved to see the rescue party disappear from view. Knowing her friends were safe she could at last make her way back to the harbour. She moved from tree to tree, away from the soldiers.

The area around the palace was now full of guards. The sergeants were shouting orders, instructing their men to search this way and that. Despite Tannus's warning, Azgoose decided to transform. Safely concealed among the trees she touched her head with her wand. She rose into the branches from where she was able to take flight. She flew above the roof tops hoping that no one would notice a large white goose and if they did, that they did not have a bow and arrow.

It was not far, by wing, to the harbour. First, ensuring that no humans were nearby, the goose landed behind some sheds close to the latrine. Azgoose hastily transformed back into herself. She hurried towards the little boat where she was supposed to be spending the night.

Soldiers were searching the harbour and all the craft that were in dock. "Have you seen two men and a young woman?" one of them asked her as she passed them.

"No, I've just been to the latrine. I've seen no one."

Back at the boat the two fishermen had been woken by the sound of soldiers searching the quay. They stood on it watching the search going on around them.

"Where have you been, Gisela?" demanded Stan. "We've been worried about you."

"To the latrine," she answered, as she climbed down the ladder and back into the boat. "What's going on?"

"The hay warden's escaped and kidnapped the princess." Bert replied loudly. Then he mumbled so that only his two companions could hear, "Must have been difficult to kidnap her with so many guards around. Any fool must know she's gone willingly. She probably organised it – her or one of her sisters. After all, there's not much that young fool could have done himself, locked in a cell with a palace full of soldiers."

They settled in the boat, keeping out of the way of the soldiers whose numbers multiplied as the night went on.

Next morning, the trio reported to the court where the clerk gave them permission to go home. The court officials were too busy with everything else going on to worry about the fishermen or the goose woman.

"What happened last night?" asked Bert

"The hay warden escaped," replied the clerk.

"That must have been difficult with all those soldiers guarding the palace."

"Someone helped them. He somehow got past all the sentries on duty and stole two uniforms. The gaolers were found asleep. The king is far from happy. You three best be on your way before he finds a reason to stop you going home."

"And thank you," added the clerk as the trio turned to go, "we are all grateful that you made the king aware of the illegal fishing that's been going on and the high prices being paid to the foreign traders. The matter is now being resolved."

He gave them a cheerful wink as they left.

The party from Grey Seal Bay made a hasty retreat back to their boat. It was a long time since the fishermen had had broad smiles on their faces, but they felt that today was the beginning of a new era. They bid goodbye to Bailiff Watson who was on duty at the quay. It would have been good to spend a little more time talking to him, but the young man was busy collecting the new ten coin tax from each of the foreign ships in port. Barrmin warships loomed in the background, ready to bar any ship that tried to leave port without paying the tax.

The little boat set off towards Grey Seal Bay. Stan had raised a small Barrmin flag at the back of the boat to show the warships that they were local people.

"It's the first time I've been proud to fly that one," he laughed, as the little flag flapped in the cold biting wind.

They sailed past the long beach next to the harbour, carefully avoiding the needles bordering the granite cliffs and the whirlpool. Up on a cliff ledge stood a black dog, which barked at the passing vessel.

"Look at that poor dog," Azgoose pointed at the creature, "it's stranded and trying to attract our attention."

"Best leave it," Bert stated firmly. "We can't feed ourselves let alone a dog. It'll get washed away in the high tide and won't take long to drown. It'll be out of its misery soon."

"I remember you saying something like that about me once. It was the day you found me washed up on your beach."

Bert was alarmed. "Did you hear me?" He had assumed the old lady was unconscious when he had spoken similar words.

"Yes, I heard you. I know I was an unwanted burden at the time, but I hope I have proven my worth since. Perhaps the dog will do the same. It could make a good guard dog. We were taken by surprise when Bailiff Baldrock arrived that morning and now that the villagers know that there are geese around, they might try to catch one for their dinner."

Bert and Stan looked at each other and without uttering a word, rowed the boat towards the cliff.

The dog jumped down into the boat and nuzzled up against Azgoose. "He's an old boy. You can see his black face turning grey, but he must have been a handsome cur once. I'm sure we can find a use for him. I think I'll call him Fido. I hope he likes goose eggs."

CHAPTER 16 - THE CHASE

Rabbart was furious. He and Jaeggar were waiting at the castle entrance for their horses and an escort of armed soldiers.

"How could someone get past all our guards without being seen? How could anyone have got into the barracks and stolen a uniform? I can understand how he got into the Western Tower dressed as a Barrmin soldier, but it's how he got in, in the first place, that I don't understand." The king was turning the events of the previous night around in his head, trying to make sense of them.

"I don't understand how he overpowered the sentry on guard outside the dungeons. He was a strong lad. I picked him for that duty myself," Jaeggar was puzzled too. "To add insult to injury, he stole my hand-picked sentry's uniform for the hay warden."

"The gaolers have yet to explain why they were found asleep." Rabbart paced the hall impatiently, listening to Jaeggar's own explanations. Although his son spent much of his time away from Barrden, it was he to whom the commander-in-chief of the palace guard reported.

"I've got them both under lock and key in separate cells for the time being," Jaeggar told the king. "That way, they can't concoct the same story between them. One of them said that he thought their supper must have been drugged, but I don't believe him.

"The only guards who seem to have seen anything were the guards on the lower wall, but they were taken by surprise. One had taken a punch to the throat from the hay warden, which stunned him. The other could only remember a stranger being dressed as one of our sentries before being knocked unconscious."

The Lady Kyrsteen approached. "I've questioned Mother Grimes. She says Luena must have somehow got hold of a key and escaped while she closed her eyes for forty winks. I've had her put in a windowless cell where it's so dark, it won't matter whether her eyes are open or closed. "She tried to tell me her drinking water must have been drugged."

Rabbart and Jaeggar exchanged glances.

"That's the same explanation given by one of the hay warden's gaolers. Interrogate all the kitchen staff," the king ordered Lady Kyrsteen. "Find out who had an opportunity to put a sleeping draught in either food or drink. Jaeggar and I must be on our way. Send a messenger if you have new information."

Hooves echoed in the courtyard. Rabbart and Jaeggar hurried to their horses.

"If we are not back, make sure you sail in time for the wedding in Avalon. I don't want Isla to miss the opportunity of meeting Edward. Let Issy help with the arrangements... and don't upset her." The king looked directly into his sister's eyes. "She is a good and surprisingly loyal diplomat. Besides, we can't afford any more problems before her father arrives. I want no upset with King Xargon. It'll be embarrassing enough explaining to him that I've lost one of his granddaughters."

"They can't get far on foot," Kyrsteen assured her brother as she watched him mount. "I'm sure you'll find them before they reach Karminesque. I'll make sure every house in Barrden is searched and send word to you if they are still in the city... and don't worry, I'll do my best not to upset Issy too much."

Rabbart and Jaeggar led their large armed party out of the gates, but once outside the city walls the army split into three. The king leading one party, Jaeggar another and a loyal captain, who much resembled them, led the third. Although each group took separate routes, all three headed towards Robin's homeland. They were followed by another large group of soldiers who also split into three. This second group would follow at a slower pace and search every homestead and woodland en route to Karminesque.

Robin and Luena sat on the backs of Storm and Thor, the two thunderbirds. They had been nervous of the big birds at first, especially as Thor had stretched his neck hungrily towards Luena, the mouse, with his beak open. However, Yzor was ready to stop the birds trying to snack on the blue-eyed rodent by giving them auroch steaks instead. Nevertheless, he and Tannus were relieved when the mouse gradually transformed into the princess.

First of all, the hair on the mouse's head turned from grey to golden. Next, the creature's long nose diminished and its face turned into that of a lovely young girl. Finally, the arms and legs lengthened and Luena's body changed back into its natural shape.

The thunderbirds seemed bemused when the mouse transformed into a young woman with blonde hair and sapphire eyes. Robin was equally bewildered, but he was also relieved to have the woman he loved looking like her usual self.

Tannus admitted nothing, although he too felt a heavy burden lift from his shoulders. He had often transformed himself into a dog, but had never before turned a human being into another creature. He'd practised the spell of transformation on Fido. However, turning a dog into a mouse was rather different from transforming a human being. He was beginning to feel very tired. He looked forward to spending a few days without the need to perform magic. Magic was fun, but it sapped his strength.

The practice sessions on Fido had proved useful though. Fido, in his mouse form, had entered the palace ahead of Tannus so that he could warn his new friend of any dangers. Accessing the palace had been much easier with Fido paving a safe route.

The warlock had originally intended to simply put the guards to sleep and help the prisoners escape that way, but Luena did not have any dark clothing. He decided that it would be easier to transform her into a small creature that would not be so noticeable – and also light enough to carry. Luena knew her way around the castle and he had instructed her to wait in the hollow of the tree. He had not considered the possibility of her being snatched by a prowling cat.

Yzor and Tannus flew either side of the thunderbirds, on their broomsticks. They knew they would be safe because the king had ordered that no harm was to come to magical beings or thunderbirds. It was cold flying through the air yet dry because the rain the birds created was beneath them. Tannus had lent Luena his cloak. He hoped he would not catch a cold because he had a busy few days in front of him.

Robin and Luena leaned close against the thunderbirds' backs – partly to feel the warmth of the feathery bodies beneath them and partly to make certain they were concealed from any watching eyes below. However, the pouring rain ensured that most folk remained indoors.

They had been flying for two days, stopping only on lonely hillsides where little shelter could be found. At last, despite the storm, Robin recognised the Karminesque countryside below. "There," he shouted, pointing to a cave in the granite cliffs, "that's Zanadoo."

CHAPTER 17 - ZANADOO

The cave in the hillside was not easy to spot, being partly concealed by straggly spindlings that grew in narrow crevices on the mountain.

Yzor gave instructions to land in the language of the two birds. He had become quite adept at speaking their tongue.

The thunderbirds landed at the entrance to the cave. As they touched the ground, Robin slid down from Thor's back and helped Luena dismount Storm. He asked Yzor to bid the birds to wait just inside the entrance to the cave, where they could not be seen. He said that he would try to find them some food.

Before beckoning the two wizards and Luena to follow him, he stroked the giant birds on which they had travelled and thanked them for their safe journey to Zanadoo. Robin did not speak thunderbird language, but the birds seemed to understand him and made soft throaty caws.

As the party made their way inside the cave, two stone men seemed to emerge from the walls of the cave. Their arms and legs were made up of stones and boulders of varying sizes, attached to a rock body that adjoined a stone neck and head. Cracks in the stones formed eyes and mouths. The peculiar men stamped the hilt of the spears they held on the ground.

Robin embraced each in turn, "Ah, Randolph! Winstone! I hoped you would know we were coming and wait inside. I was afraid you would frighten the thunderbirds when they landed."

One of the stone men spoke. His deep voice resonated against the walls of the cave. "Zan saw your journey on the birds. He is expecting you. Follow me. Winstone will stay here. He will keep away from the birds."

Tannus and Yzor exchanged glances. Luena was wide eyed with astonishment and her mouth hung open. Nevertheless, they followed Randolph, the stone man, into the depths of a long tunnel. The cave was deep and dark and lit only by a few burning torches. The stone man led the way. Luena stayed close to Robin holding his hand. The wizards followed behind.

They walked for what seemed like half an hour before they could see a light at the end of the tunnel. As they neared the light, it grew brighter until it was almost blinding.

The tunnel opened up into a large cavern lit by a wall of bright yellow glass stones. Flames writhing from the sconces on the other walls reflected on the glass stones creating a yellow light within the cavern. A bevy of women busied themselves polishing the glittering stones. They looked like fairies, but were as tall as humans and they had no wings. They took the form of silhouettes – almost transparent. They sang as they worked, creating a strange sound of sweet ethereal music.

Robin raised his hand to his eyes to protect them from the dazzling light. His companions did the same.

Joy spread across his face as he recognised the familiar figure sitting in the corner of the room. It was an old man who was robed entirely in white. Like the women, he was almost a silhouette. He appeared to be so pale that he might have been a ghost. The ancient sat beside a stone table on which a meal of bread and cheese was spread. He leaned heavily on his arm, which rested on the table, giving the appearance that the table was holding him up.

He pointed to a basket full of bread on the floor beside his chair. "Take this to feed the birds please, Randolph. Take care though. I'm not sure how tame they are."

The stone man took the basket.

"They won't harm you," Yzor told him. "They know they must not harm humans. On second thoughts, perhaps I had better go with you, they may be nervous of meeting new people."

"Thank you," responded the stone man. "As you can see, I am not human. I am a gnome. I guard Nature on Mother Earth. Sturdy as I am, I do not relish a spat with such large birds and I wouldn't want them to damage their beaks on me."

Yzor, whose legs were already tired, made his way back along the long tunnel with the gnome. He wished he had brought his broom with him instead of leaving it at the entrance.

Robin was delighted to see the old man and made to embrace him. The ancient man, however, did not seem so pleased to see Robin. He turned away from the embrace.

"Take a seat," he pointed to stone chairs around the granite table. "Help yourselves to food. Now you are here you might as well eat. You must be hungry."

"You don't look pleased to see me, Zan." Robin looked puzzled.

"Pleased that you have put your people in mortal danger?" Anger reflected in the old man's face.

"Don't you think that King Rabbart will be on his way here now to find you? Do you not realise that he will torture your family, your guardians who protected you as a child, to find out where you are? Do you not realise that he will punish them whether they know where you are or not?"

"I… I had nowhere else to go," stammered Robin. "Luena was locked in a cell and I was sentenced to hang."

"How many people do you think Rabbart will hang to find out where his daughter is? One life lost is little in comparison. You shame your people.

"A princess locked in a cell with good food and books. A lot of starving people would have regarded her situation to be a luxury."

Tannus watched the ghostly figure continue his tirade at Robin. He wondered how the old man in this cave could know so much.

"You invited two strangers here without permission. You directed two birds to the entrance of this cave. That cave is the only path left in Karminesque, leading to Zanadoo. How many people might have taken notice of the giant birds? You have put the people who protected you, all their lives, in danger. You have put the existence of Zanadoo at risk."

Robin realised the wisdom of the old man's words. "I'm sorry, Zan. I didn't realise. Everything happened so quickly… I just wasn't thinking straight."

Luena, who continued to cling to Robin's arm, just stared.

The old man turned to Tannus. "You are one of the people who have been destroying the murderous vine." It was a statement not a question.

"If you know how to kill the vine, do you know how to create it?"

"No," replied Tannus, "but Yzor my wizard companion does."

"Can he seal the entrance to this cave?"

"Yes, I should think so. He knows how to re-seal the entrance to the Forbidden Forest each time we use it."

"Ah! I thought I recognised him."

Tannus was puzzled. "How did you recognise him? Have you seen him before?"

The old man did not reply, but Tannus could feel magic oozing all around him. He did not think that Zan was a wizard so he guessed the old man was some sort of seer.

"You came here through the last remaining entrance to Zanadoo from Karminesque. The other paths were blocked many years ago. Only a few people are trusted with the knowledge of how to get here. Those people are sworn to keep the secret with their lives. Robin is one of those people. He has proven to be untrustworthy albeit that he was foolish, rather than deceitful. His guardians, the man and woman who brought him up after his real parents were murdered by Rabbart's father, also keep the secret. They and their friends will suffer Rabbart's wrath. They will be tortured in order to make them reveal the whereabouts of Robin and his princess. They have sworn to keep the secret of Zanadoo safe, but under torture they may give up our secret to save their pain."

Luena started to sob. "I am sorry. I thought only of my love for Robin and being together. I did not understand how coming here would put others at risk. I did not think. I can see now how selfish we have been."

229

"Well," Zan spoke again, although not quite so sternly. "I have a plan, but it will mean giving yourselves up to the Barrmin soldiers. Would you be willing to do that to save your family, your people and Zanadoo?"

"Yes," replied Robin. "If I have to hang to save others, then so be it."

Luena's sobs became louder and echoed throughout the cave, drowning the singing of the strange silhouette women.

Zan explained his plan.

A Story Never To Be Told

CHAPTER 18 - ESCAPE FROM KARMIN

The next day, Rabbart and his men rode into the village-town of Karmin, the capital of what was once the country of Karminesque.

The army had travelled at a rapid pace. The king was tired and dusty, but exuberant. His soldiers, who remained on permanent guard in Karmin, had sent a messenger to tell him that the townspeople had captured Robin and Luena and they were now held in the local prison.

Lionel, the leader of the town council, strode out to meet the king. A mounted Barrmin soldier, who had been posted to the town, walked his horse alongside.

"Sire. I bid you welcome," Lionel bowed his head low. "Nobody here did anything to help my son, Robin, bring Luena to Karmin. We did not know that they had tried to run away together. Please do not punish my people for Robin's foolishness. I accept that he must be hanged for his foolhardiness."

"The hay warden kidnapped my daughter!" snapped Rabbart. "She did not run away with him and you must never say that again or I will have your tongue."

Lionel fell to his knees. "I am sorry, sire, I would do nothing to cause your displeasure."

"You have captured them for me so no punishment will be inflicted on your people. I am surprised you gave up your own son though."

"Sire, it breaks my heart to do so. He is my son, but he has been foolish to think he could ever marry a princess. I must put my people before the love of my son."

Lionel bowed his head.

"Where are they?" demanded the king.

"In the prison, sire," responded the soldier, "over there on the outskirts of the village."

"Lead the way."

Before following his man, Rabbart spoke again to Lionel. "You have done well. You have put your loyalty to me before the love of your son. You will be rewarded."

"To honour my king is reward enough."

Lionel remained on his knees with his head bowed, as the guards following their king made their way around him. He appeared to be a forlorn man.

It didn't take long for Rabbart to reach the prison, which was no more than a small wooden stockade. Karmin was a peaceful place and had no need of a larger or stronger establishment.

The king hammered on the locked door with his fist, but there was no response.

"Open up!" he bellowed.

"Open up Charl," the local soldier joined the king at the door, but there was no response. "I don't know what's going on. I left Charl on guard inside."

"Ram the door!" Rabbart commanded his soldiers. A burly soldier and the local guard shouldered the wooden door until it gave way. Inside, Charl was just coming to his senses and trying to rise from the ground.

"What happened?" cried the other local guard.

"Explain yourself!" bellowed the king.

"The Princess Luena was pacing up and down. She was sobbing and I was afraid she would choke. Then she fainted. I ran to her. I intended to pick her up and lay her on the straw pallet. As I leaned over, Robin must have hit me over the head."

A broken water jug lay on the floor nearby. "He must have hit Charl with that," his comrade pointed out. "Full of water, that jug could render a heavy blow."

"There's an open window at the back," shouted the army sergeant. "They must have escaped through that. Men, get outside and start searching. Now!"

The soldiers who had entered the house ran outside, shouting instructions to others.

"What's behind here?" demanded Rabbart

"Just granite mountains," responded the local guard. "There's a path, but it's narrow. No one would risk using it."

"They would!" snapped Rabbart.

Rabbart hurried outside repeating his sergeant's orders to search every house and shed. He mounted his horse and rode to the back of the stockade. Looking towards the cliff, he was shocked to see his daughter and the man she loved about quarter of the way up the cliff. They stood side by side facing the wall, moving at a snail's pace along the narrow path.

"Come back, Luena. You are putting yourself in danger!" Rabbart bellowed, but fear echoed in his usually stern voice.

"After them!" he ordered his men.

A soldier galloped to the foot of the path, dismounted and tried to inch his way up the narrow path in front of him. He fell to the ground after a few minutes.

"Fool!" roared Rabbart. "Do what they are doing – walk sideways with the cliff in front of you. That way you will be able to find fingerholds in the cliff face."

A second soldier carried out his king's instructions and was followed by a third. They moved slowly, bit by bit, and started to rise above the heads of the army below. As they rose higher, the path narrowed. Both wore armoured waistcoats, which meant they could not lean their bodies close to the cliff. Soon, one fell and then another.

Lionel was now standing beside the king.

"Robin," he called, "that path is too narrow. Don't risk the life of the princess. Come back down!"

Robin did not answer.

"Luena," shouted Rabbart, "come back down now and I will let your hay warden live. I will have him deported to Vanddalasia as your sister's bonded servant. You have my word."

"What about me? Why would I want to return to Barrden to be bullied by Aunt Kyrsteen," shouted Luena. "I hate that woman. I would rather die than have that bitch gloat over my capture again."

"I plan to release you into your mother's care, not your Aunt Kyrsteen's. I promise you. I spoke to your aunt about it last night. She will tell you what I say is true."

"I'm sure she will," responded Luena, "but that woman is a poisonous liar. She is so accomplished at the art of telling lies that she probably believes them herself. I would rather die than continue to watch her bully my mother. My venomous aunt is not worth my mother's little finger!"

Rabbart turned to his captain. "Tell your best archers to aim their arrows at the hay warden."

Rabbart did not see the alarm in Lionel's face as he gave instructions.

"But, sire..." the captain spoke quietly. "My archers will not miss their target, but if the hay warden falls then so might the princess."

"I told them they were to aim, not fire."

Rabbart looked up at his daughter. As he did so, Jaeggar rode up beside him. Taking the situation in, he looked genuinely concerned.

"Fetch straw, mattresses, whatever you can find to break the princess's landing if she falls," Jaeggar ordered his men. The men set off, following their commander's orders.

The archers came forward, taking aim at Robin.

"Luena," shouted Rabbart, "come back down, now! If you do not do as I tell you these archers will aim their arrows at Robin." It was the first time the king had used the hay warden's name. "Come back down now and I promise he will be sent to Vanddalasia to serve your sister."

Luena held Robin's hand and lifted it high. "Look, father, we are holding hands. If your archers shoot Robin and he falls so will I."

The archers exchanged looks. None had any desire to harm the princess, but they would not disobey the king's orders.

"Don't be a fool, Lue," shouted Jaeggar. "Come down. No one wants to see you hurt."

"I have been hurt every time my father and Aunt Kyrsteen ridicule my mother," responded the princess.

Jaeggar dismounted and walked towards the cliff, examining it to see if he could somehow climb up to the ridge where the couple stood. "What's this?"

"What's what?" demanded Rabbart irritably, still keeping his eyes on his daughter.

"Look, it's the vine. It's spreading across the cliff and Luena is climbing towards it!

"Come down, Lue. For pity's sake. If you don't fall you'll be swallowed up by the vine. It's killed more than one person before now!"

The king looked around to see the plant Jaeggar was referring to. He was even more alarmed now.

"It was noticed yesterday," Lionel advised the king. "We sent for the magic people straight away. We thought they had finished clearing the weed from Karmin days ago, but this vine must have been hidden in the crevices of the rock. It's grown rapidly since yesterday."

"It should have grown rapidly," Tannus grinned at Yzor, "it's had you encouraging it to grow and it doesn't need much encouragement."

The two wizards stood in the shadow of the bindweed with their backs pressed back against the stone walls. Yzor had not only concealed the entrance to the cave with the vine, but had cleverly created a bindweed tunnel. The tunnel was gradually spreading over the pathway from the cave to the section of the path on which Robin and Luena now stood.

"How long will it be before Heather and Jonathan get here?" asked Tannus, who was not familiar with the area. Yzor had already spent time here previously with Jonathan and Heather, freeing the arable land of bindweed.

"Shouldn't be too long now. I told them to let Rabbart arrive first. It would have been too much of a coincidence if they arrived at the same time."

"And too suspicious if they arrived beforehand."

Hour after hour passed, with Robin and Luena inching sideways along the narrow path, gradually rising higher. The soldiers, including Jaeggar, made several attempts to climb the path. Each fell to the ground.

At one point, Jaeggar had started to make sure-footed progress. However, his attempt was foiled by Tannus pointing his wand, as the Barrman came into view beneath him. A twist of Tannus's wrist and Jaeggar tumbled down, cursing as he went. If it had not been for the soldiers and villagers building a bed of straw at the base of the cliff, he would have been badly injured.

A satisfied smile spread across Tannus's face. "That'll teach him to try to steal my girl."

"Are you sure the bindweed won't harm Robin and Lue?" The warlock asked Yzor.

"Positive. The weed will not harm them any more than it would harm you or me. The protective spells we have learnt are very strong. I pity any of the people below who try to touch it though. At the best, it would give them a nasty sting and at the worst, it could strangle them. Let's hope Jonathan and Heather aren't late!"

Below, unaware of the concocted bindweed tunnel, the king and Jaeggar continued to implore Robin and Luena to return to safety. At one point, Rabbart even promised his daughter that he would allow Robin to live peacefully in Karmin. Nevertheless, the couple inched higher and towards the bindweed tunnel, which grew nearer and nearer.

Someone shouted, "Look, the magicians are coming!"

The crowd looked up to see a witch and wizard on their broomsticks, flying towards them. As they came close, they circled around and hovered near the bindweed and the escapees.

"Do you want a lift?" Heather called out to Luena.

"No," replied Luena sharply. Then remembering her manners, added, "Thank you."

"What are you doing here?" asked Jonathan loudly. He was fully aware of the plan and was enjoying play acting.

"Go away," shouted Robin loudly.

Heather and Jonathan flew down to speak to the king.

"What's going on?" Jonathan asked. "We offered to give those two a lift down, but they refused."

Rabbart was exasperated. "Can you at least stop the weed growing? If you can stop the weed then perhaps you can help encourage those idiots to come down."

Heather and Jonathan flew to the root of the plant. They uttered words and waved their wands, but the weed continued to grow.

"This is different." Jonathan spoke loudly so the king could hear his words. He thought he had found a new career in acting. "It is not like the bindweed we have encountered before. It is a different species. Have you found any more like this?"

"I don't know and at the moment I don't care," snapped Rabbart. "I just want my daughter back."

Evening was drawing in, making the mute light of the cloudy sky even dimmer.

The thunderbirds appeared in the sky, bringing with them a storm.

"Tell the birds to go away!" Rabbart ordered Jonathan. "Rain will make that treacherous path more dangerous than ever."

"It's too late," groaned Jaeggar. "Look! They've reached the bindweed, or the bindweed has reached them. They are disappearing from view."

Robin and Luena seemed to be fearless of the murderous vine.

"Come back," begged Rabbart, "please."

"I'd rather die than live without Lue," were the last words Robin called out before disappearing into the weed.

"And I would rather die than go back to the Rock Palace with poisonous Aunt Kyrsteen," shouted Luena, as she gradually disappeared from sight.

Jaeggar made one last attempt to scale the cliff, but his right arm became caught in the bindweed. He screamed for help.

Jonathan had started to fly up towards the thunderbirds to ask them to settle on the cliff top rather than create more rain. But when he heard Jaeggar's cries, he swiftly turned back. He found Rabbart, Lionel and the captain of the guard desperately trying to free Jaeggar from the vine that now entwined not only his arm, but also his upper body.

"Stand back!" shouted Jonathan, as he raised his wand. "This could be dangerous."

"Please, save my son," pleaded Rabbart, as he stepped back. "I've just lost my daughter; please don't let this weed take my son as well."

Rabbart was a hard man, but tears started to form in his eyes.

Flames flashed from Jonathan's wand and Jaeggar yelled even louder. The vines entwining his arms burnt and fell away. As the weed burnt, Rabbart and the captain of the guard, together with Lionel, pulled Jaeggar free. The burnt strands of the vine crumbled away, but the main stem continued to grow.

Jaeggar's face reflected the pain he felt, but he managed to speak. "I had no idea you cared so much, father. That is the first time you have ever acknowledged me as your son in public."

Rabbart wept openly.

Heather removed Jaeggar's leather jacket and vest. Burn marks were imprinted around his right arm and chest like a tattoo, where the weed had gripped him. She uttered some words to try to heal the wounds. It eased Jaeggar's pain a little, but she explained that she was not a healer and it was best to get him help from elsewhere. The thunderbirds were circling above and rain started to pour. "Do not cover his wounds until you have some proper ointment. The cold rain will help ease the soreness," she explained. "If you have no healing lotions then best get him to a pump, where you must keep water pouring over his burns."

Lionel led a group of soldiers to the house of the local healer. They had lifted Jaeggar onto a blanket so they could carry him.

Rabbart composed himself. He stood tall as he spoke to Heather and Jonathan. "Thank you for your help. If it were not for you my son would be dead, like my daughter."

Heather looked up at the granite cliff. She was cold and wet, but stood transfixed to the spot. Her face was full of innocence and wonder.

"But your daughter died for love. What a wonderful story. It's a story that will touch many hearts and be told for generations."

"That," roared Rabbart, "is a story never to be told!" He turned to the army and villagers who remained. He stood there, drenched with rain, shouting, "This is a story never to be told! Never! Do you hear me? A story never to be told!"

DAISY BOURNE

PART THREE: THE WIZZEN

CHAPTER 19 - A WISE CHOICE?

Wormald the Wise had found a quiet location outside of Merlport for the Wizzen. He sealed the spot with an invisible wall and rounded ceiling. No human could look within or pass through the dome he had created, which he had also soundproofed. If a human walked towards the enclosure they would merely step out on the other side.

Earlier, burnt sage and other cleansing herbs had been sprinkled inside and outside the enclosure. The fragrance of herbs and frankincense filled the air inside the dome. Now the Wizzen echoed to the sound of wizards and warlocks chanting. They danced round in a clockwise circle, bending and rising, in time to their chant. Most held lighted torches – others lit their wands. A few, like Merlin, held staffs with glowing orbs. Whatever lighted instrument the wizards chose, they bobbed up and down in the dark of the night, as the wizards danced around the inner wall. A glow of different coloured lights filled the dome in which the Wizzen took place.

Some witches, fairies and elves respected the wizards' privacy, but others had concealed themselves and although they could not hear what was going on, had a partial view of the ceremony. The onlookers meant no harm, but merely wanted to watch the rare and fascinating ritual. Some could only see the glowing magical instruments against the night sky, but that was enough to keep them entertained.

Merlin wove out of the line of his circling brethren. He held up his staff that emitted a purple light around the spot where he stood. The dancing and chanting stopped. He placed his staff at his throat to increase the volume of his voice, "Thank you all for coming to this historical event. Please be seated."

The wizards found places on the ground on which to sit.

"We are still awaiting Yzor, Jonathan and Tannus," Merlin stated. "They will be here within the next few minutes."

"Are you sure of that?" asked Wormald, who had come to stand beside his old friend. "No one has heard from or seen Tannus for days. We all thought he was in the Forbidden Forest or clearing bindweed from Kerner. However, a party arrived from the Forbidden Forest today and they have not seen him either."

"Oh, yes," replied Merlin. "I am sure Tannus is very close."

It seemed that no sooner had he uttered those words, Tannus's broomstick landed in front of him, followed seconds later by Yzor and Jonathan.

"Welcome," Merlin and Wormald spoke in unison.

"We are sorry we are late," Tannus bowed his head in acknowledgement to the two distinguished wizards.

Merlin lowered his voice and gave Tannus a stern look. "I'm glad you are here and back to your normal self. I thought you were very rude to eavesdrop on our meeting with Rabbart of Barrmin. You were not invited to the meeting and had no reason to be there... or did you?"

"How did you know it was me? Let me guess, I look just like my father when I transform?"

"No," Merlin shook his head, "you have grown into a powerful wizard. I could feel your presence in Arthur's tent, just as I could feel you approaching tonight's Wizzen. Hurry, take your seat. We have a lot of business to get through and we are running late."

Then in a meaningful tone, he added, "After the Wizzen, I am sure you will wish to tell Wormald and me what you have been up to."

He raised his voice again. "Now, at last we are all here. We have much to discuss before electing a new leader of the wizards. As you know, my wife is expecting twins. Neither of us is young and I wish to stay close to my wife during her pregnancy. Helen-Joy and I do not have any other children and we wish to enjoy our twins' childhood. I expect both to have magical tendencies and will train them myself. Much as I shall miss Avalon, it is my intention to now dwell with my family in Twydell's Forbidden Forest."

The assembled wizards muttered their regret over losing Merlin's leadership, but also voiced their congratulations on his recent exchange of rings.

Merlin continued, "First of all, may I welcome Isaiah, one of the three wizarding brothers from the Forbidden Forest, who has come to watch our proceedings. Isaiah will not be allowed to vote because the wizards of the Forbidden Forest are not part of our clan. Isaiah, do you have anything to add?"

Isaiah stood. "I wish to wholeheartedly thank my brethren from Avalon for saving me and my brothers from the horrors of the Kernan mines. Personally, I would very much like to join you and become a member of your clan. Unfortunately, my two brothers have still not fully recovered. I do not think it is right to ask to join you until my brothers are well enough to make a joint decision with me."

"I take it no one has an objection to Isaiah's presence?" Merlin thought he had better check rather than presume.

The wizards shook their heads. Many said how glad they were to see Isaiah and how much they looked forward to one day meeting his brothers. Most would have welcomed a visit to the Forbidden Forest, but it was already known that few would ever receive such an invitation.

"May I also introduce Seth?" Merlin indicated an elderly man sitting next to Isaiah. "Seth is father to the three wizards in the Forbidden Forest. He has always hidden his skills and took his young boys to the Forbidden Forest, asking those who lived there to take them in. The children could not control their magic and he was afraid for their safety. Would you like to add anything more to what I have said, Seth?"

Seth stood. "First of all, I would like to thank all of you who have helped bring my sons to safety and heal their minds. I have lived in Twydell all my life, where until recently, magic was frowned upon. That's why I had to give my boys to the people in the forest. My wife is human and we have other non-magical children. It would have been unfair for them to have to live a secluded life in the forest so that's why we had to give up our boys, for their own safety.

"I've always had to hide my magic so I'm not a skilled practitioner. Now, thanks to Merlin, I can use my skills openly without fear of punishment. I would very much like to develop the power I have inherited. I would also like to join your clan but continue to live in

Twydell with my wife and non-magical children, if that is acceptable?"

"That would be wonderful!" beamed Merlin. "Can we have a show of hands, please? Those in favour of Seth joining our clan?"

Every wizard raised a hand in support of the motion.

"Anyone against?"

No hands were raised.

"Good, good!"

"Anyone else got anything to say before we elect a new leader?"

Brutuz stood up. "May I introduce Iwan – he was one of the older children who were rescued from the Kerner mines. He has come to live in Avalon. He is a very skilled young warlock and in my opinion will one day be a great wizard."

"Ah, yes, let us welcome Iwan. Come Iwan, show us a little of your magic," beamed Merlin proudly.

Iwan raised his hand; he did not need a wand to create a fireball in the sky. The burning ball whirled around and around until it fell on the dry grass below.

Brutuz and Curtuz hastily pointed their wands at the flames and cast a spell to put out the fire. It was apparent to all why Iwan had been taken away from the leafy forest. Nevertheless, the wizards applauded politely because there was no doubt that Iwan was a talented young warlock.

"Right. Now is the time for this most important and historic vote. Wormald the Wise has most generously offered to take my place as leader of this wizarding clan. There being no other nominees, I ask…"

"Tannus," shouted a young wizard.

"Tannus," shouted another.

"Are you nominating Tannus?" asked Merlin, somewhat surprised.

Wormald, who stood expectantly beside Merlin, wrinkled his brows as he sought the owners of the voices shouting for a rival.

"Yes, Tannus," shouted a third voice.

Merlin turned to look at the young wizard who had settled on the ground close by. "Tannus, do you accept this nomination?

"Yes, I do," replied Tannus, as he rose to his feet and took his place at Merlin's side.

Merlin stood with Tannus on one side and Wormald on the other. He towered half a head above both of his would-be replacements. "Then let us vote. Those in favour of Wormald replacing me as your leader, please raise your hands."

About half of the wizards raised their hands. They were predominantly the elderly wizards who had known Wormald for most of their lives.

Merlin counted the raised hands. He asked a nearby wizard to check his count. They concurred on 54 votes for Wormald.

"Those in favour of Tannus, please raise your hands."

The other half of the wizards raised their hands. Merlin cast more than a fleeting glance at Yzor. Obviously, he had expected the older wizard to vote for Wormald, but instead the herbologist supported his young rival.

There was another count and both Merlin and the wizard checking the numbers counted 55. "Ah, but that's without me and I vote for Wormald, making Wormald's tally 55. As I have the casting vote, I…"

"Wait!" shouted Curtuz, "Iwan hasn't voted yet!"

"Iwan has not been elected as one of our clan," one of the elderly wizards, who had voted for Wormald, pointed out.

"Then let us put Iwan's membership to the vote now." This time it was Jonathan, who was normally quite shy, who spoke.

"Very well," responded Merlin. "Iwan, do you wish to join our clan?"

Iwan, who was not at all shy, responded loudly, "I don't see why I can't join. You've brought me to live here so why shouldn't I be able to vote?"

The last thing that Merlin wanted was for Iwan to return to the forest, or Kerner, and work on his own as a hedge wizard. "Brethren, I ask you to cast your votes as to whether to allow the young warlock Iwan to join our clan."

About seventy wizards raised their hands.

"Against?"

All hands remained lowered.

"Abstentions?"

The remaining wizards, all older members of the clan, raised their hands.

"So, Iwan, welcome to our clan.

"I believe we should carry out the leadership vote again. Those who would like Wormald to become our leader, please raise your hands."

Including Merlin's vote, the count now stood at 55.

"Those in favour of Tannus."

This time, with Iwan's added vote, the number of Tannus's supporters swelled to 56.

"Tannus is our new leader," Merlin shouted, although there was no joy in his voice. "I wish Tannus the very best of luck and wisdom in his new role and hope you will all support him."

Clapping and applause rose from the younger wizards. Despite his disappointment, Wormald joined the applause and soon his followers joined in. Only a few very old wizards shook their heads and kept their hands still.

Tannus stood tall, as he addressed his audience. Even though he was tired from performing one magical trick after another, day after day, and his long journeys in the North, he looked alert and handsome.

"Thank you for your vote of confidence in me." He waited till the cheers that met this statement had died down. "I vow that I will do my best to be the leader you wish me to be. I hope that in my new role, I will be able to rely on Wormald's wise counsel."

Wormald nodded graciously. "Indeed, Tannus. You have won this vote fairly. I promise that I will do all I can to support you in your new role. Indeed, it would be unwise for any of us who did not vote for you not to support you, for that would be a road to self-destruction."

The white-haired wizard levelled his gaze at those who did not applause Tannus's election as leader.

Tannus went on to speak of his future intentions. He said he hoped the wizards in the Forbidden Forest and the young warlocks who now dwelt there would eventually join the clan. He went on to say that the need to persuade humans to respect their magical counterparts would always be foremost in his intentions. He gave thanks to Wormald for the outstanding work he had done in ensuring that all wizards were offered training in defensive spells, adding that he hoped the training would continue.

There were murmurs of approval from all within the walls. A noticeable look of delight spread across Iwan's face at the mention of training.

The new leader went on to tell the Wizzen that he had been away in the North, not only to check on the spread of bindweed, but to also find out more about the people who lived there. He praised Yzor and Jonathan for the good work they had done in their progress of clearing the bindweed from Barrmin.

Tannus continued, "My travels in Barrmin have deepened my mistrust of the King of Barrmin. We are here tonight in this Wizzen where all that is said remains secret, unless we agree otherwise. Wormald has woven magic spells into this Wizzen enclosure, which will cause any one of us who reveals our secrets without permission to suffer self-punishment. What I am about to say must remain secret and must not, unless agreed, be discussed – even with our sister witches."

Although it was not necessary to do so, all members of the Wizzen raised their wands or staffs spontaneously and repeated their oath of secrecy. They did so to confirm their respect for the confidentiality of the Wizzen.

Tannus went on, "Rabbart has three most beautiful daughters. They and his wife are good, honest people. One daughter will shortly be married to Duke William of Vanddalasia. She and the Duke may one day inherit the Vanddalasian throne.

"Rabbart recently offered Isla, his eldest daughter, to Prince Edward as a bride. It is true the marriage would have strengthened the bond between Avalon and Barrmin. However, I now believe Rabbart's true intention was to hasten King Arthur's departure and once the couple had children, he would murder Edward too. His plan was to eventually take over the kingdom of Avalon and annex it to Barrmin.

There were expressions of anger all around. "Fortunately, Edward is promised to Daisy and their wedding will take place soon – too soon for Rabbart to cause Daisy any harm and too soon to stop the wedding. But he may now see Derrick of Twydell as a future prospect for Isla. King Frederrick is old and Derrick may inherit the throne of Twydell soon. Princess Rosalie of Avalon is promised to Derrick, but Arthur has let it be known that he regards her as being too young to marry yet. I believe that Rosalie's safety could be at risk."

Rosalie was a popular girl and more angry murmurs rippled throughout the Wizzen. Some members of the clan looked towards Merlin and Wormald, expecting one or both to comment. Both looked very grave, but remained silent to allow Tannus to finish his tale.

"I stress, Princess Isla is unaware of her father's plans. Neither she nor her mother know anything of Rabbart's intentions."

"What about this Duke William of Vanddalasia?" asked one wizard? "How safe is his life? You say he might one day take the throne with Rabbart's daughter as his queen. Is Rabbart likely to finish him off and take over Vanddalasia?"

"It's possible," agreed Tannus, "but even if he did, I think he would find it difficult to control William's bride. Delphine is a very strong character. He would have to get rid of both of them and then act as regent for any children they have. Strangely enough, Rabbart is fond of his daughters. I don't think he would harm any of them.

"I believe our strategy must be to protect Rosalie. If anything were to happen to her, it would pave a clear path for Rabbart to offer Isla's hand to Prince Derrick."

"Why can't we warn King Arthur or King Frederrick about Rabbart's scheming?" asked a wizard.

"Because it could cause a war, which is something we do not want. Even with the Twydell army and our magical spells, I doubt whether we could defeat the might of Barrmin."

"Then why are we clearing their land of the poisonous bindweed?" several voices asked the same question.

"We were unaware of Rabbart's plans at the time we started to free his country of the murderous vine that engulfs it. We should continue with our work because the people who live in Barrmin are starving. They are not to blame for their king's greed. They are innocent victims.

"Let me make a few suggestions and then we can discuss what to do. We could get rid of King Rabbart of Barrmin, but if we did, who would rule in his place? Princess Isla is next in line to the throne. She would be a good but inexperienced ruler. She would naturally have her mother Queen Issyluna's support. Issyluna would be a perfect queen if her husband allowed her to be, and she is loved by her people. Issyluna would be a good adviser to Isla and help her rule.

"But I do not believe that King Rabbart's sister would allow either Isla or Issyluna to rule. She would most likely try to take the throne for herself or Rabbart's illegitimate son, Jaeggar. She brought Jaeggar up and is like a mother to him.

"It will be interesting to meet King Xargon of Vanddalasia. It will give us an opportunity to form an opinion as to whether he would support his granddaughter if she inherited the throne."

"It sounds as if we are meddling in the affairs of other countries!" stated one old wizard.

"I have no wish to start a war, which is why I propose that the information I have brought from Barrmin remains a secret. I seek only to protect Princess Rosalie. In my opinion, the best way to do that is either by bringing forward the date of her marriage to Derrick or by getting rid of Rabbart. If we were to get rid of Rabbart, and Kyrsteen or Jaeggar were to take the throne, I am not sure whether they would continue with Rabbart's plans. I should add that Rabbart is currently seeking a wife for Jaeggar and he is looking for a prospective wife either in Avalon or Twydell."

Several brethren stood to speak, but Merlin cut in, "The news you have brought us is indeed worrying, but it does not surprise me. I do not like Rabbart and do not trust him. However, I do not believe we should meddle in the politics of other countries. If we were discovered murdering the king of another country, then our kind would be perceived with the same mistrust and hatred as we suffered in Briton. Better we protect Rosalie, but keep that protection a secret."

There were murmurs of approval.

"Very well," agreed Tannus, "let us put it to the vote." However, there turned out to be a lot more questions and discussion before the vote was finally cast.

Eventually, the Wizzen voted in favour of protecting Rosalie and not to interfere in Barrmin affairs. They also expressed a need to keep King Rabbart's activities under review, with regular meetings of the Wizzen so that they were all kept informed.

"Right," said Merlin. "Well, we did have an agenda. I think our discussion on spells of protection is well overdue, but first we should discuss a plan of protection for Rosalie. The two topics link quite nicely. We may need the help of a witch or two and a few fairies, but I think it can be done. Naturally we will need the Wizzen's agreement first."

"Ah," interrupted Tannus, "I have not told you about Princess Luena and Robin the Hay Warden yet. I think I had better tell you that story first."

The Wizzen became silent again. What was Tannus going to tell them this time?

He started off by telling the Wizzen that Robin was really a prince of the land once known as Karminesque. Then he told the story of how Robin and the Princess Luena had come to be locked in the palace cells and how he had helped them to escape.

The new leader told them that he had met a witch in Barrden, but despite questions, did not reveal her name. He explained how the witch and Yzor had helped to rescue Robin and the princess. He described their escape to Karminesque and how Rabbart now believed his youngest daughter to be dead. He then added, "And this is the biggest secret of all, but remember my brethren, we are sworn to secrecy within this Wizzen. Robin and Luena are in a mythical place called Zanadoo. I cannot give you an exact location, but you now know that it is near the village-town of Karmin. I cannot tell you about the small part of Zanadoo I have seen, for I am sworn to secrecy by a different oath."

"What did we say earlier about not meddling in other country's affairs?" raised one of the older wizards concernedly, who had not voted for Tannus.

Others shook their heads. They were worried that Tannus's actions might have saved the young couple, but if ever discovered, could cause serious repercussions for all who lived in Avalon.

"I understand your concerns," Tannus stated firmly. "I admit that in retrospect, I should not have intervened in Rabbart's treatment of his daughter or subjects. However, I do not apologise for going to Barrmin and finding out more about the King of Barrmin or his plans."

Some wizards sounded their approval. Others stated that they were glad Tannus had taken it upon himself to find out more about the Barrmin king and his family, but he had taken his actions too far.

Wormald the Wise spoke for the first time since the vote to give Tannus leadership of the wizarding clan had been cast. "It seems as if young Daisy is safe now, as her marriage to Prince Edward is imminent. Nevertheless, if it was discovered that Rabbart was involved in a plot to murder the Princess Rosalie, might that not lead to serious repercussions? Would Arthur and his family not wish to take action? What about Derrick of Twydell? Would he not want to take vengeance over the loss of his loved one? I am glad that we have this information because by saving Rosalie, we may be preventing a war. You have given us valuable information Tannus and for that, I thank you.

"You have also shown yourself to be a brave, young man, however, by interfering in the King of

Barrmin's family affairs, the time may come when you are proven to be a foolish one."

"Well, what has been done is done and cannot be undone," Merlin stated finally. "What is clear is that we have a brave new leader and whether you wholly agree with his actions or not, we are grateful for the insight into Rabbart's plans. Now I think we should discuss how to protect Rosalie, and leave the rest of the agenda for another meeting. Do you agree, Tannus?"

"Yes," agreed Tannus, who continued by putting forward some ideas to protect the Princess of Avalon. With a plan of action finally approved and agreement to involve some witches and fairies, it was expected that Tannus would close the meeting. However, before he did, Tannus had one more revelation.

"I mentioned earlier that I had met a witch in Barrden. The witch I met was none other than Azgoose!"

This final statement was met with tumultuous cheers and applause. Azgoose had become a well-respected witch since taking a leading role in helping to defeat the Trajaens at the Battle of Merlport. No one thought she could still be alive after her fall into the ocean.

Even though the spot in which the Wizzen took place was supposed to be soundproofed, the cheering was so loud that the magical beings outside became aware of the sounds of celebration. They wondered what had caused so much appreciation that the soundproofing spell could not conceal the ovation within.

Tannus continued, "She is alive and well and living in a place called Grey Seal Bay, where she is caring for a human family... three young children who call her 'granny!' She uses an alias and calls herself Gisela the Goose Woman. Azgoose, or Gisela as she is now known, wishes to stay where she is for the time being. Nevertheless, we may see her again soon."

Merlin and Wormald, like all their brethren who knew Azgoose, were delighted. The night had not run as either of them had expected, however, this final piece of news was indeed good.

At last the time came to close the Wizzen. The opening rituals were reversed. The brethren danced in an anti-clockwise direction uttering the words of the chant they had used to open the event – but backwards. Wormald removed the protective walls. The starlit sky started to fill with broomsticks heading in all directions – north, south, east and west.

As expected, there were those who lagged behind chatting to friends or simply not wanting the event to end. Many would have liked to have spent more time with Tannus. They wanted to find out more about his trip to Barrmin and what had happened to Azgoose, but the new leader avoided them all, even Merlin and Wormald. He was tired and anxious to get home to rest in Esmerelda's arms. The young warlock hurried away as soon as it was polite to do so.

PART FOUR: THE WEDDING

CHAPTER 20 - PRINCESS ISLA'S VISIT

Tannus and Esmerelda sat on the grassy hill above Avalon, close to Edward and Daisy's new house. The modest home had been finished and Daisy was inside with a number of female helpers, dressing for the wedding.

"The Barrmin ship is in sight!" shouted Esmerelda. Daisy stuck her head out of the open window. She looked a strange sight with her hair half pinned up and the other half falling loose on her shoulders.

"So Isla has definitely not heard about her sister yet," Tannus commented, as he saw the yellow and red flag flying high on the ship's mast. "Look, the Barrmin standard is flying high. It would be at half mast if they thought Luena was dead."

"Well, she isn't dead. You know she's not, although you won't tell me the whole story!"

"I'm sworn to secrecy." Tannus kissed her neck. "Please, don't try to make me break an oath."

"Very well, keep your lips sealed and your oath unbroken."

Esmerelda added, "I was going to send a jar of ointment to Jaeggar, but if Isla and her aunt don't know that he's been injured, I will have to save my healing balm till the news is broken."

"You're teasing me. I'm sure there are lots of healing balms in Barrden."

"None as good as one prepared by the Queen of the Witches!"

Tannus ignored her. "Look there are the little boats going out to greet her."

Esmerelda and Tannus watched as a flotilla of small boats, waving Avalon and Twydell flags, rowed out to the elaborate ship that was weighing anchor. The Barrmin ship was putting down a landing craft, which made the little Avalonian boats look like toys. It was similar in shape to the Trajaen longboats, but smaller.

The Queen of the Witches turned and waved to Daisy, who was still leaning out of the window, before mounting her broomstick. Tannus and Esmerelda flew down to the village and joined the formal welcoming party. They took up their allocated positions. Prince Edward decided to stand beside them.

King Frederrick and Queen Elise had arrived the previous day and set up a large and very grand marquee on the outskirts of Avalon. Their guards had spotted the Barrmin ship as it sailed into sight. They too were hurrying down in their carriage to meet the Princess of Barrmin and her aunt.

Isla and her aunt stood at the front of the craft, which contained an armed guard who stood to attention on either side of the boat. A second landing vessel bringing armed soldiers followed. Isla smiled and waved to the people in the little boats that surrounded her. Lady Kyrsteen stood stock still, looking straight ahead.

As the landing craft reached the sand, Avalonians ran to the beach to welcome the visiting princess and her aunt. Four Barrmin soldiers lifted Isla ashore on a chair fixed on a board, with handles at each corner. Kyrsteen simply marched ashore. She wore her customary black leather jacket and trousers. Her well-fitted trousers were tucked inside her thigh-length boots and she carried a sword at her side.

Kyrsteen was flanked by armed soldiers. She ignored the people welcoming her, as if they were not good enough to deserve her attention. At the edge of the beach, one of the soldiers bent down to clean the sand from her boots.

"She doesn't look very friendly," Esmerelda commented.

"She isn't," responded Tannus.

"How do you know?" asked Edward.

Esmerelda and Tannus exchanged glances.

"Well, do you think she looks friendly?"

"No, I don't. Fancy coming to my wedding dressed in black and wearing a sword. And why does she need so many armed guards?"

The four soldiers carrying Isla came behind the Lady Kyrsteen who shielded her niece from view. They put the chair down on the path and as the king's sister moved forward to meet her hosts, Isla became visible to the rest of the welcoming party.

Edward gasped as he caught sight of the slender young woman stepping away from the wooden platform. She wore the Barrmin colours – a bright red velvet cloak with a dress of shimmering yellow silk, studded with small rubies to match the larger ones in her necklace and earrings.

"I think you're standing in the wrong place." Esmerelda told Edward. "You're supposed to be next to Derrick."

"Bossy boots," Edward muttered, as he made his way to his allotted spot.

"Well, she really is as lovely as Rabbart told us she was," commented Esmerelda. "It seems he doesn't lie about everything."

First of all, King Arthur introduced Kyrsteen and Isla to Gilda who, unable to walk, was hovering on her broom. Next, he introduced the Elf King and Queen, followed by their Fairy counterparts. Allarond and Farainne sat at the front of Gilda's broom whilst Maud and Selogon floated above them.

Kyrsteen just stood and laughed at the witch and her broomstick passengers, as well as at the fairies fluttering above.

Arthur looked horrified at the insult. Isla, realising her aunt's mistake, rushed in front of her, stressing how pleased she was to meet them all and shaking them each by the hand.

"I really am delighted to be here," Isla had the same musical voice as her mother and a genuine smile on her lips.

"My father has told me so much about you. I have longed for this visit since receiving your kind invitation. Thank you so much for all the work you have done in ridding our land of that awful bindweed."

Arthur beamed. He was a well-travelled man, but he had never seen such a lovely young woman before. "Well, meet the people who have been clearing your land of that cursed weed! This is Merlin, the mighty sorcerer. He has long been leader of our wizards, but I am sorry to say he has now retired."

Merlin took the princess's hand and kissed it. "A pleasure to meet you," he said with a broad smile.

However, having observed Kyrsteen's insult to his friends, he decided to totally ignore her.

"Merlin has been busy clearing the weed from your land," Arthur stated, "but Tannus here, the new leader of the wizards, has been helping to perform the same job in Kerner."

Tannus clasped the princess's hand and brought it to his lips. "What an honour to meet such a charming lady."

Tannus also ignored Kyrsteen. Kyrsteen looked puzzled, not realising how her earlier behaviour could have been so offensive.

"And this is Queen Esmerelda of the Witches," Arthur continued.

"Oh, your grace, how delighted I am to meet you. I have heard so much about you!"

"You have?" Esmerelda looked at the princess quizzically with her soft, moss-green eyes.

"Jaeggar, my father's adviser, has commented several times on your exquisite eyes. He says you can make them change colour."

Esmerelda laughed. She turned her head towards Tannus who was looking a little irritated at the princess's comment. The Witch Queen's eyes turned to a sparkling emerald and emitted a green, heart-shaped image that floated towards her lover.

Tannus laughed as he carelessly caught the green heart shape in his left hand. The heart disappeared, but he kissed his hand on the spot on which he had caught it.

"Oh, how amazing! Will you do it again, please?"

"I'm sure Queen Esmerelda will show you more of her tricks later," Arthur gently touched the princess's arm and moved her forward to meet King Frederrick and Queen Elise of Twydell.

"I am so very pleased to meet you and the Lady Kyrsteen," Frederrick shook the princess's hand and then moved swiftly to her aunt. He had recognised the discomfort that had been felt by the magical people who had arrived to welcome her and the foolish woman's lack of understanding of the insult she had caused.

"I do hope that this is the beginning of a long and fruitful friendship between our two countries," Frederrick looked up at Kyrsteen who towered above him.

Queen Elise and Isla greeted each other warmly before Arthur ushered her towards the two waiting princes.

Prince Edward of Avalon and Prince Derrick of Twydell stood side by side. Kyrsteen was pleased to note that both stared at the lovely young woman in front of them. Both greeted her warmly. Both greeted Kyrsteen with cool respect.

Arthur turned to the Lady Kyrsteen, "Now the only people you have not met are my daughter Rosalie, and Daisy. Rosalie is helping Daisy prepare for her wedding. You will meet them both shortly. In the meantime, if you would like to travel with King Frederrick and Queen Elise in their carriage, we will arrange some refreshment before you take your places in the tiered seating. We have found a nice spot for you where you will be able to see all that is going on. I'm afraid there is no grand palace in Merlport, or indeed anywhere in Avalon. Therefore, the wedding will be performed in the village square."

"A good job it's not raining," commented Kyrsteen, looking up at the sky.

The weather had not been good for the past few days, but it seemed as though the sun was shining on those who deserved it because it shone brightly, casting its warmth over the late afternoon.

Everyone was surprised to see Kyrsteen step inside the carriage ahead of her niece. After all, Isla was a princess and although Kyrsteen was also a princess in her own right, the king's daughter should have had priority.

"What an unpleasant woman," muttered Derrick. "No wonder she has never been married. Who would want a wife like that?"

Edward laughed. "Her niece is nice though. I wonder what her sisters look like. I can't believe either of them could be as lovely as Isla."

"I don't think that's the sort of comment you should be making on your wedding day!" Derrick patted his friend on the back as they walked together to the village square.

The whole village stood around the square waiting for the announcement that Daisy was on her way. They took refreshments while they waited.

Fairies and elves had helped themselves to food from the tables and started to settle on the roof tops or on the banisters of the tiered seating. Willy and a group of carpenters were busying around making sure the seating was secure.

The giants had turned down the invitation to the wedding, but a few of them had gathered on the hillside to watch the proceedings below. They had sent barrels of cider as a wedding present and said they would plant some apple trees in Edward and Daisy's garden to start an orchard for them.

Kyrsteen looked up nervously as the echo of the giants' footsteps resounded in the village below. She looked around to make sure her bodyguards were close by. Isla, on the other hand, was looking up at them pointing excitedly, as did Queen Elise, who had been talking to her.

Esmerelda and Tannus were taking the opportunity to scold Merlin for staying for the wedding instead of returning to his wife in the Forbidden Forest.

"I'll only be away an extra couple of days and Edward had specifically asked me to officiate. Wormald says he doesn't mind me taking over again at the last minute." Merlin stuffed a large portion of apple pie into his mouth as he finished speaking.

"But Helen-Joy needs you at home. Promise you will return first thing tomorrow morning," Esmerelda pleaded.

"Well, I must say that I am considering staying a little longer and sailing up to Barrden with you all. It would be nice to call in and see Azgoose again. I would also like to meet Queen Issyluna, her father King Xargon and…"

Tannus interrupted. "I can understand you staying an extra day or so for the wedding and you must be disappointed not to be travelling to Barrden, as we all know that you enjoy your trips, but I have a message for you and you must take it seriously. I ask you to tell no one."

He turned to Esmerelda, "I must bid you say nothing of what I have to tell Merlin."

Merlin and Esmerelda looked at the serious expression on the new wizard leader's face. Both nodded their agreement to the secret they were about to be told.

"I was asked to give this to you. It is a gift for Helen-Joy, but first you must show it to Lennox."

Tannus handed Merlin a pendant. The pendant consisted of what appeared to be a clear stone, set in a gold surround. However, as Merlin took the jewel it glimmered a pale yellow and then a light green, as it caught the light at different angles.

"What is it?" asked Merlin. "Where did it come from?"

"It is a stone called zanite. I am sworn to secrecy. I am sorry I can say only two other things. First, that we must take a more careful look at the Kernan mines. Second, that you must show the jewel to Lennox. Lennox too has been sworn to secrecy, but when he sees the gift for Helen-Joy, he will know that he and his mares can tell you about their journey to the Forbidden Forest."

Merlin looked puzzled. "Is that all you can tell me? Is this something to do with you taking Robin and Luena to safety in Zanadoo?"

Esmerelda was more concerned about the instructions to look more carefully at the Kernan mines. "Are you telling me that there are more of our kind and children being forced to work in the mines?"

Tannus put his arm around her. "If that is what I thought, I would be in Kerner by now. No, I believe it is something else. I also believe that the message is urgent.

"Let Lennox tell you his story, Merlin. He knows more than I do and I think Helen-Joy may do so too. Perhaps they can tell you what we need to know about the Kernan mines. Don't forget what that man said, the one who brought the children to us, about the children not being needed any more because they had stronger creatures working in the mines."

"I'm intrigued…" Merlin was about to say more, but a horn sounded in the distance.

"Ah, Daisy is on her way. I must officiate. Thank you, Tannus." He slipped the pendant into an inner pocket of his colourful best gown. "We'll talk again later."

"I have no more to say. I have told you how we saved Robin and Luena and took them to Zanadoo, but I can tell you no more. You must speak to Lennox and you must waste no time in doing so."

Merlin nodded and hurried off to a dais that had been set up at the end of the square. Visitors were shown to their allocated places in the tiered stand. Kyrsteen and Isla were led to the royal box where they were joined by the royal family of Twydell. Gilda flew up to the box on her gilded broom, with Allarond and Farainne as passengers. The elves hopped on to the railings whilst she stood her broom alongside Esmerelda's in the corner. She took a seat beside Elise who patted her friend's hand warmly. The fairy royalty fluttered down, settling themselves beside their elf companions.

Kyrsteen looked bemused and looked around to see where her bodyguards and other Barrmin soldiers had placed themselves.

Isla, however, smiled happily. Her aunt sat beside her on one side and Derrick on her other. The prince and princess chatted amiably.

The orchestra of fairies and elves had come from the Forbidden Forest with all their instruments. To start with, they had been rightfully nervous about the prospect of travelling outside their forest home. However, when Merlin told them that they would travel in the safety of the Twydell royal carriage alongside the king and queen, they were pleased to accept the invitation to play at the wedding.

Merlin touched the musical instruments with his staff so that when the orchestra started to play, the strange ethereal music could be heard across the village square. Elves blew delicate notes on their reed flutes while fairies tapped chains of snail shells to make them tinkle in tune. Musicians bowed their violins making the silk spider strings hum while cellos were strummed for deeper notes. Only those who had been to the Forbidden Forest had ever heard such a strange, enchanting sound. The whole audience ceased their excited chatter and listened in silence.

As the haunting music played, the sound of hooves and the jangle of wheels could be heard on the road. Six white horses pulled the golden carriage of Avalon into the square. Arthur stepped forward to help Daisy alight. Tannus, who was best man, was there to meet Rosalie. The golden carriage then drew away. Avalon may not have had fine palaces, but no other country could better its golden carriage.

"That's my girl," Derrick whispered to Isla, "that's Rosalie, my intended."

Isla took her eyes away from the scene in front of her for a while. "You're a lucky man," she murmured, "Rosalie looks lovely."

Rosalie wore the same blue dress as she had worn to the wedding of Princess Jeanette and Prince Steven. In fact, having nothing else to wear she had had to make do, but this time a crown of blue roses adorned her dark hair. In her hand she held a bouquet of the same azure blooms.

Daisy, meanwhile, wore a white silk dress decorated with every type of real flower that could be found so late in the year. She wore a crown of red roses and held a bouquet of the same flowers, which was so long it almost trailed on the ground. The two lions, Leo and Sybil, also alighted from the carriage. It appeared that they were taking the place of page boys.

Arthur was not Daisy's father, but as she had no family of her own she had asked him to escort her. The old king had accepted the request with a great deal of pride. Now he led her to the dais where his son, Prince Edward, waited.

Tannus, who had taken Rosalie's arm and led her to the platform, left her standing behind the bride as he took his place beside Edward. The lions sat on their haunches beside Rosalie and seemed to be taking an interest in all that was going on.

Everyone in the royal box and all in the vast crowd looked on as the exchange of rings ceremony took place. Merlin had raised the voices of those taking part so everyone could hear the happy couple taking their vows. Some magical beings took to the air to get a better view.

Isla and her aunt watched in awe. Even Kyrsteen smiled as she watched the fairies fluttering in the air above her.

At the end of the ceremony, Derrick stood up abruptly but turned to Isla, "I'm going down to see Rosalie, would you like me to introduce you?"

"Yes, please," the Barrmin princess replied eagerly. "I'd love to meet her!"

"You should stay here," snapped Lady Kyrsteen. "You don't know who else is down there. Your father would never forgive me if anything happened to you."

Isla looked at her aunt. She was obviously quite shocked by her words.

"Who is likely to hurt her?" asked Esmerelda, who was sitting just behind the Barrmen and Twydellers. "Surely you don't think that any of us would harm Princess Isla? If we meant you any harm then we would not be clearing your land of bindweed."

Kyrsteen looked confused. The last thing she wanted to do was to say something that would stop the good work the Avalonians were doing in Barrmin. She was silent for a few moments while she struggled to find something to say. At last she said, "There are giants here. I saw them sitting on the hillside. The giants are the enemy of Barrmin."

"But as you said, they are sitting on the hillside. If they were to make their way to the village, then I can assure you that you would hear them coming and feel the ground tremble long before they arrived." Esmerelda smiled, but her sparkling eyes betrayed the anger she held back in her voice.

Kyrsteen conceded with a curt nod and Isla followed Derrick down the stairs.

Esmerelda hopped smartly onto her broom and dropped gracefully to the ground. By the time Derrick and Isla had reached the bottom step, she was standing there waiting for them with a grin on her face and a hand on her hip. "Hello, haven't I seen you two before somewhere?"

Isla burst into peals of laughter and threw her arms around the Witch Queen. "Oh, I am having so much fun! I feel like I'm in a wonderful dream. I just hope nobody pinches me and wakes me up!"

Esmerelda returned the girl's hug. "Come along and meet the lovely bride and her equally lovely bridesmaid." She took Isla's hand and led her across the square to be introduced.

Isla could feel her aunt's malicious stare, but for the time being she could not care less.

"Let's send a drink up to your aunt and the royal Twydells," said Esmerelda, who could also feel the glare of Kyrsteen's eyes. She tapped a jug of red wine with her wand. The jug lifted itself off the table and hovered while the witch tapped three goblets with her wand. The jug filled the goblets with red wine. Esmerelda then sent the three goblets soaring into the air. One of them almost crashed into a passing fairy, but the little winged person just managed to avoid the flying vessel. The goblets landed on the railing in front of Kyrsteen, Elise and Frederrick. Elise and Frederrick took their drinks and raised them in their hands to thank Esmerelda. Kyrsteen was not sure what to do, but eventually copied the Twydellers.

Esmerelda continued to be host by filling little goblets, which looked as if they had been made out of hazelnut shells, with apricot wine. She sent the wine to the fairies and elves in the royal box. As the tiny goblets flew towards them, the fairies and elves raised their wands to create sparks in the sky, marking their gratitude.

The other magical beings, taking the fairy and elf royalties' actions as a cue, imitated them. Soon the darkening sky was filled with glittering sparklets of every colour imaginable.

Isla clapped her hands with joy and other humans followed her example.

The orchestra's ethereal music came to an end and the local band took to the stage. Their music was more jolly and soon the whole village was dancing. Isla took turns on the floor with Merlin, Derrick, Edward and Tannus.

Isla could feel Kyrsteen's watchful eyes and knew her aunt's spitefulness would be festering. However, for the time being she was enjoying herself and didn't care.

"I can feel the ground trembling beneath my feet," she told Tannus, as they danced. "Am I imagining it? I'm sure I have not had so much of your delicious apricot wine that it could have such an effect."

"No. You are not imagining it and you're not tipsy. It's the giants dancing. Look, you can just about see them." Tannus pointed in the direction of the hillside.

In the brightness of so many wands and glowing staffs, the giants were just about visible in the soft light that had been cast. They danced a merry jig as they waved to the crowds below.

"The giants are our enemy," Isla said, but she did not look alarmed.

"They are really very friendly, as long as you don't cut their trees without permission. They have even supplied most of the cider for tonight's festivities. Perhaps we could take you to meet them tomorrow. It could be the start of a new friendship." Tannus could not imagine that the giants would fail to like Isla.

"We have to return tonight," Isla responded, with a hint of sadness.

"Tonight? Surely not!"

"I'm afraid so," Isla attempted to put an upbeat tone to her voice, "not just my aunt's orders, but those of my father too."

"I understand. It is such a pity that your mother and sisters could not come. I would have loved to have met them." There was a hint of mischief in Tannus's eyes as he spoke. He had, of course, already seen Queen Issyluna and her daughters before, while in the disguise of Rover.

"They will be delighted to meet you when you come to Delphine's wedding. I can't wait to tell my mother and sisters about my visit to Avalon!"

The mischief in Tannus's eyes was replaced by a hint of sadness. He knew that when Isla returned home she would be told that her sister, Luena, was dead. He wanted to tell her that her sister was alive and safe, but he knew he could not.

A Barrmin soldier approached Isla. "The Lady Kyrsteen is ready to leave. She bids you hurry. She has heard the giants on the move."

"Oh, they are only dancing..." Isla started to protest, but as she looked across the square, she saw her aunt standing with her leather travelling cloak already across her shoulders. Another guard stood beside her holding Isla's red velvet cloak.

"It seems the night is over," she told Tannus, "but it will remain in my memory forever."

Tannus gave a slight bow.

Arthur came forward, determined to escort Isla to the beach. He had hoped to have been able to spend more time with the girl. "It is such a pity that you have to leave, but your aunt is adamant that you must leave tonight. I assure you, the giants mean no harm, they are simply enjoying themselves... and hopefully their merriment is not inadvertently causing any damage to Edward and Daisy's new house!"

The ground continued to shudder as the giants danced.

"My father has ordered that we must return tonight," Isla smiled. "He thinks only of our welfare and is very protective. However, I will tell him about the friendship you have won with the giants. Perhaps one day, Barrmin and the giants will make peace."

Merlin dimmed the sound of the village band whilst the goodbyes were said to the Barrmin guests.

As Isla gave Esmerelda a warm hug, she caught sight of Kyrsteen's glare. Deciding not to test her aunt's temper any further, she gave modest handshakes and soft kisses on the cheeks to the rest of the Avalonian and Twydell royals. However, she was aware that Edward held her hand just a little longer than the others, as she looked into the depth of the dark pools of his eyes.

Others may have missed the look that passed between the Princess of Barrmin and the Prince of Avalon, but the Lady Kyrsteen did not.

Later, as their fine ship sailed away from Merlport, Isla stood at the aft watching the glow in the sky around the little village, as the wedding party continued into the night. She stood, imagining herself to still be there, until Merlport drifted out of sight.

THE END

Epilogue

Bert and Stan hauled in their catch. Silvery mackerel glistened in their net. Geese flew down and pecked at the cockles and smaller fish that had been caught up in the net.

Two wheelbarrows full of fish were trundled back to the little shack that served as Stan's family home. After taking one each, they wheeled the barrows to the narrow path that led to the village. The children had been told to stay at home with Hubert and Fido. A villager seeing a dog, however old the cur might be, might see a roast dinner instead.

Azgoose was keen to see the village she had heard so much about in Hubert's stories. However, the path was still blocked by the stones that had fallen when Bailiff Baldrock had tried to take the geese.

"I told you it would take hours to clear this lot," Bert grumbled. We should have left the fish in the net till we could clear these rocks.

"No, it won't," Stan replied, "not if Gisela uses that little stick of hers."

Azgoose froze on the spot. Stan smiled at her. Bert looked at both of them with a puzzled expression on his face.

"I told you the other day that I thought Gisela, if that's her real name, was a witch. Don't you remember, Bert? When I said all the things that seemed to happen to us lately must be magic?

"I was first suspicious when I saw Bailiff Baldrock's donkey stumble and the crates of geese smash open, yet none of the geese were hurt. Then

Bailiff Grimshaw fell off the quay, but the quay wasn't wet or slippery. The night Princess Luena and Robin the Hay Warden escaped, Gisela was missing. She said she had gone to the latrine, but I know she wasn't anywhere near the latrines because when the guards woke us up, I went there myself to look for her."

"I thought you were joking." Bert looked at the other fisherman then he turned to the old woman. "It would be wonderful if you really were a witch, Gisela."

"Yes, it would," agreed Stan. "If you say you are not a witch, then of course we will believe you. But if you really are a witch, then Bert and I would promise to tell no one. We won't even tell Hubert and especially not the children, just in case they let it slip to their friends in the village. I'd love to tell them about how you sent Grimshaw tumbling into the sea, but even that would be a story never to be told."

"If Gisela is a witch, I promise to tell no one," Bert raised his right hand and spoke in a solemn voice. "If I break this vow may the sea take me and drown me in its depths."

Stan raised his right hand and repeated the same words.

Azgoose simply smiled. It was a relief to no longer have to hide her secret to everyone in Grey Seal Bay. She took her wand from her waistband and muttering her magic words, rolled the rocks to one side.

The local people had resorted to eating termites, spiders and anything else they could find that seemed edible. The sight of two barrow loads of fresh fish brought welcome relief and exclamations of thanks.

No payment was sought. The look of gratitude on the faces of the villagers was reward enough for the two fishermen and their witch friend.

Characters

List of main characters, in alphabetical order:

Ajax: green dragon; husband of Blitzen

Alexander: the blacksmith's son (usually referred to as Alex); brother of Andrew; friend of Edward

Alfred: an elf

Allarond: King of the Elves

Andrew: the blacksmith's son; brother of Alexander; friend of Edward

Arthur: King of Avalon (formerly King of Briton); husband of Gilda the Witch; father of Edward and Rosalie

Azgoose: a witch who can create clouds of goo

Bert: a fisherman from Grey Seal Bay (son of Hubert)

Big Stan: see 'Stan'

Bizzbuzz: a wizard who specialises in making honey

Blitzen: blue Dragon; wife of Ajax

Bramble Family: Bertha (Great-grandmother Bramble), mother of Nora (Grandmother Bramble) and Maura; Nora (Grandmother Bramble), mother of Dilly, Dally and Sally; Dilly Bramble, wife of Jerry; Dally

Bramble, wife of Garod; Sally Bramble, wife of Isaiah and mother of Heather

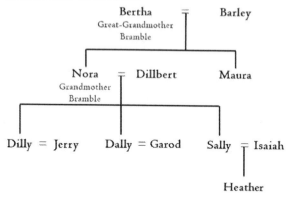

Brutuz: a large, muscular but kindly wizard; brother of Curtuz

Comet: Merlin's white stallion

Connie: the baker's daughter

Curtuz: a large, muscular but kindly wizard; brother of Brutuz

Daisy: the last of the Brewins

Delphine: Princess of Barrmin; daughter of Queen Issyluna and King Rabbart lll; granddaughter of Xargon, King of Vanddalasia; engaged to Duke William of Vanddalasia

Derrick: Prince of Twydell; son of King Frederrick and Queen Elise

Edward-Arthur: illegitimate son of King Arthur (usually referred to simply as Edward)

Elise: wife/consort of King Frederrick of Twydell (given the title of queen at the time of marriage)

Elvira: Queen of the Witches; all her witches migrated to Avalon

Esmerelda: Queen of the Witches (after Elvira); daughter of Elvira

Farainne: wife/consort of Allarond, King of the Elves (given the title of queen at the time of marriage)

Frederrick: King of Twydell

Gilda: one of the first witches to migrate to Avalon; she later married King Arthur; mother of Rosalie

Greatog: former leader of the giants; killed in an earlier battle with the Trajaens; father of Zog

Helen-Joy: a soothsayer

Hubert: a retired fisherman; father of Bert

Isaiah: see Bramble family

Isla: Princess of Barrmin; daughter of Queen Issyluna and King Rabbart lll; granddaughter of Xargon, King of Vanddalasia

Issyluna: Queen of Barrmin; wife of Rabbart lll; daughter of Xargon, King of Vanddalasia; mother of Isla, Delphine and Luena

Iwan: a young warlock rescued from the Kernan mines

Jaeggar: adviser to King Rabbart lll

Jeanette: Princess of Twydell; daughter of King Frederrick and Queen Elise

Jeffrey: King of Kerner

Jonathan: a young warlock who specialises in plants (herbologist); son of the wizard Yzor and a half-witch

Lennox: last of the British unicorns

Luena: Princess of Barrmin; daughter of Queen Issyluna and King Rabbart lll; granddaughter of Xargon, King of Vanddalasia

Maud: Queen of the Fairies; married to Selogon

Merlin: powerful wizard who organised the migration to Avalon; adviser to King Arthur

Rabbart lll: King of Barrmin

Robin: a hay warden from a land once known as Karminesque

Rosalie: daughter of King Arthur and Gilda the witch

Selogon: husband/consort of Maud, Queen of the Fairies

Shirley-Poppy: wife/consort of Jeffrey, King of Kerner (given the title of queen at the time of marriage)

Stan: a fisherman from Grey Seal Bay, father of Young Stan, Harry and Harriet (the Harries)

Steven: Prince of Kerner; son of King Jeffrey and Queen Shirley-Poppy

Tannitus: powerful wizard; father of Tannus

Tannus: powerful young warlock; son of Tannitus

William: a Duke of Vanddalasia

Willy the Wood Wizard: wizard who can talk to trees

Wormald the Wise: wise old wizard

Yzor: a wizard who specialises in plants (herbologist); father of Jonathan

Zog: leader of the giants; son of Greatog

About the Author

Daisy Bourne was born in England in 1917. Nothing much is known about her real parents except that their lives were changed dramatically by the First World War. At the age of six, Daisy was unofficially adopted by a farmer and his wife. They changed her name and took her to Canada.

There are several similarities between the real Daisy Bourne and her namesake in this book. To a  small child, Canada, with its heavy snowfalls, huge forests and grizzly bears must indeed have seemed like some kind of new world. Although Daisy loved Canada and the farm on which she lived, she was not happy and ran away. She returned to England at the age of 16. In later life, she took up farming again. She also enjoyed her garden and preserving much of its produce. This is where the similarities between the real Daisy and the character in the "*Tales of Avalon*" series end.

I am proud to use my mother's birth name as a pseudonym when writing the *Tales of Avalon* series. My ambition is to one day write the story of the real Daisy Bourne. In the meantime, I will continue to complete the *Tales of Avalon* series.

A note from the Author

I love hearing from my readers. If you would like to contact me, please use the link on my website: TalesOfAvalon.co.uk or message me on my Facebook page: *Tales of Avalon* series

If you enjoyed reading this book, why not recommend the Tales of Avalon series to your friends. But please suggest that they start on Book 1, right at the beginning of the tale, so that they do not miss out on any of the adventures.

DAISY BOURNE

More from the Tales of Avalon series

*T**he New Land* is the first book in the *Tales of Avalon* series. It was published in 2016.

What happened to Arthur, King of the Britons, after he was allegedly killed on the battlefield? Legend has it that Merlin, the mighty sorcerer, put the king's body in a boat and set sail for a mysterious place called Avalon. However, many Britons refused to accept that Arthur was really dead and believed instead that Merlin had taken the king to a place of safety. There have been many theories as to the whereabouts of Avalon, but none have proven to be accurate.

The New Land tells the story of how Arthur, magical beings and other Britons who feared for their lives sought refuge in a far-off land. They hoped their new home would be a place where magical beings and humans could live together in peace and harmony. Did the travellers find the new life they so desired? Well, they certainly found a land full of surprise and adventure.

The Avalonians soon find that they have to form new and unusual alliances in order to protect themselves against an unexpected enemy.

If you like stories about witches, wizards, fairies, elves, giants and unicorns, you will enjoy this book.

The Land of Twydell and the Dragon Egg is the second book in the *Tales of Avalon* series. It was published in 2016.

What happened during Merlin's trip to Twydell? Who, or what, did he meet? *The Land of Twydell and the Dragon Egg* describes the wizard's extraordinary adventures in Twydell and the people and creatures he meets there.

As he flies across the countryside on his broomstick, he is puzzled to see a long line of people leaving the capital of Dalton and heading towards the outlying villages. Entire families are fleeing the capital. They look ragged and downcast and appear to be taking their possessions with them. As he approaches Dalton, Merlin is shocked to see billowing smoke and that large parts of the city have been destroyed by fire.

The wizard learns that the devastation has been caused by a pair of dragons that have lived near the city for many years without any problem. King Frederrick is bewildered as to why the dragons should suddenly seek to attack the Twydellers, for no apparent reason.

The Exchange of Rings is the third book in the *Tales of Avalon* series. It was published in 2016.

The Exchange of Rings follows on from *The New Land*, the first book in the series. It describes the preparations for the wedding of Princess Jeanette of Twydell to Prince Steven of Kerner. Rosalie is excited at the prospect of meeting Derrick, Prince of Twydell, who many hope will be her future husband. The weddings are an opportunity for each county to build new alliances.

Everything seems to be running smoothly, but news is brought that wizards who have been missing from

Twydell's Forbidden Forest for many years, are being held in a Kerner prison. It is also revealed that fairies and elves have been similarly treated with cruelty by Kernans. The magical people of Avalon are furious and some want to take revenge on Kerner.

King Arthur of Avalon, Merlin the wizard and their new found ally, King Frederrick of Twydell, try to resolve the situation. They are concerned that revenge will be the beginning of war.

The allies hope that a solution can be found when the King of Kerner is forced to ask the magical people of the Forbidden Forest for help.

Lennox's Story is the fifth book in the *Tales of Avalon* series and is to be published early in 2018.

It tells the story of Lennox, the last unicorn in Briton, and how and why he made the decision to travel to Avalon. In *The New Land*, Lennox left his fellow travellers on the beach and headed straight towards the scent of other unicorns drifting from the Great Forest. We do not see him again until he greets Merlin at the entrance to the Forbidden Forest in *The Land of Twydell and the Dragon Egg*. How and why did Lennox travel through Twydell? What secrets has Lennox yet to tell about his journey to the Forbidden Forest and how is it connected to the zanite locket that Tannus has given to Merlin? Who are the strong creatures who work in Kernan mines? All is revealed when Lennox's magical story is revealed.

Edward's Story, the sixth book in the *Tales of Avalon* series, is planned for publication in 2019.

Is Princess Rosalie safe from King Rabbart's scheming? Will he murder the young princess before her marriage to Prince Derrick? You will have to read *Edward's Story* to find out.